Sea Horse Lodge

Sea Horse Ranch
Book Two

Natalie Keller Reinert

Also by Natalie Keller Reinert

Briar Hill Farm
Foaling Season
Friends With Horses
Outside Rein

The Ocala Equestrians Collection
Alex & Alexander: A Horse Racing Saga
The Eventing Series: A Three-Day Eventing Saga
Sea Horse Ranch: A Beach Read Series
Ocala Horse Girls: A Romance Series
The Hidden Horses of New York: A Novel
Grabbing Mane: A Duet Series
Show Barn Blues: A Duet Series

Catoctin Creek: Sweet Romance
Sunset at Catoctin Creek
Snowfall at Catoctin Creek
Springtime at Catoctin Creek
Christmas at Catoctin Creek

Learn more and find bonus stories at nataliekreinert.com

Chapter One

I NEEDED THIS ride.

Wow, did I ever need it! I put a hand on my horse's warm neck, looked around, and breathed in the scent of salt and flowers. *Mmm...* that was the good stuff!

I was the luckiest girl in the world; sometimes it just took a canter on the beach to remind me. And my timing tonight was impeccable, because it didn't get more beautiful than this in the Florida Keys.

A rich blue dusk was falling across the islands, these tiny clusters of coral reef capped by twisting mangrove roots and thick, glossy green leaves, but there was still a pink shimmer above the western horizon. Above those last remnants of the sunset, one tiny, perfect star hung from some unseen picture hook in the sky.

I looked at that star between my horse's pricked ears and couldn't stop a grim smile from pulling at my lips. Showing the way to Key West, that star, like a trap for unwary travelers and runaway teens.

Not for me, though. I didn't want to go to Key West—not tonight. I was happy out here in the out-islands, forgotten or undiscovered, how ever you wanted to look at them. I didn't need the throbbing crowds on Duval Street; the bars spilling onto the sidewalks and the passersby spilling onto the roads, the pounding nightclubs and the constant flood of *Margaritaville* from the souvenir shops, drenching everyone with its drunken blues.

Not tonight, anyway.

Reggie tugged at the reins; my horse had his own ideas about where our night ride should take us. I let him splash into the shallow water, startling a great blue heron taking in a little night-fishing. The bird lifted from the lapping waves, all six feet of her dangling in our path for a moment before her huge wings took her off into the darkness.

Reggie snorted and wheeled on his haunches.

He'd always been a spooky little horse.

I leaned forward slightly and let him run. There was nowhere for him to go; in twenty strides we'd be at the end of this little beach, and the rocks lining the channel between the islands would turn him. Three more jumps after that, and we'd hit the thick jungle shielding the beach from the shell road through the islands, its leaves and vines lush with early summer heat and rain. Reggie would come to his senses quickly.

Or maybe I'd fall off again, and he'd do a few laps up and down the beach while his brain figured out what was going on. Reggie took a while to catch up with current events, and I was still a pretty novice rider. He turned back to the water, jumped a small wave, and I felt my balance waver.

Before Hell and Dammit Cay, before Sea Horse Ranch, before spring, I'd barely done more than pet a school friend's horse.

My whole life was so different then.

Now I took care of a stable of horses every morning before breakfast, rode a few horses a day, and led rides through the jungle to this beach. I was a ranch-hand. A ranch-hand on an island in the

Florida Keys. And my parents said hitch-hiking was just going to get me killed!

Reggie wheeled again and went rushing up the beach, his breath snorting from his nostrils. I balanced myself carefully in the cheap Western saddle we used for our beach rides. Nylon and fake leather. Plenty of grip. I was not going to fall off. I went through my riding position checklist. My heels were down, my eyes were up, my hands were steady—I was missing something. Ack! What was I missing?

This time, when Reggie saw the rocks rising up at the end of the beach, he swerved hard to the right, leaving the shallow water and thundering up the slight slope of the beach. The white sand glowed beneath the luminescent blue dusk. Reggie turned again as the thick wall of jungle loomed ahead, and then he bucked, and coarse beach sand went flying everywhere.

I spit out a mouthful of it and pondered how I'd ended up sprawled on the beach while Reggie went cantering away. Heels, eyes, hands...what else? What let me down?

"You have to learn to read his mind," Lou called, pushing aside a palm frond and stepping onto the beach. His voice was full of suppressed laughter. What a good boyfriend, I thought sarcastically. I mean, he was, but some sympathy would have been nice at this particular moment. I struggled to sit upright, the sand sliding away beneath my hands and making me look like a clumsy foal.

Lou stood over me, rubbing his dark beard and smiling, like he was considering whether he should bend down and help me up. Or just let me clamber to my feet under my own steam.

I was annoyed, but also appreciative, if that makes sense. Lou knew I wasn't looking for a knight in shining armor. He hadn't popped out of the jungle to save me. It was just timing.

He always had such good timing.

"Do you want help up?" he asked. "Or are you going to stay down there a while?"

"Oh, give me a hand," I said with a little sigh, reaching up one hand. He grasped my fingers in his, the callouses of his fingertips brushing against my palm. My heart lurched a little, like it did every time I touched those rough ridges of skin, the marks of his craft. When he felt like doing it.

Lou had been holed up in his bedroom playing guitar all afternoon, and I'd been so happy about it, I'd gone off to make sure I didn't accidentally leap into his room, scream congratulations, and scare him out of his work.

We had a record due in six months, and I was learning some serious hard truths about Lou's work ethic. This was a man who had produced a DIY record with a friend which had become an indie sensation, but when given actual deadlines and requirements, he suddenly developed a burning interest in fishing, boating, carpentry, oil painting—oh, *anything* that wasn't working towards said deadlines.

Men, I know.

With his assistance, I got back to my feet, my bare toes sinking into the cool sand. (Yes, I rode in bare feet. Lou's mother taught me to ride, and she said flip flops were dangerous in stirrups, much better to go without.) With a quick little movement as I straightened, Lou tugged me to his chest and wrapped his arms around me.

I savored the quick embrace, ignoring that it was an almost self-conscious show of affection. Lou'd been a bit distant this summer, tending towards brooding in his room or quietly gazing out at the green waters of the Gulf. I knew not to expect a perfect emotional state from a man like Lou, who had a habit of disappearing and had broken his mother's heart more than once. So I let him do his thing, figuring that if he was writing music, then he might be going wandering in the depths of his imagination. I just hoped he'd find his way back soon with some real hits to share.

We'd definitely need one hit if we were going to keep Rivers McLean, my producer "friend"—it's important to keep the quotation marks when referring to anyone in the music business as a friend—happy and requesting more music from us.

And I wanted that more than anything. More music. A career as a musician. Not as a backup singer, disposable, like I'd been before. I wanted *my* name up in lights.

I know, I know, me and everyone else, right? But we had this deal, which had started as a simple request for a single and had turned into a full record. Lou's name as reclusive artist Silvery Star preceded him. We could *do* this.

I rested my chin against his chest and listened to his heartbeat. It seemed as slow and steady as a horse's.

Speaking of horses—I looked up, wondering where Reggie was.

Lou stepped back and gave me a once-over. "You didn't bust anything, right? Nothing broke, nothing bleeding?"

"The sand saved me," I told him, sweeping my arms around dramatically. "Everyone should learn to ride on the beach. Like falling on a pillow."

He lifted a skeptical eyebrow. "I've fallen off here, too, and I'd say it's a little harder than *that*. And where do we think Reggie is...*oh*, good. Here he comes."

Sure enough, my little mustang came tripping up to us, his ears pricked, the skin around his dark eyes all furrowed with concern. He pushed his nose against me and ruffled his big nostrils, blowing hot air and not a small amount of snot along my bare arm.

"Hey, goober," I told him, sliding a hand beneath his chin until I could clutch the reins. "You gotta let me back on. I'm not walking through that jungle in my bare feet."

Lou made a mocking *snick* sound with his tongue. "Can't believe you ride in bare feet. Just like my mom."

"And who taught me to ride?" I countered. Crystal wasn't exactly a conventional horsewoman or a certified riding instructor, but then again, there was nothing normal about our lives on this isolated little island, ten minutes and a world away from the tourist-laden strip of asphalt called the Overseas Highway—also known as plain old U.S. 1. The point being that out here, riding barefoot was perfectly acceptable. And I still rode in a helmet!

Most of the time.

Not tonight, but most of the time.

Lou chuckled as he took the reins from me. "Okay, cowgirl, mount up. I'll walk you two back to the ranch to make sure there's no more funny business."

Reggie snorted again.

"I mean from you, especially," Lou informed him.

With Lou holding Reggie (relatively) still, I swung back into the saddle with ease. At least *that* was something I'd gotten much better at since my early days here. With my bare feet once again secure in the stirrups, we walked together into the dark jungle which stood between us and the road. This had been the site of a planned eco-resort years ago, and the lush foliage wasn't native to the Keys, but it sure liked the humid, hot weather here.

The path was wide enough to allow Lou to walk at my side; one of his duties around the island was keeping our riding trails manicured so paying customers didn't get scratched by thorny vines or find themselves face-to-face with a harmless, but enormous, banana spider. I hoped nothing especially alive and creepy-crawly was on the move yet tonight. We knew this trail well enough to walk it blindfolded, but the jungle was still a spooky place after dark. As I thought about it, something crackled deep within the thickets of vines and shrubs.

Reggie's ears flicked back and forward.

Lou's hands closed on the reins again. I felt the pressure travel to my hands through the leather and tried to breathe a little easier, hoping to send my little horse some reassurance. I needed to stay on top until we got back to the road. Okay, maybe riding out here after sunset hadn't been the best idea. At least, not barefoot.

But I'd just really needed to get away from everyone on Hell and Dammit Cay.

It was sad, but true. I needed the break.

As if he'd heard my thoughts, Lou spoke up. "The islanders making you crazy again?"

I shrugged, then realized this was a useless gesture in the darkness. "It's not anything I should complain about," I said. "Everyone means well. They just—"

"They just rely on you for everything? And you're worn out with it?"

"That's not true. I mean, it's not—the only—"

He chuckled at that, a rueful sound, and I gave up the back-pedaling. Because it *was* true, and we both knew it.

I was basically the caretaker of Hell and Dammit Cay these days. If anything went wrong, the three full-time residents of the little island —Marchant, Crystal, Stacy—turned to me to figure out a solution.

I'd brought this on myself. I'd figured out how to stop developers from turning this jungle into a series of tile-roofed villas with luxury boats on lifts out back. I'd used my connections in the live music business and my ability to sweet-talk artistic temperaments to create an art and music festival which had raised awareness about our island

and brought public opinion against the county's impending approval of that development. And I'd organized the reclusive artists of neighboring Little Bucket Key into an organized artist's colony, complete with weekly residencies and monthly festivals on Hell and Dammit Cay which brought in passing tourists who wanted to take a piece of the eccentric Florida Keys back home with them.

It was a lot of work to organize all that. And it was an ongoing thing. The initial success of the art and music festival made the island into an increasingly busy place.

We'd brought in sand to improve the beach along Hell and Dammit Cay's rocky shores, and the trail riding, photoshoot, and wedding business at Sea Horse Ranch was taking off. Since I was officially in charge of barn chores and leading trail rides, the increase in business was taking a lot of my time and energy.

As for the artists, we'd built a collection of little studios amongst the sabal palms on Stacy's quadrant of the island, and each week a new artist spent a few days there dabbing or sculpting or drawing while tourists watched and bought souvenirs. It was only a few hours of time for them but it seemed to require incredible investments of *my* time in fixing their issues, which ranged from needing a new fan to not enough ice in the cooler I provided, filled with drinks and snacks each day, to easels not put away properly, to curious tourists getting too close and crowding them at their work.

And when it wasn't the businesses calling on me, it was the residents. Marchant, the old salt who lived in the blue house with a Persian cat and endless dreams of sailboats, often wanted company or to talk about wild business ventures. Crystal, who had picked me up from the side of U.S. 1 that sunny morning when I walked away from Key West and my old life as a backup singer, seemed to think my youthful energy was a bottomless well she could draw on whenever she had a new idea about fencing, or needed something from the post office, or wanted someone to give an artist a talking-to about driving too fast on their way to residency hours.

Stacy—who of all of them was the one I would have expected to be the most help, because she had run her own business as an artist successfully for so long and because she occasionally went to the mainland and interacted with non-islanders—placed every art festival question or problem in front of me. She regarded the Little Bucket Key Artist Colony as my invention and my responsibility, even though she'd been so instrumental in helping me make it happen.

And that was fine. It was all just fine.

But then there was Lou.

Was it wrong, or even surprising, that I often wished I could run away from Hell and Dammit Cay and find my own island, some outcropping of coral and mangrove I could split with Lou and no one else?

It *felt* wrong. Because I loved it here. I loved Hell and Dammit, I loved Little Bucket, I loved driving up to the main island in our community, Cutlass Key, and getting cinnamon rolls from the Slutty Mermaid, a pub so local it didn't even have a sign (to keep the tourists out), and I loved running errands to Big Pine Key or even Stock Island and occasionally, very occasionally, the big island of Key West, driving the narrow road and its many bridges across the blue-green shimmer of Florida Bay, the Gulf of Mexico, and the Straits of Florida swirling together in tropical tranquility.

I loved riding our herd of mustangs and even leading the tourists on their trail rides. I loved sunsets over the water. And I loved Lou, Crystal's son, with his menacing black beard and sensitive dark blue eyes and his brooding silences, sardonic smiles, and brilliant bursts of musical genius. I loved that we were writing an album together (or at least, we were supposed to be).

I looked down at his dark head as we emerged from the jungle and Reggie's hooves found the firm bed of crushed coral and shell which served as roads out here on the islands. There was a lingering luminescence in the air which would hang around for a while after dusk, thanks to all this shallow, clear water surrounding us. It was just enough for me to see the quiet contentment in his gaze as he glanced up at me, and I thought that tonight, at least, Lou was happy.

And that was enough to keep me happy.

For now.

Chapter Two

I KNOW, I know. Cry me a river, Katie LeBlanc. Tell me another story about how you live on a tropical island with your boyfriend, a bunch of artists, and a herd of cute ponies, and that's just tearing you apart.

I get how it sounds.

And yes, the island life is good. So good. After all, Hell and Dammit Cay is about as remote as an island can get without requiring a ferryboat, and with the waving palm trees, the shimmering blue-green waters, and the wonderful people who live here, it's a little piece of heaven on earth. The island's short strands of sand aren't exactly the glimmering white beaches your average beachcomber dreams of, but the water which gently laps against Hell and Dammit Cay's shores are crystal-clear and home to dolphins, sea turtles, wading birds, and innumerable species of fish.

We even manage to make messy human living look carefree and tropical. The four houses, once identical but now painted in their own bright colors, stand on stilts above a storm surge tide, each looking over their four quadrants of the island, all looking over the sea and the scattered out-islands through wide sliding-glass doors, which make inside and outside one and the same on breezy days. And the charming little huts recently added in the center of the island are home to colorful, eclectic works of art from Little Bucket Key's artist colony.

And of course, there are the six mustangs of Sea Horse Ranch. No, they're not native or anything—sometimes I think the only things native to Florida have scales and sharp teeth. But Crystal brought them here and hid them away in this oasis to create a beach-riding business which quickly hit a brick wall when she realized the island had no beaches...which we've recently rectified with several truckloads of sand and the right to continue using the jungle beach on Little Bucket Key.

All in all, this was the perfect secret island...and I knew I was lucky to land here. Things could have ended very differently for me. When I walked out of the gingerbread fantasy of Old Town Key West and put out my thumb along the Overseas Highway, I was definitely playing with fire. *Anything* could have happened, most of it bad. But I was depressed and not thinking clearly. I'd just been booted out of my boyfriend's band after a year on the road singing backup, all because of one booing crowd. Had it been past time to leave him and that life? Oh, without a doubt. But Katie LeBlanc's mama didn't raise a quitter.

(That's an oversimplification—my mama would have loved it if I'd given up The Bombers a lot sooner.)

Anyway, it turned out okay. I wasn't picked up by a serial killer and chopped up in bits. Instead, Crystal Linney, Lou's mom, found me and brought me back to this island to help with the horses.

And...the rest is history. That day, a part of me already knew I'd be happy to stay on Hell and Dammit Cay forever.

But forever's a long time, and the horizon was starting to look mighty appealing.

It wasn't just the responsibility. It was my itchy feet. It was the same twitch in my toes that had taken me away from the tiny Gulf-side town of St. Bart Bay, Louisiana and on the road traveling with a small-potatoes band boasting a helluva charismatic lead singer. I just hadn't expected my wanderlust to crop up again so quickly.

Not that I wanted to disappear for good, but oh, I just wanted to leave for a little while. I wanted to explore new roads, learn new tides, find new hideaways.

No, this wasn't about responsibility—not entirely—it was the pirate in me. My dad always liked to say we LeBlancs were descended from bayou privateers. We settled in St. Bart Bay to get some sleep, he'd say, but the days were for sailing the open waters of the Gulf, or exploring the hammocks and canals of the salt marshes. Maybe that was what I craved now. Instead of the open road, maybe the answer was out on the endless wave—

"Hey, LeBlanc, you getting off that pony or what?"

Shaken right out of my daydream of fair winds and far places, I looked down at Lou. In the yellow glow of the bug lights above the barn doors, his profile was sharp as a hawk's. His eyes were amused. "You wandered off on me," he said. "Go somewhere nice?"

"Yeah, I guess I did," I replied, shrugging. I slipped out of Reggie's saddle and looked around for my flip flops. They were by the feed room door, right where I'd stepped out of them earlier. I poked my feet back into them while he walked Reggie to the horse's open stall door. The other horses, already in the barn for the night, looked through the screens covering their open Dutch doors and neighed their greetings.

"Hey, babies," I told them, walking down to Reggie's stall with a horse cookie in hand for my good boy. Halfway there, though, a brilliant flash lit up the night, arresting me in my flip flops for one astonished moment. Then thunder shook the sand beneath my feet and the horses all ducked backwards from their windows, startled.

"Whoa," Lou told the horse urgently. I heard Reggie's hooves bang against the back wall and hustled back into motion. Reggie usually sensed storms before they arrived, but this one seemed to have just materialized over our heads, so he was justifiably alarmed.

Poor Reggie. Florida was like that sometimes.

"Let me hold him," I said, slipping into the stall and pulling the door closed behind me. Reggie stood in the corner, watching me with wide eyes. I showed him the cookie and his nostrils flared. He leaned forward eagerly, and as another flash of lightning illuminated the blue-green water outside his back window, he gobbled up the cookie and crunched away, his ears flicking back and forth.

"Cookies to save the day," I told Lou.

His beard split into a toothy grin as he uncinched the light saddle, tossing it over his arm and leaving me to take off Reggie's bridle. "I would work for cookies, too," he said, standing in the stall door to make sure the horse didn't spook and make a break for it.

"Finally, we found something you'd work for," I joked in reply.

Oof. Lead balloon. Lou's expression darkened, and he walked out of the stall just as the first drops of rain clanged against the metal roof.

"I know," I told Reggie as I slipped the bridle over his ears. "It's not funny when I say anything to him. Anything that implies he might not be working as hard as he should be is strictly off limits."

Reggie pushed his head against me, looking for more cookies.

"That's it," I said, patting his neck in farewell. "Eat your hay. Have a good night. Love ya mean it."

I could have stayed in his stall and poured out all my frustrations and no one would have heard; the rain was thundering down on the roof now, like someone had just dumped an enormous cosmic bucket over the island. The only thing I could hear over it was actual thunder, which was slamming around the barn with ferocity. But Reggie didn't need to hear me complaining about my boyfriend. It would put him off his feed. He was only human, after all.

So I latched the stall door behind me and pulled the screen closed, then walked along the covered aisle to the tack room, trying not to wince *too* much whenever lightning flashed. The sky was pulsing with electricity. The whole island was lit in shocking white with each streak of lightning, and the water seemed to glow with neon light. A stiff breeze whipped up and tousled my loose hair, raising goosebumps with its unexpected chill. These Keys thunderstorms could be a full sensory experience, especially at night.

Lou was in the tack room at the end of the barn, standing in the doorway and watching the rain pour off the metal roof, forming roiling pools along the edge of the aisle. He stepped aside as I approached, silently giving me enough room to shove past him. I tossed the bridle onto its hook, then turned and gave him a smack on the shoulder. "Don't sulk," I said.

"Not sulking."

"You are."

"Nope, I'm just thinking."

"About what?"

"How annoying you are when you put on your busy-bee routine.."

I crossed my arms across my chest so I didn't hit him again, because it would be for real this time. "You better apologize for that," I demanded.

He glanced down at me and I saw the crinkles around his eyes. He was hiding a smile behind that black beard of his. "Okay. I'm very, very sorry, girlfriend."

"Thanks, boyfriend." I tipped my head against his shoulder. "But maybe you could just admit you get mad every time I mention our deadline, even in passing?"

"Because we'll get it done."

"But we're so behind."

"We'll get it done. Things always get done, by the end. Haven't you noticed that?"

They got done because I did all the work.

"But what you don't understand," I began, straightening up again, "is that I won't have all day and night to do this with you when you suddenly feel like putting in the work. I have the horses, I have the artists, I have whatever else everyone on this island wants from me. So if you decided to suddenly do everything in one marathon recording session, Lou, I wouldn't be able to do that. We need to work on this album in daily sessions. Together. Or it won't get done."

He was quiet for a moment. Then he said, "I just need you to stop worrying and trust the process."

I sighed and bit back a sharp reply. This was my future career as a musician on the line. I was working on so many things for so many people all alone; I needed Lou for the one thing I really wanted for myself.

Group projects were a bitch.

Together, we watched the rain pound down. The lightning eased up a little, but the downpour only intensified. "It's getting harder," I said eventually.

"That's what she said," Lou snickered.

Okay, that deserved a punch. I buried my fist into his shoulder and he howled with mock pain. "So violent! This is abuse!"

"Don't be such a dork and bad things won't happen to you."

"What's the matter with you tonight?" He sounded hurt. Maybe I'd hit him a little too hard. Cleaning up after horses and building up beaches had me fit and strong for the first time in my life. He rubbed his arm and pouted. "When did you get so discerning about your jokes?"

"I don't know. I guess I'm just tired. Lou, I have so much going on, all the time, you know?" I felt like a broken record, repeating myself again and again. But he just didn't seem to recognize how much I was doing here. How I'd taken on the responsibility of this place, like I was mayor and city council and social worker and department of commerce all at once. No one expected anything of Lou; no one ever had. He was the prodigal son; he ran away and then he came home and Crystal killed the fatted calf, which in the Keys was grilling lobster.

The golden boy slipped his hand around mine and squeezed my fingers reassuringly. "Listen to me. Trust me. We're going to get the songs ready for recording in time."

I nodded, but I didn't believe him. We were in a rut. We had two songs ready to record. We needed at least ten. Better yet, fifteen. Lou didn't know Rivers McLean the way I did. Rivers was a nice guy, but he was savvy and wouldn't let us skate by on Lou's previous fame as anonymous indie-techno darling Silvery Star. The plan was to out Lou as part of our publicity next year…along with an album of ten to twelve *perfect* songs which blended our talents. Lou was amazing at arrangements and beats; I was a (hopefully) gifted lyricist.

I opened my mouth to say we had to buckle down and finish a song tonight, but before I could, a bolt of lightning flashed so vividly I saw stars. Thunder cracked a moment later, driving the words right out of my head.

"This is *nasty,*" Lou marveled. "And getting nastier. Wanna make a run for the house?" He craned his neck to look down the aisle. Past the barn and another few dozen feet away, the staircase of Crystal's house beckoned.

Welcoming light streamed from the windows of her yellow house on its spindly stilts, beckoning to us in the distance from behind a hedge of fuchsia-blooming bougainvillea. But there were at least forty feet of exposed, flat ground and a staircase of slippery wooden steps standing between us and safety.

"Ugh, I don't know," I said. "Maybe it would be safer to just stay here."

Then, I heard an odd ping.

"What was that?" I looked around. "Was that your phone?"

Lou plucked his phone from his pocket. "Huh," he said, flicking at the message on the screen. I watched his face as his brows came together. "Uh-oh."

"What? What is it?"

"It's a marine warning," Lou said, "And it's *really* localized."

I took out my phone just as it got the memo and pinged as well. I read the message. "Lou, why does this specifically say 'Hell and Dammit Cay' on it?"

"It's amazing what radar does these days," Lou said, squinting into the dark rain. He looked across the island, towards Marchant's side of the island. "A waterspout just south of Hell and Dammit Cay means it's right over there, I guess?"

Waterspouts are just tornadoes on water, and I don't mess with them. I started running, confident Lou would follow. Maybe heading for a house wasn't the best idea; maybe we should have stayed in the barn, which was at least all on the ground level instead of high up on stilts. Bad in a storm surge, good in a wind storm. But everything in me was screaming, *Get inside, get inside!* So I ran away.

But I was met at the foot of the steps, rain streaming down my face, by Crystal. Wearing cut-offs and a faded pink tank top, flip flops on her feet and nothing at all over her faded yellow hair, she screwed up her lined face at me and said, "We got to get to

Marchant's dock! The old fool was out on his boat, and I don't know if he got back before this storm."

"He was *sailing?*" Lou demanded. "After dark?"

I had no words. Only speed; I was faster than Crystal, so I turned and raced across the island, abandoning my own cheap flip flops somewhere along the way.

Chapter Three

I HEARD THE waterspout before I saw it, a horrible rushing, sucking sound that didn't make sense to my brain. Around me the wind rose sharply, then fell off again, in short, strange gasps. As I pelted through the scruffy grass between Marchant's house and the water, lightning lit the sea in front of me and there it was.

A thin, ghostly finger of pale water stretching from the surface of the earth clear up to the heavens, its base rimmed with white mist as it trailed through the water, heading back out to sea.

The lightning gave me just a half-second to absorb the sight before it was lost in the darkness again. I was glad I couldn't see it. I didn't want to see that again. Not ever. Not so close to land, anyway, Maybe way out to sea. Going away. Quickly.

I stumbled to a halt right before my bare feet slapped on the wooden planks of Marchant's dock and stared into the rainy night. Now I wanted to know where it was. I could hear it; I could feel it— a burst of cold wind seemed to shove me forward, and I slipped on the wet dock. Lightning flashed again and revealed the waterspout was zipping away from us at a serious clip now. And I also saw

Marchant, sprawled on the dock next to his sailboat. Whether he'd fallen on slippery boards or collapsed from shock or injury was immaterial. I was off again, running, with Lou and Crystal panting just behind me.

I dropped to my knees next to Marchant, but before I could check his pulse, Lou and Crystal were lifting him by the arms. I went with their program, grabbing his feet, and the three of us hustled him back to land. He wasn't a heavy old man, our Marchant; he was seventy years old and while he was incredibly hearty for his age, he'd still thinned with age. His mop of curly white hair was plastered to his head by the downpour, his stubbly beard was dripping, his breath came quiet and so slow it frightened me.

But he was a salt of the first order, and when we draped him over his dark blue sofa, Marchant woke and began to splutter, first in astonishment and then in annoyance as we wrapped him in layers of towels and blankets. Crystal was eager to swaddle her old friend like a baby and I let her lead the way; no one else here had known Marchant as long or as well as she did. She held down his arms and shoved a pale blue duvet over his chest and he finally subsided, while his Persian cat, Bluebeard, purred heroically in his lap, putting up with his foul mood like a nurse dealing with a difficult patient.

Finally, Crystal was satisfied he was too trussed up to escape and sat down on the sofa next to him. She folded her arms across her chest and gave him an icy glare, saying, "You shoulda come in before the weather blew in and that's all there is to it."

"I was *heading* in," he protested, his rusty voice squeaking a little. "That storm blew up outta nowhere."

Crystal was unconvinced. "No storm blows outta nowhere, you've said it yourself. There's always signs."

"Well, I couldn't see the signs. It was *dark*."

"And what were you doing out in the dark?"

"Heavens, woman, I wanted to look at the stars!" Marchant blustered.

"The *stars,*" Crystal mocked, not giving him an inch. "You old fool. You coulda seen the stars from your damn porch."

"Not like out on the water," he asserted. "It's different on the water and you'd know if you ever went out with me."

Crystal waved a dismissive hand. "I don't need to go out there to look at the sky. I got all the sky I need right here."

"Well, I do," Marchant asserted. "I like it out there."

They looked at each other for a moment, their argument already out of steam. Keeping Marchant off the water would be like keeping the sun out of the sky.

I glanced over at Lou, eyebrows raised: *Can you believe these two?*

He shrugged in reply, but his eyes were twinkling with suppressed laughter. Fair enough; we'd spent enough time giggling about the dynamic between these two in the past. I just didn't think tonight's circumstances were very funny.

"Marchant," I asked suddenly, "what happened to you out there?"

He looked at me from beneath bushy brows. "I slipped and fell. All that wind—"

"If the waterspout turned towards the island, you'd be dead," Crystal snapped. "And we'd all be dead for chasing after you."

"Woman, I coulda handled myself!"

Crystal snorted and looked around the room at us: *Can you believe this guy?*

A lot of annoyed looks were going around tonight, but no one was addressing the real issue. At least, not as I saw it.

I chewed at my lip, gathering the courage to ask, then finally just letting it all out in a rush. "Um, have you considered it's not safe for you to sail alone?"

Everyone's eyes swiveled to me, and I felt my cheeks warm. Had I really just asked that? Did I really just imply Marchant shouldn't be sailing without some kind of minder? I'd better watch myself, or I'd be right back out on U.S. 1 with my thumb up.

Crystal shook her head at me.

"Of all the absurd—!" Marchant was red in the face behind his fuzz of white whiskers. "For God's sake, all of you, *all* I did was stay out to sea a little too long. That storm wasn't on the radar when I went out. Wasn't even thought of. It blowed up outta nowhere. Ask anyone. Ask the dag-gone Coast Guard fella I saw out there, toodling around in his speedboat tryin' ta catch some drug dealers. *He* didn't see it comin', neither."

"Well, I guess I will ask him!" Crystal snapped. "Who was it you saw, was it Pat?"

"I don't know who it was," Marchant replied sulkily. "Looked like a new guy."

"Oh, I wonder if they transferred Pat." Crystal was distracted now. "He was saying it might be time. Guess we oughta head down to the Mermaid and catch up on news."

"Who's Pat?" I asked, befuddled by the rapid change in conversation—but definitely relieved the focus wasn't on me anymore.

"Our local Coast Guard man," Crystal replied. "I mean, there are a lot, but Pat's the one who sees to our area. The Coast Guard are like the cops here. They sneak around after druggies, look out for Cuban rafts, that kinda thing. Sometimes a party boat catches fire and they go out and rescue the people on board."

Marchant barked with laughter. "Remember when those Yanks from Boston took out that pontoon boat into a tropical depression? Squall dang near flipped them over and their booze blew overboard? Boy, they was glad to see a Coast Guard boat!"

"Pat dragged them in, but then he took them out the next day and made them pick up all the bottles that washed ashore," Crystal laughed. "Oh, that was funny! I bet they never come back here again!"

"Here's hoping," Marchant snorted, slapping his knee. "Dang old fools!"

My eyes met Lou's once more, and he lifted his eyebrows. There was nothing old Conchs like Marchant and Crystal bonded over quite like fool tourists from up north. Looked like they'd already forgotten their fight. And my gaffe of a comment about sailing alone. So much the better. I decided to beat a retreat while I was still ahead.

"Well," I announced, standing up. "I guess I'll be heading home. It's late and I'm tired. Crystal, we have three riders at two o'clock tomorrow, right?"

"It mighta been two riders at three," she said. "Better check the appointment book. It's in the kitchen."

"Right." I glanced at the brass ship's clock on the living room wall. Ten past nine—how did it get so late? I still needed a shower, something to eat, and hopefully a few minutes to hear what Lou had worked on today. If anything.

With any luck, I might get five or six hours of sleep before I got up to feed the horses and start all over again.

It would have to be enough.

"Marchant, I'm glad you're okay," I called, heading for the door to the porch.

"I'm fine," he replied. "An old salt like me is bound to get caught in a few gales from time to time."

"Or waterspouts," Crystal said mildly.

"Or waterspouts." Suddenly, Marchant's bravado seemed to drop. His jaw sagged and his eyelids drooped as he looked at the floor.

"Y'know, for a moment there, I thought I was getting sucked right into the sky."

"We *all* thought that," Crystal reminded him crossly.

"I looked past that old spout and out to sea and I thought I was goin' to my grave," Marchant went on. "Too soon, though. Too soon. I've still got things I want to do."

"Of course you do," I said soothingly. "Which is why we want you to take care—"

"The sailboat lodge," he said. "Crystal, you remember that old idea? Put some boats out on the water, have folks to stay overnight, teach them to sail and love the water? Like what you do with the ponies out there. I always wanted to do that. Never found the way. Too late, now."

Crystal shifted on the sofa, her jaw crossing as she thought. "It would be a big undertaking," she offered finally.

"Nah, we couldn't do it," Marchant sighed with regret. "That's the sort of thing you gotta have a lot of money and experience and time for, and I ain't got a single one of those things."

"You have plenty of time," Crystal told him. "Time ain't your problem."

He grinned at her. "Woman, I'm seventy years old. Time is definitely a problem!"

"Oh, you're a young seventy," she said, waving a hand at him. "Practically sixty-five!"

"That's true," Marchant reflected. "Must be all the salt in the air. Preserved my old bones. Well," he went on, brightening, "maybe I can still do it, then. Maybe I can!"

Well, maybe Marchant had plenty of time to start a hotel on a couple of boats, but I sure didn't. I edged out of the living room, thinking of tomorrow's agenda.

"You're a fool for a boat," Crystal told Marchant as I went out the door.

"I know it," Marchant replied, almost sadly.

I paused, my hand on the sliding glass door's handle as he continued, "and all I ever wanted to do was share that feeling with someone else."

I slipped and skidded down the steps, which needed pressure washed. I added it to my mental list, then went straight back to thinking about Marchant's oddly emotional line about sharing his love of boats.

He didn't mean sharing that feeling romantically, although we'd all had our guesses about Marchant and Crystal. They'd be adorable together. But she was an avowed singleton, averse to talking about the disappearance of Lou's father ("He was no good anyway, I shoulda known he'd never stick around.") and uninterested in the attentions of various Conchs who bought her beers at the Slutty Mermaid ("All these men have to offer a woman are fish guts and dirty dishes.") If Crystal had ever been in love, she didn't seem very interested in repeating the adventure.

No, when he talked about sharing his love of all things related to the sea, Marchant was talking about his dream of his hotel.

And now I had a new problem to chew on as I picked my way between the sharp seashells on the sandy path between our houses. Because, of course, my brain wouldn't just let go of this. I couldn't just move on. Didn't have enough to do. No, I needed to zero-focus on this kind man's fondest wish, and figure out how to make it happen.

But was there even any point?

I mean, Marchant wanted to start a *sailboat* hotel. I never heard of such a thing before he first mentioned it, but I'd done a little casual research since then and found that renting nights on sailboats wasn't that uncommon. You anchored the boat and provided an inflatable to get to it, or you had it tied up at a dock for easy access, and you filled the cupboards and provided housekeeping and boom, people spent the night on your boat and felt very island-y and bohemian about their vacation choices.

What Marchant wanted to do was in that vein: anchor two or three sailboats just off his dock, keep folks overnight in them, and perhaps teach them to sail—or merely let them appreciate the pleasures of sleeping on the quiet waters of Florida Bay. He did it himself quite often, bunking down in his boat instead of upstairs in the house, with Bluebeard disapprovingly stalking along the deck, keeping watch.

It sounded kooky to me, but I suppose I shouldn't have been quick to judge. After all, I was here to tend a herd of horses on a tiny island; additionally, I had personally overseen the construction of multiple temporary artist studios to convince the outside world we were a legitimate artist's colony. Something in the air or the water of the Florida Keys made the kooky into the normal. Nothing expected ever happened here. Just crazy, unsuitable, wild things which fascinated tourists and made every day a bit of an adventure.

Sometimes *too* much adventure, I thought wearily, climbing the stairs to Crystal's house. And that was why it was confusing when every day seemed so much the same. Like all the kooky adventures bled into one. Maybe what I was really missing was boredom, a touch of normalcy.

"Not likely," I muttered, letting myself into the house.

Lou and his mother came upstairs while I was in the shower. When I heard their voices in the living room, I quickly toweled off and pulled on a bathrobe, hoping Lou would set up his laptop and synths to show off some work from the day. I was annoyed to see him sitting at the rattan breakfast table near the kitchen window, playing with his phone and drinking a beer.

"Lou, I was hoping you had some music for me tonight," I said, looking around for Crystal. But the light under her closed door indicated she'd already gone in for the night. Good. That gave me more room to talk to her son the way I wanted to. "Didn't you say before you'd have some work done every day—"

"I don't today," he interrupted. "Sorry."

"But what's the hold-up? I'm sorry, I just don't understand." I took a beer from the fridge and sat across from him, tapping his hand. He didn't look up from his phone. I tried again, evening my tone as best I could. "Lou, I don't want to repeat myself over and over, but if I'm going to manage everything on the island the way I have been, you *have* to be responsible for taking the lead on the music. We have a contract. We have deadlines. These things can't be moved—"

"Are you worried I'll sink your musical career, Katie?" He glanced up at me, his expression amused. "Is your ticket to fame not as certain as you thought?"

"Well, it would be nice if you at *least* did your share!" I retorted.

"It's not that simple," he said. "Sorry. Guess I can't be your free ride after all."

The *free ride* part annoyed me, but it was the *after all* that scared me. "What are you talking about?"

He got up and went into the kitchen, his back to me. He looked like a big, lumbering bear who didn't want to be bothered before hibernation.

Well, nice try. I happened to *love* bothering bears. If by bears we are talking about my broad-shouldered, moody boyfriend.

"Lou," I persisted, getting up and going after him. "Lou, please tell me what's going on, babe. I can help."

Of course I could help. I helped everyone, all the time.

"Please ask my mom," he sighed. "I don't want to talk about it. Even with you."

"No, I'm not going to ask your mom," I informed him crossly. "You're twenty-seven years old and you can tell me your own problems."

Lou's eyes flicked to the kitchen counter, and I saw, amongst the junk mail and bills scattered there, a square envelope. The kind a greeting card would come in. I picked it up. The envelope was still sealed. "This? An unopened card is the problem keeping you from fulfilling our contractual obligations?"

He looked at the tiles.

I glanced over the return address. "Wait—is this—"

"It's from him," Lou said gruffly, his eyes suddenly glittering. Tears? Oh, surely not tears. "It's from my *dad*."

"Oh!" The syllable that escaped my lips was involuntary; I knew no one talked about Lou's father. I knew no one expected him to show up again. I knew no one wanted him or missed him. But maybe that last assumption was incorrect. Lou might have wanted a father many times—and knowing there was one out there, one who wasn't willing to raise him or be there for him, must have been awful. I faltered for real words, but instead I just reached out, took his hand, and gripped it tightly.

"I haven't opened it," he said, looking at the envelope.

"I can see that. Do you want me to?"

"It's not even addressed to me. It's to Mom."

"Does she know about it?"

"I don't know. Yes? Probably? I brought home the mail and left it here; that was hours ago."

I looked at her closed bedroom door. "Maybe that's why she went to bed early. And why she was so ready to fight with Marchant."

Lou freed his hand from mine and snatched at the offending envelope. "I'm going to open it."

"You don't want to open her mail."

"I do," Lou said, his eyes still glittering dangerously, and he ripped open the envelope.

Chapter Four

THE NEWS IN the card didn't go over very well with Lou. Which was probably the real reason Crystal left it and went to bed early. Not because she didn't want to face the return of her ex. Because she didn't want to face *Lou* when he found out.

I couldn't really blame her for hiding in her bedroom, either, and leaving Lou to me. She'd already done the hard work of raising her moody son alone. I guess she figured if I signed on for girlfriend, I could take up some of the tough stuff. And sometimes with Lou, it felt like it was *all* tough stuff. But he was worth it.

Most of the time.

Tonight, there was simply no dealing with him. He took out the card, read the message, and put it down. Then he went into *his* room and shut the door. Quietly, not slamming it. But I must say the slam felt implied, and maybe if Crystal hadn't gone to bed, he would have shaken the whole house down. But one thing I will say for Lou, he wouldn't wake his mother.

And then there I was, alone in the kitchen, while the two Linneys hid beneath their covers.

So much for hearing any new music tonight.

I sighed and picked up the card. A cartoon manatee sunning itself on a beach on the front; inside, just a few lines: *Hello Crystal, I hope you don't mind if I come by now that I'm back in Florida. See you sometime in July? - Arnie.*

My fingers tightened on the thick paper. No mention of Lou. No apology for disappearing twenty-some years ago. Not even a phone number to stop him from coming. Just planning to drop by as if he was an old neighbor passing through on his way to Key West.

For a moment, I was as angry as Lou was.

Then I made myself shake it off. I couldn't join the pitchfork and torch crowd. It wasn't my battle to fight. I had to be the quiet, logical one.

As usual.

Man, the way my parents would laugh if they knew I was the level-headed one on Hell and Dammit Cay!

They were pretty impressed with the work I'd done here, though, so maybe their impressions of me were already changing for the better. No one had been happy with me for leaving St. Bart's Bay to be a backup singer. And they hadn't exactly been thrilled to learn I was masquerading as a ranch-hand on a tiny Floridian island. But the news of the festival, and the way I'd saved our islands from development, had gone over very well.

I thought about them for a moment, just happy that I had a nice normal family dynamic—a mom and dad who generally liked each other, the ability to go back for holidays but without the need to live at home—then took out my phone and tapped a quick message to my mom.

Been too long! Love you Mom!

Her reply bubble appeared immediately, as I knew it would. I could picture where she was at this very moment. She was sitting in the living room, in her favorite spot on the cushy old sofa I'd grown up with. Iced tea on the table, an ignored murder mystery on the TV. Candy Crush on the phone. Dad drowsing in his easy chair. A scene so aggressively normal, so classically typical, it almost hurt to live with—but it was nice, at the same time, to keep as a memory of home.

Her reply was characteristically kind: *Love you baby girl! How's your island?*

A smile creased my lips. *My* island. How things had changed. Six months ago,   before Hell and Dammit Cay, she would have responded with something like, "You coming home yet, daughter?" She wasn't a fan of my choice to follow the leather-clad Justin around the country, playing small clubs and festivals with his band.

In her defense, it hadn't been my best choice. But at least it had led me here. To a found family I loved as much as my biological one—how many people could say they had two wonderful families?—and to Lou.

I looked at his closed door again. The light was out. With a sigh, I typed, *Everything is great! Just thinking of you.*

Maybe everything was not great, but it was close enough. For now.

The options had been two riders at three o'clock, or three riders at two; the appointment book had been inconclusive. (Crystal had just written *TRAIL RIDE* across the boxes from noon to four.) What I got was two riders at two o'clock, while I was still grooming the horses we'd need. I had five horses in the barn—three for the potential riders, one for me as a guide, one for Lou as the tail. I liked to have a tail, so no one disappeared in the jungle or went for a gallop down the shell road through Little Bucket Key. The last kind of publicity we needed was a runaway horse racing up the Overseas Highway, with or without their rider still in the saddle.

Two lanky kids jumped out of an SUV, but their parents kept driving, rolling up to the parking area for the artist studios. Another kiddie-ride situation. This happened a lot; my website skills were not advanced, but I had figured out how to deny a reservation without anyone over eighteen years of age on the booking. In turn, parents just paid for a spot and then didn't take it.

Not a problem; I'd take them out as long as at least one of them was over age thirteen and seemed in control of the other. These two, red-headed and close in age, looked fairly sedate. I checked the mobile sign-up app I'd put together for the trail rides, found the parents had already signed releases and paid online, and then waved the kids over.

"Justine," the girl said, walking over. She glanced at her brother. "And Carter."

Justine, huh? I hid a wince; that was still painfully close to my ex's name. "Hey, you two," I said, getting it together. "Have you ridden horses before?"

"Yeah," Justine said authoritatively. "I can ride horses, like, really good. And Carter is okay."

"I'm better than *okay*," he insisted. "I'm really good, too."

"Well, if you're really good, we can canter," I told him. "And if you're making it up, we'll find out really fast."

"How?" Carter asked, suspicious.

"You'll fall off," I said. "And we'll make you walk home."

Both kids seemed to think this was fair.

I put the ponies in cross-ties underneath the stable overhang and let the kids go over them with brushes; I found assigning grooming duty was usually a good test of the riders who claimed they were experienced enough to canter on the beach. There was only room for a dozen or so strides of canter, so running away wasn't an issue, but flopping out of the saddle could be if a person didn't know how to ride the back-and-forth, rocking-horse gait. We sometimes got experienced riders who didn't know how to groom, but more often we got non-riders who claimed they were experienced horse-people, then backed away when confronted with a curry comb.

Justine set aside a glass Coca-Cola bottle she'd had jutting from her back jeans pocket and reached for the brush box.

"Where'd you get the glass bottle Cokes?" I asked, curious. My ex, Justin, had always been going on about Mexican Coke in glass bottles. But he was something of a snob. I only drank Diet Coke and since I'd come to Hell and Dammit, hardly ever saw soda unless it was going into one of Stacy's impeccably crafted cocktails.

"We stopped at the Slutty Mermaid," she explained, giving her brother a pointed look. Carter smirked back at her. She grinned. "I shouldn't have asked the name of the place, I guess. My parents weren't too pleased."

"You actually went inside?" I was impressed with her bravado— her entire family's, in fact. Few tourists were brave enough to open the windowless door of the long, nondescript building alongside U.S. 1. It was the only business on Cutlass Key, but there was no sign out front, or any way of knowing what was inside. Tourists sped past, never giving the faceless business a second glance.

And the natives liked it that way; otherwise, the local bar and grill would be swarmed with out-of-towners pretending to be real, local Conchs on their drive to and from Key West, and obviously that would kill the local vibe. The Slutty Mermaid was a Lower Keys institution, and the rarest of endangered species: a roadside bar the tourists hadn't found. Yet.

"Well, I had to pee," Justine said, picking up a curry comb and giving Ruby a pat on the neck. The red-and-white mare regarded her with quiet approval. Justine began to brush her, adding, "We didn't know if there would be anyplace to go here. And there were cars parked out front. It was clearly open for business. Why? Should I not have gone in? Did I break a rule?"

"Not really," I admitted. "I just know it looks kind of scary from the outside."

"Seriously," Carter piped up. "Haven't they ever heard of a sign?"

"They don't want to be found," I said, setting the saddles out on the racks by the cross-ties. "Locals only. I don't even go alone. I guess I haven't lived here long enough to feel like I belong."

"Wow, I had no idea." Justine picked up a body brush and paused by Ruby's head, letting the mare lip at her fingers. "Will she bite me?" she asked, forgetting all about the Slutty Mermaid. "Can I give her a sugar cube or something?"

"We have horse cookies for afterwards," I assured her. "I'll get the saddles on and we'll head out as soon as you're done grooming."

"Almost done," Carter called, brushing Bart frantically. The gelding snoozed on the end of the cross-ties, letting the ropes hold up his head.

"No rush," I said. "Y'all were here early."

"Oh, that's our mom's fault," Justine informed me airily. "She wanted to see the mermaid art lady."

Well, that explained while the adults went straight on to the studios.

With the children momentarily occupied, I sent a text to Lou, hoping he was awake. I hadn't seen him all day, but he was supposed to come down and lead this ride with me. We always liked to have two out-riders when possible, a guide and a tail, to make sure no one got into trouble while out of our watchful gaze. He'd probably set an alarm to come downstairs right at three and help me out, but there was no way I was going to amuse these two on the ground for an hour. We were going to get tacked up and get out on the jungle trail as soon as they were done grooming.

The ride is already here, I tapped. *Come down and let's get them mounted.*

The text sat on delivered. I watched and watched, willing for the message to change to *read*.

Nothing.

I sighed, perhaps a tad dramatically.

Justine looked up with interest. "Is there a problem?" she asked hopefully, sensing something interesting was up with the perfect radar of a teen.

"No problem," I said. "What do you think of Ruby?"

"I love her," Justine said, leaning her head against Ruby's neck. The mare's dark chestnut mane fell around the teen's red hair and made them look like two of a kind. "I can't wait to ride you, Ruby!"

Carter wanted to be included. "Bart, Bart, I love you, Bart!" He pressed his face against Bart's nose and the horse snorted. "Oh, Bart, gross!"

I liked these kids. They definitely knew their way around horses. "Okay, you two," I said. "I'm going to grab my horse and get him ready."

Reggie was waiting at his paddock gate, ears trained on me as I approached. I knew it was the carrot in my hand he was excited for, but I pretended his low nicker and eager expression were because he enjoyed my company so much. "At least someone does," I told him, slipping his halter on. "Goodness knows my boyfriend doesn't seem keen on me now."

Just normal grumps, I thought, for someone who hasn't seen their significant other since the night before. When they live in the same house.

The kids were all ready to tack up their horses. I tied Reggie and sent Lou another text, even though the first one was still unread.

Then I looked around, craning my neck to see if his blinds were open.

"Looking for someone?" Justine asked. "Can we tack up? What's wrong? Can't we start yet?"

A lot of questions.

"Just waiting on Lou," I said. "My partner."

"Lou..." She looked at me closely, pressing a finger to his chin as if she was trying to recall something. "Wait a minute, do you mean Lou *Linney?*"

I was too surprised to keep a poker face.

Justine's jaw dropped. "Lou *Linney* of *Silvery Star?*"

"How on earth did you know that?" I protested.

"Because I heard Monica talking about him! It's him? The rock star?"

"No, he's not a—wait, who is Monica?" And why was she talking about my boyfriend to this teenager?

"The bartender," Justine explained eagerly. "At the Slutty Mermaid. After I peed and I went to pay for the Cokes. She asked where we were going and I said Sea Horse Ranch, and she said, oh where Lou Linney lives, and I said I guess so, and she said oh you don't know him, and I said no never heard of him and she said, do you know Silvery Star, and I was like, of course—"

"That's fine, I got it." I held up a hand. Reggie mistook it for my cue to back up and I hustled to stop them before he used up the slack in the cross-ties and panicked. And just then, Lou arrived.

He was wearing his saltwater cowboy outfit, blue jeans and Hawaiian shirt and red neckerchief under a sand-colored Stetson. I liked Lou best as a sunburned Conch, in cut-offs and t-shirt, but there was no doubt he wore this costume very well and at the sight of him, Justine just about melted into a little puddle next to Ruby's hooves.

I couldn't really blame her. When Lou dressed up nice, whether in a slim-cut suit for a business meeting or in a pressed button-down shirt and good shorts for a trip to Key West or like this, for a trail ride with clients, he really brought his A-game. I mean, there was nothing wrong with Lou in salt-stained khaki shorts and a tattered old t-shirt, but the man cleaned up entirely too well for his own good.

Certainly for *my* own good.

As for poor Justine, she was too young for this display of rampant male sexuality. I wanted to tell him to go back upstairs and put on one of those awful old t-shirts he wore around the ranch for chores.

"Y'all talking about Monica?" he drawled, in an accent that wasn't his. "Thought I heard someone say her name."

"You know this person?" I struggled to keep my voice neutral. "I didn't know there was a new girl at the Slutty Mermaid."

Carter tittered. Justine shot him a look.

"Forget it," I told them. "Carter and Justine, saddles on. Then, let's go get pictures and then get you mounted, okay? Lou will tack up Reggie and his horse, then we'll all go out."

I always enjoyed our trail rides, but on this one, all I could think about was the new girl at the Slutty Mermaid. For the first time, I realized I hadn't talked to another woman my own age in months. And now, I was hoping this bartender, Monica, was worth talking to.

And also that she didn't have any unrealistic ideas about Lou. If she knew so much about him, she knew he was taken, right?

Would that stop her from making a move?

After all, there wasn't anyone our age in this cluster of islands at all. If she'd showed up hoping for a Florida Keys fling, she must be sadly disappointed by the gray-beards and mid-life crises propping up the bar in the dark recesses of the Slutty Mermaid. This little outpost of the Lower Keys was no Key West, and we liked it that way...but I was starting to see how the average age of the local citizens could weigh down a person under thirty.

Huh. Maybe that was where my itchy feet were coming from. Maybe I just needed a night out now and then, not a whole change of latitude, the way I'd been thinking lately.

We reached the beach on Little Bucket Key, and the kids squealed with delight, the way I knew they would. Lou and I reined back our horses and sat them in the shade of a banyan tree while the kids took Bart and Ruby into the rippling waves. His brooding silence next to me seemed to drown out the splashing water and the kids' laughter. I tried to wait him out. I was good at waiting him out.

I...couldn't take it anymore.

"Lou," I ventured, "you think you might want to drive up to Cutlass Key later and have a drink?"

He turned his head slowly and raised his eyebrows at me in slow motion, for maximum dramatic effect, before drawling, "I thought we were imprisoned on this island until you were satisfied with the amount of work we produced."

I bit my lower lip. "Seriously? That's what you think of me asking you to do your job?"

And, we were fighting already.

"I write music when it feels good. You can't force it."

"Oh, don't give me that old 'the spirit has to move me' bullshit," I sighed. "Justin liked to say that, too, but it doesn't pay any bills, Lou."

"I don't exist to make sure your old pal Rivers is making money."

"This is not about Rivers," I bit out. "Although he *is* giving us a chance when he doesn't have to—"

"Giving *us* a chance?"

So rude. I would have loved to have reached over with both hands and shoved him out of the saddle. I was mad enough that I was pretty sure I could do it, too. But with the kids here, I had to behave. So I just sniped, "I didn't realize you had a record deal for a second Silvery Star album," and grinned when his brows came together. Score one for Katie.

"Maybe I wasn't in a hurry to put out another record, anyway," he said. "I could probably make more money if I DIY'd it, you know."

"You're ignoring the point," I informed him. "Which is that I asked you if you wanted to go get a drink. At the Mermaid. We don't even have to turn onto U.S. 1 to get there."

"We can get a drink," Lou agreed amiably, further frustrating me —why hadn't he just said that in the first place? Why the song and dance? "But first, maybe we better rescue the boy."

He nodded at the beach, where the drama was going down.

"Oh dammit," I swore, nudging Reggie into motion. Bart was buckling his knees in preparation for a roll in the water, and Carter was tucking himself into a tiny ball on top of the nylon saddle, his face screwing up in anticipation of certain death. "Just hang on a second and jump off if he goes down," I bellowed. "You're gonna be fine!"

Chapter Five

"Do you really *know* her?" I demanded.

Lou shook his head. "Just heard about her."

I eyed the new bartender and wondered if he was telling the truth.

Monica was everything you could ask for in a bartender at a roadside bar on a lonely out-island. Dangerously pretty, with dark beach-bum curls cascading down her back, a slightly upturned nose sprinkled with freckles, deeply tanned skin and a surfer's long, lean muscles. She was wearing cropped black leggings and a loose tank top, which sagged suggestively when she leaned over the bar.

Which, I was surprised to notice, I could actually *see*.

The few other times I'd come into the Slutty Mermaid, it had been nearly pitch-dark inside and patrons had been serving themselves from behind the bar. Now there were lights—dim lights, but lights nonetheless—and with the prospect of being served by a human, I realized an air of normalcy had invaded the previously anarchic local bar. No wonder Justine had felt comfortable enough to come inside when she'd opened the door this afternoon.

"Afternoon," Monica said cheerfully as we sat down at the bar. "What can I get for you?"

I noticed she didn't recognize Lou. So, she'd been repeating what someone else had told her when she'd informed Justine that a famous rock star lived at Sea Horse Ranch. I wondered who it had been. Not that I knew everyone around here or anything, but these islands were the kinds of places where folks kept their secrets. The Keys weren't known for being particularly law-abiding, after all. People knew not to ask too many questions.

I guessed Monica had the kind of pretty face that could get away with acting a little too curious, and none too discreet.

Lou ordered a couple of draft beers and I smiled and nodded, simultaneously agreeing with his order and making sure Monica realized we were a couple. She gave me a careful once-over before pulling glasses from beneath the bar.

Grudging respect. I'd accept it.

Then I said, "You must be Monica."

She glanced at me from beneath a strand of lusciously curling hair. "I sure am. But I don't know your name."

"Katie," I said. "And this is Lou." I watched her closely for a reaction.

Sure enough, her hand bounced just a little on the beer tap. But she recovered herself neatly, putting two pint glasses in front of us before she let her curious gaze stray to Lou. She took in his dark beard and thundercloud expression, then glanced back at me. I resisted running a hand through my hair, trying to flatten the flyaways. I knew it was frizzy; it was always frizzy. The real question was, why *wasn't* Monica's hair standing on end? What did she know about humidity and hair that I didn't?

She set beers before us and then took a sip from her own. "Nice to meet y'all." Her southern drawl was smooth, not overpowering—like sweet and unsweet tea mixed in the same glass. "I'm still just getting to know the locals around here."

"How do you know we're locals?" I challenged.

Lou shot me a questioning look.

Monica just shrugged, unconcerned with the edge to my tone. "You just have that look," she said sweetly. "Also, you have a streak of something on your arm that looks like a horse was rubbing on your arm, so I guessed you were from the little horse ranch down the road."

Lou guffawed while I swiped ineffectually at the long, greenish-black mark on my upper arm. Reggie must have rubbed his nose on me and left a surprise for later. Nice of Lou to mention it. Maybe he was a little *too* used to my being covered in horse dirt.

"You know about horses," Lou said once he'd stopped snickering at me. "You'll fit right in. Come down to Sea Horse Ranch some time."

"I'd like that," Monica replied, giving him a dazzling smile. "When I get a day off, maybe I will. This job is pretty much my whole life right now, though. I'm not complaining! I'm happy to have it. But eventually someone else is gonna have to cover the bar so I can get up to the grocery store and stop living on chicken wings."

She didn't look like living on chicken wings was hurting her any. But maybe that was just the jealousy talking. I studied her perfect skin. No, not jealousy. She was just beautiful.

Lou was saying something about the Slutty Mermaid never having bartenders.

"It was running fine," he said. "Wasn't it?"

"Maybe it was losing a little money," Monica suggested, lifting her eyebrows. "I hear Conchs are just as honest as they have to be, but they're not above borrowing a few beers between friends. Well, they borrowed a couple too many, apparently."

"So you're the new cop on the island," I said.

Lou and Monica both gave me an identical look. It said, *Really?* Nothing else.

Yes, really, I told them telepathically, and then aloud I said, "So how did *you* get the job?"

"Through a friend of a friend of a friend," Monica said, shrugging. "The last one in the chain is the owner of this place."

Lou looked up. "Really? Who's the owner of the Mermaid?"

"Arnie Morehead," Monica finished. "You know him?"

I shook my head, but my reaction must have gone unnoticed. Because when Lou pushed back his barstool with an ear-splitting screech, every head in the bar swiveled to see what was going on. And we all watched in silence as Lou went storming out of the bar, silhouetted momentarily against the gleaming golden sunset outside, and then let the door slam behind him.

"Well, damn," Monica said after a moment, surprised but not particularly upset. "What climbed up his backside?"

"I don't know," I lied, still blinking at the closed door. I heard a truck door slam and the sputtering motor of Lou's truck. "But I think I'm just about to get abandoned here," I added, sliding my purse strap over my shoulder.

Before I could reach the door, though, the sound of gravel under tires told me Lou was already gone.

Monica followed me to the door, and we watched the truck hurtle west. He was going the wrong way. The turnoff to Little Bucket Key was to the left of the Slutty Mermaid's sandy lot. So why did Lou turn right? Where could he be going? There wasn't much between us and Key West. If he actually went down to the Southernmost City, after all the whining he'd done at me earlier...

"Does he know Arnie?" Monica asked, her husky voice cutting into my irritated thoughts. "Maybe they don't get along? I know he never comes down here anymore."

"They don't get along," I said grimly, remembering the name on the card. "I can't tell you why. It's not my story to tell and I don't know the half of it, anyway."

"Well, damn." Monica sounded genuinely regretful, possibly because there was some juicy gossip out in the world she couldn't access. "I feel really bad for upsetting him."

"Oh, you couldn't have known, not with him." Suddenly, I felt more charitable towards Monica. Maybe because it was just nice having another woman my age around, especially when Lou was acting like a bear with a sore head. "All I know for sure is, now I'm going to have to walk the whole way back to Hell and Dammit Cay. I better get going."

"Oh, don't walk," Monica said. "I'm getting off work in half an hour and I'll drive you home. This place closes itself still." She laughed. "It's the craziest place I've ever been, but I like it."

"Are you sure? You probably live in the opposite direction."

"I kind of do, yeah. I found a little place to rent further up Cutlass," she admitted. "But it's only a couple of miles back to your island, and I don't mind, really. I admit I've been curious about the place, anyway."

"It's nice," I admitted, following her back inside. "Very small. Just about enough room for the houses and the horses and the artist fairs on weekends."

"How did Lou Linney end up there?"

I glanced at her as she took up her post behind the bar. "How long have you wanted to ask that?"

She had the grace to look down, swiping a cloth along the bar. It was already the least sticky it had been in years; the damn thing would probably fall apart without old drink rings holding it together. Her voice was low when she finally replied, "I'm sorry. When he hired me, Arnie told me not to pry into the locals' lives. But I live here, too. How long until I'm a local?"

I sighed. Because I liked her, despite her blatant curiosity. Despite how pretty she was. She was so beautiful, I thought, feeling just a little despondent about it. Beautiful girls were hard to trust. Or maybe it was just my experiences on the road that had convinced me of that. It was a cutthroat world out there in the realm of small-time rock clubs.

Could be that everyone in the islands was a little more chill, though.

"Lou's mom owns the ranch," I explained finally.

"So that *was* him." Her hand stilled on the bar.

I remembered there were no publicity photos of Silvery Star. His rise to (relative) fame had been completely anonymous. Until we'd played a gig together at the festival in late May, he'd been a faceless indie wonder.

"That was him," I said. "Walking out on his girlfriend."

"Oh my god—is Lou your *boyfriend?*" Monica exclaimed, not sounding chill at all. "You're actually seeing Lou *Linney?*"

I didn't care for the way she said his name, like he really was a rock star, like he wasn't just a guy with a single underground hit record. Silvery Star wasn't exactly a household name, unless the household was a college dorm room. There was no need to act like I was dating a member of The Beatles here. "Yeah," I said, shrugging. "He's my boyfriend. And we're working on a record together," I added. "I'm a singer-songwriter, too."

"Wow," Monica sighed, truly awed. "That's so cool. I had no idea. You guys seem like normal locals, you know?"

"We are and we aren't," I said thoughtfully. "In a lot of ways, I guess we're just like you. Outsiders, let in by the grace of very kind relatives. Or in this case, adopted by nice locals. Lou's mother took me in and hired me as a ranch-hand when I needed some help getting back on my feet." I didn't plan on telling her *how* I'd ended up needing help. Getting kicked out of The Bombers was going to stay in my back pocket until I was firmly established as a singer. Then it would make a great anecdote for interviews.

"A ranch-hand!" Monica was enchanted. "Okay, yes, I definitely need to check out your island. Please and thank you."

"Of course," I said, forgetting I'd ever been threatened by her. Or at least shoving the idea into a dark corner of my mind. "Now tell me what you did to get yourself exiled to Cutlass Key."

Monica laughed and poured herself a Coke from the soda jet. She sipped and thought for a moment. "Where to begin? I used to be a hotel concierge in South Beach."

I lifted my eyebrows. "A fancy hotel, I'm guessing?"

She nodded. "The *fanciest*. I worked my way up all along Ocean Drive. It was a crazy career, but I thought I loved it. I was always getting asked to send limos to pick up drunk movie stars or sneak drug dealers in through the back to meet with personal assistants or find vegan tacos at two a.m. for some random singer..."

"So you met famous people?"

"Mostly their assistants and their dealers," she admitted with a laugh. "I really got into it because I wanted to own a hotel of my own. Not like a big fancy one, obviously, but a little place, like the ones here in the Keys. I just wanted to understand what people really wanted, but all SoBe taught me was people wanted excess and to be spoiled like, beyond the norm. So I kind of changed my mind. I quit my job and I was just bopping around Key Largo, working at some dive places, when my dad's buddy came down to do some snorkeling.

I showed him around the island and took him to some reefs and we got to talking about work, and he suggested I decompress down here. Said his friend needed a bartender to class up his bar." She laughed again. "Here I am, classy as hell."

It was a crazy story, but the Keys were full of people who lost the thread of their lives on the mainland and came down here to decompress and start over again. I was one of those people. Stacy was one of those people. In these islands, you were either born a Conch or came here to learn the wisdom of their ways. Mainland notions needed to be left at the bridge over Jewfish Creek. Once you hit Key Largo, you better be ready to live on island time. And that meant more than just mixing up a margarita at nine a.m.

Also? Monica's story was giving me an idea.

"So, how much did you learn about running a hotel?" I asked her. "Was it all drug deals and limo runs?"

"Oh, that's the cool thing about being a concierge," Monica answered, eyes sparkling. "You work with *everyone* in the hotel. Food and beverage, rooms, entertainment, you name it. I could absolutely run a hotel with one arm tied behind my back at this point. The question is, do I really want to? That's what I hope I figure out while I'm hanging out here, you know?"

"Right," I agreed. "This is a good place to figure out what you really want. Do you think you might give me some tips, though? I happen to know someone who could really use an expert's help putting together a hotel idea."

Now Monica looked very interested.

I had a feeling she wasn't going to take a lot of time to figure out what she really wanted to do.

"Come back to the island with me," I suggested. "Or, I mean, give me a ride home. And we can talk more about it there. I think you should see this place."

Chapter Six

BY THE TIME Monica's Jeep tires were coaxing a song out of the Humming Bridge, I was starting to doubt my initial conviction that she and I should help Marchant's sailboat hotel come to life. If I poured my efforts into Marchant's dream, what would be left over for me? Especially when Lou was becoming increasingly unreliable at holding up his end of the record deal bargain.

Maybe this should be Monica's gig.

If I could convince her to take it.

Who wouldn't want it, though? She'd meet Marchant and everything would be easy after that.

And Monica was delighted with everything about Hell and Dammit Cay. The ponies, obviously, but also the four houses on their stilts ("They're identical but they're all different, I'm obsessed!" she gushed) and the strip of beach we'd put in along the east shoreline, behind Crystal's house and the barn ("This white sand is gorgeous, so much nicer than anything else around here!"). She praised the little round studios we'd built beneath the palm trees on Stacy's side of the island, admiring the way they fit in so naturally, and she had nothing but nice things to say about the oceanic blues of Marchant's house.

Then I took her up the stairs. "You have to meet him," I assured her. "Marchant is one of the true treasures of the Keys."

"It's about time someone recognized my charms," a husky baritone rumbled, and Marchant himself came out of the house, his chunky Persian cat cradled in his arms.

Monica's eyes were like saucers as she shook his fingers—the only appendages not full of fluffy cat—and introduced herself to the old Conch. Marchant's white stubble and deeply tanned, leathery skin somehow worked perfectly with his shy smile and friendly blue eyes; he was like a Keys Santa Claus. You couldn't help but like him the moment you saw him, and he always seemed to feel the same way in return.

"Sit down and have a beer, lovelies," he said heartily, depositing the cat onto one of the wide outdoor sofas dotting his wraparound porch. "The cooler is freshly stocked. I'll just get us some fish dip and crackers."

Monica sank down next to the purring cat as I pulled two dripping wet beers from the cooler next to the sofa. "Don't be scared of the fish dip," I advised her. "It's the caviar of the Keys."

"It's fine," she laughed. "I'll try anything once."

And by the look on her face when she tried Marchant's smoked mullet dip, she'd be back for more. He looked gratified as she dug a second cracker into the creamy dip. "Made it myself," he assured us.

"You're a cook?" Monica asked.

"Oh, anything to pass the time," Marchant sighed, looking wistfully out to sea. "Water's rough today and the ladies here expect me to stay close to shore when there's a chop out there."

"They're just looking out for you," I told him. "They like you. Plus, if you're lost at sea, this house will get sold and we'll have to get used to a new neighbor. No one wants that."

Marchant chuckled. "That's fair, I guess. But what will y'all do if I get my motel up and runnin'? I guess then there'd be new folks all the time."

I was secretly pleased he'd brought up his motel idea, but I kept my face severe and replied, "We'll have to vet every single reservation to see if they're our kind of people."

"That's why I'll keep it small," Marchant said seriously. "Real small. You know I only want three or four little boats. Five or six at the most."

"It jumps from three to six real quick," I said, grinning.

"What motel is this?" Monica asked, looking between the two of us. "A motel with boats? I'm so intrigued!"

I'll bet you are, I thought, helping myself to another little pile of crackers. *I'll just bet you are.*

Then I sat quietly and let Marchant talk himself hoarse about his pie-in-the-sky sailboat hotel.

"Thanks so much for introducing me to everyone," Monica said as we walked back to her car. "I love this place. What's going on with that house out there, anyway? Is it for sale?"

I glanced at her; Monica was looking at the unfinished house on the far corner of the island. "It's not done inside," I told her. "Probably all rotted from the weather."

"So, no one will just let me camp in it and become an honorary Hell and Dammit Cay resident, is what you're saying."

"Sadly, no. But you can come back and visit. Marchant likes you, Crystal likes you. I think Stacy would if she were here." Crystal had come over while Marchant and Monica were discussing the logistics of hotel websites—or rather, while Monica was explaining how online reservation systems worked and Marchant listened with wide eyes. Stacy was back in Miami, dealing with another art gallery emergency. That was about the only thing that took her off the island these days. "Or," I added coyly, "you could help Marchant get his hotel going and move here to run it."

"Run his sailboat hotel?"

"Yes, wouldn't that be fun?" For a moment, I thought I had her hooked already.

But Monica laughed. "It's a cute idea, Katie, don't get me wrong, but I didn't come all the way down here to run a hotel! I wanted to find myself and decide if there's something else out there for me *besides* hospitality."

"Don't you think 'finding yourself' is a little cliche?" I persisted. "Besides, this is the kind of opportunity that feels more like fate than anything! You have the knowledge, Marchant has the dream..."

"And that's great, but who has the start-up cash?" Monica lowered her voice and looked around the island. "Forgive me, but I don't foresee a lot of extra money coming outta locked safes in these houses. This place is a little beat-up, don't you think? Charming, but not what it takes to start a business like that. It would cost a fortune to get the boats, do them up right for guests, plus we'd have to get insurance and occupancy permits and a million other things in order. It's a *huge* undertaking."

"So you don't think we could do it." This wasn't what I wanted to hear.

"It's not a case of *could*," Monica told me. "It's a case of *can't*. It can't be done. That's what I'm telling you."

I felt my blood pressure rising, and suddenly, I wondered why I was listening to Monica at all. She didn't know everything. She was a former concierge, not a hotel owner. She'd never run a business in her whole entire life! But the folks here on Hell and Dammit Cay *had*. Stacy was an artist; she ran her own business with her paintings, right? Crystal ran Sea Horse Ranch, and maybe it wasn't making her a million dollars but it hadn't closed, right? Still here, still ticking! That should count for something. Certainly more than the opinion of one negative Nancy from the mainland, with precisely zero hours of experience managing her own company.

"Well, I think we *can* do it," I informed her, my jaw jutting mutinously. "I think if we all work together, we can make it happen. That's how the art festivals started up, you know. A group effort." *Led by me,* I thought smugly. At least, at first, it had been. "And now we have a thriving business for both islands."

"Well, if you're determined to do it, I won't try to change your mind," Monica said, shrugging. "And I'll consult however you want. But I'm not giving up my particular path right now. I'm going to stick to bartending, okay?"

"That's fine," I said, feeling generous now that I'd decided her opinion wasn't worth anything. "You bartend and we'll come up and pick your brain about hotel-running."

"It's called hospitality," Monica laughed. "And yeah, you've got a deal."

Well, apparently I was going to start a sailboat hotel!

I leaned against a paddock gate and watched the horses inside pick at the remains of their hay. Things often made more sense when you just stood and watched horses for a while. There was something about their slow, deliberate movements and their general lack of concern about anything besides eating, which put the noisy, demanding outside world into perspective.

But no answers came to me.

Just the troubling reality that one more problem on Hell and Dammit Cay had been added to my already overflowing plate.

And I couldn't just run for the neon arms of civilization every time I had a problem, either. That was what Lou had done, right? He'd gotten news he didn't like, and he just took off, the same way he'd done before I'd come here. But Lou belonged to this island. He'd always be welcomed back as a prodigal son.

I had to work for my right to be here—at least, the way I saw it, I did.

Besides, I *wanted* to get things right; I *wanted* everyone on this island to be happy. And by god if Marchant needed a sailboat hotel to be happy, then it was just going to be my problem until it got done.

"No big deal," I told the horses. "I can do this on top of everything else."

The horses nosed through their hay and said nothing.

I'd take it as an agreement.

Now, the pressing question was to figure out where Lou had gone and figure out a way to make him come back. I would have to rely on him more than ever to take the lead on our record. Surely, I could make him understand that if I was spending my time making his mother and Marchant happy, he could spend his time catching up on *our* dreams. Lou was not an unreasonable person.

Most of the time.

I walked out to the bridge, waving hello to Roger and Rogerina, the iguanas who lived on the rocks along the canal separating our island from Little Bucket Key. It was a short stretch of confined water which opened up onto the broad, green reach of the Gulf of Mexico.

The evening was waning, and the sun was close to the water, an intensely golden light surrounded by flickering thunderclouds.

Between me and those storms lay the loud, crowded island of Key West. Could I find Lou in the mass of drunken tourists heaving around that island every night? Or should I just wait for him to come home?

I went back to the house and trudged upstairs, still mulling over the question. I found Crystal sitting at the wicker table in the breakfast nook, her eyes on her phone. She glanced up at me. "You heard from Lou?"

"Not yet," I admitted.

She sighed and put her phone down. "I don't like it when he up and disappears," she said. "It's his old trick. He senses some trouble, and he runs away. That's how he ended up in Chicago the last time."

"Well, he made his Silvery Star record up there, so it wasn't all bad," I suggested, but I could feel a flutter of trepidation in my chest. Was Lou really a chronic runner? Was this more than just getting away from the island for a few hours? Surely he would be back before bedtime, and Crystal was just making his absence into more than it really was.

"But he wasn't Lou when he was doing Silvery Star," Crystal said, shaking her head at me. "Not Lou Linney of the Lower Keys, anyway. He was Louis A. Linney of Chicago."

I sat down across from her and tried to follow her line of thinking. "You're saying he thought of himself as someone else entirely up there?"

"It sure seemed that way. Whenever he'd leave, everything about him would sound off," Crystal explained. "When he'd call me, his accent would be different. The way he'd use words, even. I know he went by Louis in Chicago. But no one down here ever called him that. Marchant used to say he was tryin' on someone else's skin when he went away from the Keys. I was hopin' he was done with all that, though."

Crystal tapped her fingers on the glass-topped table between us and looked at me with her kindly, faded blue eyes. "I thought with you here to steady him, maybe he'd left all that behind. But it's only been a few months, and he's already on the hop again. I always think maybe he doesn't want Louis and Lou to get mixed up...maybe now that his secret is out, that's what he sees happening. And maybe he sees his father coming back as part of that, like the news is out and Arnie's coming for his share."

"You think that's what is happening?"

"No," Crystal said. "Arnie ain't a bad man. Useless, maybe, but not bad. He's not coming to try to get his hands on whatever he thinks Lou's got. But if his coming keeps blurring the line between Louis and Lou, maybe that's enough to confuse the boy into leaving."

"But why would he still need Louis?" I asked, my words coming slowly as I tried to follow her explanation. "If he's here now, if he's finally home and we have a record deal and he's ready to make a go of it with me...Oh." I swallowed. "You're saying he's not ready for any of that."

She reached across the table and took my hand in hers. "Sometimes it can take boys a long time to settle," she said.

"He's not a boy," I choked, rubbing my free hand across my stinging eyes. "He's a grown man."

Crystal's smile was sad. "You know as well as I do those two words don't hardly mean anything when you stick them together. He's only as grown as he thinks he is, and I don't know that Lou has ever really gotten over his childhood."

"I'll go get him in the morning," I said. "I'll give him tonight to figure it out."

"Good plan," she said, patting my hand. "I think we all just need a little time to get used to the idea of Arnie coming back."

I was feeding the horses when I remembered that I hadn't told Crystal the real bombshell about Lou's father. That the missing man from her past was the absentee owner of the Slutty Mermaid. Did she know?

Maybe she knew.

Crystal was a dark horse.

Chapter Seven

THE NEXT MORNING, I took Crystal's truck to Key West with her blessing, parking it in the hulking parking garage near City Hall in Old Town. I wasn't good at her stick shift transmission, and the truck ticked quietly after I'd turned it off, seemingly relieved I was done torturing its gearbox. "Sorry, truck," I told it. Crystal said the truck liked it when we talked to it. I figured there was no harm in playing along.

Out on the humid streets of Old Town, I dodged puddles from another morning rain storm along with clusters of coffee-seeking tourists. Although on second glance, it was evident not everyone needed a caffeine injection to start their day. Some of them were already clutching frosty plastic glasses. It was funny, the way vacations with any hint of a tropical vibe seemed to involve non-stop alcohol. Put people near a beach and they had to hit the booze; I'd seen it all over while touring the country over the last year.

The nice thing about this visit was that Lou wasn't actually hiding from me. I knew where I was going. In a text, he'd told me exactly where he'd crashed last night, so I was able to walk with confidence up a few narrow streets, banyans and hibiscus crowding me from the sidewalk to the asphalt, before pausing at the overgrown garden gate of a shotgun-style Conch cottage. Restoration clearly wasn't high on the mind of whoever owned this little piece of nineteenth-century paradise; the tiny porch was speckled with peeling white paint, and the screen door looked like a relic of the 1950s. A gray cat sat on the porch steps and licked her white paws, glancing at me as she worked.

I double-checked the address and then opened the leaning gate in the battered picket fence, startling several lizards and a small bird just inside on the shattered paving stones. Palm fronds and orchid leaves brushed against my arms as I entered the shadow of the miniature front yard; two steps and I was on the porch stairs, the cat uttering a rusty meow as she stepped aside to let me pass.

I faced the screen door, noticing the rips in the old netting, the dents in the aluminum framing, and took a deep breath. I could *do* this. I wasn't afraid of Lou; that would be ridiculous.

But I was a little afraid of failing.

Crystal had told me her son's disappearing acts were serious. He left because he couldn't handle what the world was asking him to do. If he couldn't face the possibility of seeing his father again, would I be able to convince him to come back to Hell and Dammit Cay? Or would I have to wait it out, the way Crystal had been doing for so many years? Sitting alone in her house on stilts, wondering when her darling boy would come home?

I couldn't do that; couldn't be that person. But at the same time, I loved Lou, *and* my life was hopelessly wrapped up with his. I lived in his mother's house. I was supposed to be making a record with him. I could manage the island affairs on my own, but everything had Lou all over it.

It would make a terrible mess if we tried to split it all up.

Not to mention what it would do to my poor heart.

I took a breath, steeling myself to knock on the door...and then it opened, and there was Lou, standing behind the screen in a shadowy hall. His familiar shape in this unfamiliar place was so comforting, I felt tears spring to my eyes. But I blinked them away, and if anyone asked, I'd say it was allergies.

He looked me up and down, and I saw his cool eyes soften. "What are you doing here so early in the morning?" he asked, pushing the door open to let me in.

"It's nine o'clock," I retorted, stepping inside. There was only a hint of air conditioning, and a rumble down the hall told me this little cottage had a window unit, not central air. Truly a relic of another age in Florida. "I fed the horses two hours ago, took a shower, and hopped in the truck. Good morning."

Lou followed me down the hall. Four doors opened on either side, lined up evenly, then the hall ended in a back door with an opaque louvered window. Palm fronds tapped against the pebbled glass and I had a feeling there was no pool or barbecue out there. Just a little square of jungle. I followed my ears to the air-conditioned room and found a small kitchen with ancient fittings and a tiny breakfast table. I sat down and waited for Lou to join me.

He leaned against the growling old fridge instead.

We looked at each other for a long moment.

"Whose house is this?" I asked finally.

"A friend's," he replied, shrugging.

"What kind of a friend?"

"An old one."

"Is this your dealer's house?"

Lou laughed. "What? No. You know I don't—come on, Katie. I haven't gone off the deep end or whatever it is you're thinking. I just can't be around home for a while. Not if he's going to turn up."

I sighed. Was our relationship still too new for me to demand all the dirty details on his dad? I felt like it was. In a lot of ways, we'd moved fast. But there were still plenty of deep, dark holes in each other's psyches we weren't ready to share yet.

Still, he'd made certain commitments to me, with me, that I couldn't just drop now. "I need to know you're coming back to the island," I told him, and I watched his gaze drop to the peeling linoleum.

"I'll come back when she's gone," he said.

"Who?"

"Monica."

"*Monica?* What did she do wrong?"

"She's his spy," Lou told me, deadly serious.

"Whose?" I demanded, although I already knew what he was thinking.

"His," Lou said. "My father's. You think it's a coincidence she knows him and she shows up, then he's coming? No. She's been here gathering intel on me."

Oh, boy. "I don't think that's it. Monica's a super nice girl who is trying to figure out what she wants to do with her life. Kind of like I was, a few months ago? When your mom took me in? You didn't think I was a spy."

"Well, my *dad* didn't hire you," Lou pointed out. "My mom did. And I trust one but not the other, so..."

This was a tough point to argue. Fortunately, I'm good at arguing. "But *you* never told me your dad owned the Slutty Mermaid," I told him. "So I made all my initial assumptions about Monica without knowing that part, which gives me a more clear view of her. And I think she's nice."

"I didn't know about my dad owning it."

"Seriously?"

"Seriously." Lou ran a hand through his hair. "The Slutty Mermaid has just always been there. When my mom moved to Hell and Dammit permanently, my dad was already long gone. If I'd known he owned that place, I don't think I would have come back."

My heart thumped erratically. He couldn't be thinking of abandoning the island just because of his dad. Could he? I reached out a hand, hoping he'd take it. "Come on, Lou. We can figure this out. It's not like your mom is going to be all lovey-dovey with him, right?"

Lou shrugged, ignoring my outstretched fingers. "I don't know, Katie. What is my mom going to do? That's up to her. We didn't talk about him. We still don't. Maybe she doesn't care that he took off and left us. Maybe she secretly sees him sometimes. I don't know."

"There's no way Crystal is secretly seeing the guy who left her," I scoffed. "Come on, she's *way* tougher than that."

And, I thought, she's probably pretty in love with Marchant, even if they're not making any moves on that front.

"I'd like to think so," Lou said. "But—"

He was interrupted by a loud crash outside. I leapt up from the rickety chair, but Lou barely moved. "What the hell was that?" I demanded.

"You mean the garbage truck?" he drawled. "It's trash day."

I sat back down, glaring at him. There was another crash outside, but I distinctly heard glass bottles tumbling and the groan of a truck motor. "Well, well, aren't we civilized in Old Town."

"You're just mad you've been living on an island for four months and forgot what the real world sounds like."

"Hardly," I sniffed. "What's the point in the real world, anyway?"

Lou scowled, and he turned around, pouring himself a cup of coffee from a dilapidated Mr. Coffee on the counter. "Spoken like one of my mom's true disciples," he remarked.

"And what's that supposed to mean?"

Lou sipped his coffee elaborately. Evidently, that was meant to be his answer.

I wanted to storm out so, so badly. But of course, I couldn't. We needed a reconciliation and an agreement on how we were going to move forward, today. There wasn't time to mess around. Rivers was waiting on our record. We had six months. That much time should have been forever, but it was our first time recording together, and with Lou squirreling around like this, I had no way of knowing how things would play out.

But I wasn't going to let him ruin my chance of getting a record out. He could have a nervous breakdown about his father *after* we approved the final mix.

I stood up. "Take me to breakfast," I commanded. "I want the whole story, and I want to know when you're coming home."

Lou put down his coffee cup and sighed. "Fine."

The street outside smelled like hot garbage. The cat was gone. I wondered where it lived. Lou opened the rickety garden gate and waited while I stepped onto the narrow sidewalk. "You have a place in mind?" he asked.

"No," I replied. "I don't know Key West very well. Do you?"

"I know a thing or two about it," he said. "Come on. It's a walk, but I know a place."

We walked in single-file along the cracked sidewalk until it ended, then side by side in the narrow street. The garbage smell faded and was replaced with the heavy perfume of tropical flowers. Shotgun cottages and narrow Queen Anne houses with stacked front porches and elaborate wooden gingerbread did their best to hide behind thickets of palm trees and bougainvillea. Now and then, a chicken ran past us or picked at gravel in the street. The air was heavy with humidity, and low gray clouds slid through the blue sky, constantly threatening us with a tropical downpour.

"It's so much hotter and stickier here than on the island," I remarked. "The houses block all the breeze, I guess."

"And the asphalt soaks up the heat," Lou agreed. "Yeah, the two places really don't compare."

"I'm so glad we put all that effort into the music festival and the artist colony," I said, hoping to remind him of the great things we'd already done together. Surely, Lou could remember that we could do *anything* as a team? And also that we owed Rivers a tremendous debt for putting on the music festival in the first place...we couldn't let him down by failing to get an album recorded.

He didn't say anything, and we walked in silence through the muggy streets until he paused at an old wooden porch. I looked up. *Cuban Deli.*

Ten minutes later, I was swatting away a nosy chicken while I ate my way through the best egg and sausage sandwich I'd ever eaten. It was an effort not to moan about how good the sweet Cuban bread was, or how fluffy the eggs, or how spicy and snappy the sausage. But I managed to keep things family-friendly.

Lou drank a Cuban coffee, inky dark and well-sugared, and jiggled his leg in a way which suggested he really didn't need the extra caffeine. He looked up and down the street constantly, and watched a tourist train ding-ding its way past like it was a crocodile on the way to eat him. I revisited my initial assumption that he was on something. I'd never seen relaxed, laid-back Lou so tense before.

This couldn't all be about his dad, right?

Hooves rang out on the pavement, and we watched the Key West mounted unit saunter past, the officers looking comfortable in the saddle despite the swampy atmosphere. I eyed Lou, wondering if he'd get more squirrelly in the presence of law enforcement, but he just watched the horses with interest, making a few comments about their shoes, before turning back to his coffee. He'd been quiet for our entire breakfast. The whole story, whatever it was, hadn't come out.

Bribed with eggs and Cuban sausage. He really knew me too well. But the silence was killing me.

"Lou," I finally blurted, "please just come home with me."

"I need some time," he said. He paused, swirled the dregs of his coffee. "I'm sorry. I really am. I just have this thing about—the idea of him makes me crazy. I know you need me, and I don't *want* to abandon you with everything we had planned. I'm trying really hard not to."

My heart began a crazy thudding dance against my ribcage at the word *abandon*. So, there was a part of him, a not so small part, that really was ready to pick up and leave the Keys? This was not the information I needed this morning.

"You can't let him drive you away from your home," I told him. "We'll tell him to leave! Everyone's on your side, Lou. Not his."

He looked up at me, his eyes boring into mine. "But that's not true, is it, Katie?" A statement, not a question. "He owns the Mermaid. Which means that people around us still know him. And *like* him, I'll bet. People on Cutlass Key, even on Little Bucket—"

"But not on Hell and Dammit," I interrupted, leaning forward. I slipped a hand over his; his skin was cold and damp. The feel of it made me want to take him home and tuck him into bed, bring him tea and cookies. And then go out with a hunting rifle and tell Arnie to take his sorry ass back to the mainland. "Not on *our* island, which is where it counts."

He nodded, his eyes drifting away from mine and sliding over the tourists on the sidewalks. He couldn't stay here; this carnival atmosphere wasn't him.

"Take some time," I said. "But you have to come back soon. Please."

"Okay," he sighed. "Soon."

At least he was coming home, I thought. Assuming I could believe him. We finished our breakfast in silence.

After we'd tossed our cups and plates, Lou offered to walk me down to the Southernmost Point, just a few blocks away, but I declined. There were enough tourists here without me gawking at a photo-op, and anyway, I had work to do. He walked me back to the parking garage and gave me a kiss before I got into Crystal's pickup.

I drove back to Hell and Dammit Cay, feeling like a failure.

Chapter Eight

With Lou sticking it out in Key West, I had no choice but to move forward on the things I *could* work on alone...or with Monica's help. Still determined to work on the sailboat hotel concept without getting Marchant's hopes up prematurely, I enlisted her to join me on a hunt for the boats themselves. "Can you see if you can find a guy from the customers at the Mermaid?" I asked her, stopping in on the way home. "A boat guy?"

She promised she would, and a few mornings later I drove up to the Mermaid to meet her for a cinnamon roll and conspiracy.

"So, I found a guy," she said, sliding into a booth beside me. She took a big bite of her cinnamon roll. "God, these are delicious," she said around a mouthful. "Sheila won't tell me her secret."

"Sheila?"

"Sheila makes the cinnamon rolls," she explained. "She lives down Cutlass Key on Triggerfish Terrace. Brings them every morning."

"Sheila's a goddess."

"Mm-hmm."

For a few moments, we just abandoned ourselves to cinnamon rolls.

"So, you found a boat salesman?" I asked at last, licking cream cheese icing from my fingers.

"I remembered one I knew about, actually. I was doing dive shop work in Key Largo before I came here, remember? Well, I met a ton of boat people. And I forgot before, but Arnie has a great hook-up with a dealer up in Islamorada. We should go up there and talk to him."

"To the dealer or to Arnie?

"The dealer."

I considered this. "The problem is Arnie's the connection. You know he's Lou's father, right?"

"Oh, is *that* what's going on?"

"Going on?" I asked, feigning ignorance. She must mean why Lou was still gone.

"Yeah, people are talking about Arnie coming back like it's going to blow the palm trees out of the ground. Everyone's like 'when Arnie gets here' and then they start whispering. They're not sharing with me." Monica tapped her fingers on the table, drumming out a little tune. "I'm new here, I get it. But I can't help people if I don't know what's going on."

We picked at the remnants of icing on the plate between us.

Finally, Monica sighed and sat upright, with the air of a person who needs to get on with her life. "Look, I think this guy is worth talking to. Maybe Lou doesn't have a good relationship with his dad, but my dad has known his friend Charlie for twenty years, and Charlie has known Arnie for at least as long. So it's kind of like *I've* known Arnie for twenty years. You get me?"

"No," I said. "I'm almost positive that's not how it works."

"It's introduction by association," Monica said enthusiastically.

"You just made that up."

"Come on, Katie. I wouldn't steer you wrong. And you wanted a boat guy."

I wanted a local boat guy who would cut us a deal, not some dealer in Islamorada. Hell, I could have driven up U.S. 1 and stopped at every boat dealer between here and Upper Matecumbe myself. I didn't have to get Monica's help with *that*.

But she'd sort of tried to help. Baby steps, right? If this guy didn't pan out, she'd have a better idea of the under-the-table island deal I was looking to make.

"Fine, okay," I said. "I can go on your next day off. But we cannot tell Lou, not ever."

"Sure," she agreed. "Let's go tomorrow. You want another cinnamon roll?"

Of course I did. That decision, at least, was pretty simple.

The boat dealership was off a shell road in Islamorada, on a scrubby section of Plantation Key lined with canals leading to Florida Bay. It was clearly set up for houses to move in as soon as the lots could be sold. We were so close to Key Largo, I felt like we were practically on the mainland.

I let Monica drive us in her cherry-red Jeep, and with the top down and music blaring, I felt the tiniest bit like a tourist roaring up the Overseas Highway with salt wind in my hair.

It wasn't the worst feeling, I guess. I hadn't been able to let loose in a while. Responsibilities, horses to feed, artists to placate, the usual. When Monica put on some Taylor Swift and started belting out the lyrics, I found myself joining in.

Yeah, I felt good.

The islands and canals flashed by. We passed all the sights: the huge signs around Big Pine Key warning us to drive slow and avoid killing the tiny, foolish Key Deer who wandered the streets and grazed in the parking lots; the long oceanic stretch of the Seven Mile Bridge; the grim beauty of the Art Deco monument to the workers lost in the Labor Day Hurricane of 1935 on Upper Matecumbe Key.

And then we were pretty much there.

Islamorada was like a mainland beach town stretched out along either side of U.S. 1. There was an airport, a Publix, cross-streets, subdivisions. A park with baseball diamonds and an aquatic center. It was kind of crazy how much stuff people could wedge onto one narrow strip of coral and sand. And a stark reminder of what was at stake when I worked to protect our islands from further development. I didn't begrudge the people of Islamorada their thriving town, but it wasn't the kind of island I wanted to live on, either.

Monica had lived near here when she'd worked on Key Largo, so she pointed out a few favorite places, like a coffee shop with good drinks and a tap-room with local beer. Then she made a few quick turns, and we were back in the scrubby mangroves and low trees that grew native on the Keys. An iguana scurried across the road, half the size of Roger, but clearly without his good-natured personality. Monica turned into a wide parking area of crushed white shell. A hand-painted sign read: *Parking for Pelican Boat Customers Only.*

"Here we are!" she announced.

I looked over the scene. Beyond the parking lot and a line of stringy queen palms, a high wooden privacy fence guarded the boat dealership from...prying eyes? Boat thieves? I wasn't sure. I could see a few boats up on lifts and the backside of a metal warehouse, but nothing else. A dog began barking.

"You sure about this place?" I asked warily.

"Oh, it's fine," Monica assured me. "I called this morning. He's here."

"Does he have a name?"

She hopped out of the Jeep. "Marlin."

"Marlin?" I stared at her. "That's a fish."

Monica put a hand on her hip and tossed her hair. I realized she was planning on using her looks to get us a great deal. The barking dog and the privacy fence had me wondering if that was such a good idea. She shook her head at me and said, "We're in the Keys, Katie. Marlin's one of the most normal nicknames you'll find. Honestly," she continued, turning and walking towards the gate. "You'd think you were new around here."

Maybe I was, I thought. I'd been sequestered on Hell and Dammit Cay for most of my stay in the Keys, but Monica had been out here with the live ones, diving and drinking and making deals. Maybe Monica, the supposed outsider, was already more of a Conch than I'd ever be.

Monica's Marlin surprised me. He wasn't a wild-eyed conman. He was a nice guy in shorts and sandals, with sun-faded hair and a sunburned neck. And he welcomed Monica like a daughter. Which I found suspicious, because she'd said she knew *of* Marlin through Arnie…who she supposedly didn't know in person either.

Suddenly, I realized Monica's stories did not add up.

But it was too late to do anything about it now. We were through the board fence, the dog was sniffing my shoes, and Marlin had ushered us into an air-conditioned office attached to the warehouse building. I looked around his wood-paneled office, draped with taxidermy fish trophies and one extremely impressive LEGO Camaro which was kept in a dusty plastic case, presumably to keep small children from dismantling it, while Marlin hugged Monica and exclaimed about how pretty she was looking.

"So glad y'all got up here to take a look," he exclaimed once he was done hugging her and shaking my hand with unfettered enthusiasm. "I have two boats I think are just the ticket for your client. Nice, roomy living quarters. Heads need replacing, but, for you guys? I'll do it at cost."

"That's so nice of you, Marlin," Monica enthused. "I knew you'd have just the thing."

"Well, come on, then," he urged us. "Let's go have a look."

We crunched along the crushed shell paths between the boats. There were dozens, of all sorts: pontoon party boats, deep-sea fishing boats with tall towers and sophisticated radar systems, square little house-boats never meant to leave their docks. And sailboats, of course, the prettiest and most complicated way to cross the waters. Marlin produced a small stepladder, and we clambered onto an attractive boat with a navy-blue hull and gorgeous wood and brass fittings.

Too expensive, I thought, walking along the curving deck. A nice size, though. Two bedrooms. A salon. A tiny kitchen. It was probably exactly what we needed.

"The one next to it is practically identical," Marlin said, waving his arm to take in the neighboring boat. "We can look at it if you want, but here's what you need to know..."

Marlin launched into his pitch.

When he landed on a number, I burst out laughing.

Monica stared at me in shock. Marlin's face was dismayed.

"Come on," I chuckled. "You can't be serious."

Marlin gave me a wounded look. "I don't see the problem. That's an excellent deal."

"Mr. Marlin—"

"Just Marlin," he interjected.

"Mr. Marlin," I repeated, not going for the folksy charm at all, "Let me be clear with you. That's twice what I'm interested in paying."

He pursed his lips. "You ain't finding anything for a better price in these islands."

"Then I guess I'll look on different islands," I retorted.

No, I don't know what I meant by that. But it sounded nice and final.

Marlin shook his head. "I was trying to make a nice deal because you're family and all, but if this is the way you're gonna treat me—"

"Family?"

Monica blushed. Oh, good lord, what did she tell this man?

Marlin looked between us, confused. "Well, sure, we're family, ain't we? You're Arnie Morehead's—what is it, cousin? I forget."

"No," I said coolly. I wasn't about to be related to Lou. Not even for a handshake deal on a sailboat. "Not related to anyone in the Keys, as far as I know."

"Arnie ain't in the Keys," he muttered. "At least not yet. He's still over in Naples—"

"*Marlin,*" Monica hissed. "Stop it."

The boat dealer hushed up.

"I'm out of here," I declared. "Y'all are up to something." I was halfway down the ladder before I remembered that, once again, I had no ride. I really needed to start driving myself places.

Luckily, Monica was hopping down after me. "Come on, don't be mad," she cajoled, chasing me across the shells. "I was just trying to get us the very best deal I could."

"Which is sad," I told her. "Because it still sucked." I came to a canal lined by a concrete seawall and stopped. The green water lapped a few feet below me, stirred by the tide and a swirling of fins in its depths. Someone fed the fish here.

"Well, boats are expensive. I did what I could." Monica sat down on the seawall, flicking away some ants. I glanced behind us; for some reason, the boat dealer was giving us some space. Maybe he thought Monica could talk me into the boats if we had some time alone. Bless him. In the budget I'd drawn up for the motel, his offer was already taking up twice the money for the whole project. When I looked back at Monica, she gave me a tentative smile. "Okay, maybe you don't want everyone in the islands to think you're related to Lou. I can see where I went wrong."

I barked out a laugh despite my irritation. "You think?"

She giggled. "Kissing cousins not your thing?"

"Well, the way Lou's behaving right now, I'm not kissing *anyone,* whether they're related to me or not."

Monica sighed and looked at the fish gathering below our feet. "I wish he'd give Arnie a chance."

"When were you going to be straight with me and tell me you knew him? Instead of playing this friend of a friend of a friend game?"

She kicked the wall with her heel. "I was going to tell you."

"Really."

"Yes! I just didn't know we were going to be friends at first, that's all." Monica's smile was endearing now, luring me out of my annoyance. "You know, I thought you guys were just coming into the bar to get a look at me, and I didn't want to get mixed up in any trouble with Arnie, or the Linneys, you know. He told me when he sent me down to the Mermaid that the Linneys weren't gonna like having him around."

"He sent you?" I asked, thinking her wording was getting weirder and weirder. "What exactly is your relationship with this guy?"

There was silence for a moment. The fish scattered, distracting us, and a moment later a gray dorsal fin pierced the water's surface. Then another. Dolphins fishing in the canals. We watched them bob past just a few feet away from us, their blowholes puffing each time they surfaced.

I really loved the Keys.

Monica stirred next to me. "Arnie's my boss," she said finally. "He owns a lot of places besides the Mermaid. He owned the dive shop up in Key Largo, too. He sent me to the Mermaid because of some trouble up there." She nodded towards the north, indicating Key Largo.

"Trouble? What were you guys doing, selling drugs?"

"I had a stalker."

Oops. "Damn, I'm sorry."

Monica shrugged. "It happens. I had a stalker before, when I worked in Miami. He used to sit in the lobby until security kicked him out. Night after night. Then he found the employee door—we ended up calling the cops, and he had a million warrants, so they took him in and that was the end."

"Jeez."

"He was wanted for murder," Monica said, so matter-of-factly I was sure I'd heard her wrong.

"What?"

"Yeah." She kicked her heels again. The dolphins were heading to the open water beyond the boat lot. She watched them wistfully. "That's why I left the hotel, actually. I just—it didn't exactly pay well enough for that kind of visibility, you know? Not like I was one of the celebrities staying there and I could get a private bodyguard to keep an eye on me."

"So, how did you find the place in Key Largo?" I asked, trying to move the conversation along, even though there was a *lot* I wanted to unpack about this concierge gig of hers.

"Arnie offered me the job," she said. "He really is a friend of my father's friend, Charlie. I didn't make that up. Charlie was in Miami on business and he looked me up to check on me, and I said I wanted out of the city, and he asked if I wanted to work in a dive shop. He knew I could dive," she added. "Because we all went to Mexico on a big vacation when I was a kid, and that's where I learned it. So anyway, Arnie hired me and Charlie told him the whole story, and Arnie worked really hard to protect me. Too hard, maybe. He didn't like the way guys looked at me."

"So he sent you to be a bartender?"

She shrugged. "He said the people in Cutlass Key were good and wouldn't bother me."

I nodded at that. She was right, as far as I knew. And if we couldn't trust the tourists, well, that's why there was no sign on the bar. "It's not easy being as pretty as you are, is it?" I asked her.

Monica tugged her knees to her chest and hugged them. "It's not, actually," she admitted. "That can be hard to explain to people, though."

"Well, gorgeous," I sighed, "maybe we should get you back to Cutlass Key and away from all these ravenous beasts in the Upper Keys. What do you say?"

"Agreed," Monica said, hopping up. She held out a hand to me, and I took it, brushing sand off my bottom with my other hand.

I really liked Monica. And no, I didn't believe everything she said about Arnie—I thought she was leaving something out, something about Lou. But maybe I was just being a little too suspicious. Maybe my year on the road with The Bombers had made me into a grittier person than I'd realized. I'd give her another chance, I decided. I was still short on friends, and it seemed like Monica could use one, too.

Chapter Nine

IT WAS LATE afternoon when we got back to Hell and Dammit Cay. Roger was sitting in the middle of the bridge, and it took several minutes to convince him to climb back onto his favorite rock.

"Weirdo," I said, coming back to Monica's side of the Jeep once the iguana was relocated and gazing balefully at us from his rock. "You want to stay awhile? I'm going to take care of the horses and then I think we're having dinner at Marchant's tonight."

"How do you know?"

I pointed to the pirate flag hoisted above the house. It flapped in the fresh afternoon breeze with vigor. "He used to just come out and wave it when he wanted to have someone over, but now he puts it up the pole as a signal."

"Oh, that's too funny. Now I have to stay. He won't mind?"

"He loves everyone," I said. "That's why I'm working so hard to help him get his hotel off the ground."

Monica drove the Jeep forward and parked it along the paddocks. She hopped out and walked with me to the barn. "I need to get on one of these ponies some day soon," she said, as the horses walked to their paddock gates, ready to start talking dinner.

"We'll definitely go on a trail ride," I assured her. "I have a quiet week next week. Want to come out on your next day off?"

"Oh, that would be amazing!" She paused as a tall, red-haired woman biked down the shell road behind us. "And who was that?"

"Steph," I replied, waving to the woman. "Steph O'Reilly. She's this week's artist in residence. Does mermaid artwork."

"I love mermaids! Why didn't you tell me?"

I grinned. "We weren't busy enough already? She'll be here tomorrow. Come back and talk to her."

"I'm going to," Monica vowed, sounding serious. "Here today, back tomorrow, then again next week...I'm practically living on Hell and Dammit Cay, now! Pretty soon, y'all will just tell me to grab my overnight bag and stay. If I play my cards right," she added slyly.

I glanced sidelong at her, but I didn't have the heart to correct her.

Hell and Dammit Cay was not open to new residents. Even really, really pretty ones.

We went up to Marchant's porch once the ponies were fed, and we'd had quick showers, changing in my bedroom. Monica was delighted with my faded watercolors of shorebirds and the bent bamboo furniture. "This entire house is like *The Golden Girls* set," she gushed. "I'm obsessed."

"I didn't do any of it," I admitted. "I just showed up and stuck my clothes in the dresser drawers."

"You're so lucky," she said, admiring the flamingo painting hanging on the wall opposite the windows overlooking the water. "My little efficiency in Cutlass Key is nothing like this. Just a studio with a galley kitchen. The walls are brown wood paneling and there's mold around the sliding glass door. And of course, it's not on stilts, so if there's a hurricane warning, I have to go to the mainland or find someone else to stay with. But," she added, turning around. "Maybe I can stay here!"

"If there's a hurricane warning," I said. "But let's not speak that into existence. I'm from Louisiana, you know. I've been in a few too many big 'canes." I pulled a clean t-shirt over my head and knotted my hair into a quick bun. "Okay, let's go see Marchant. And I think Stacy is home, too. You have to meet her."

Stacy was up at Marchant's, her bright pink blouse and skirt contrasting wildly with his blue decor. Crystal was there, too, drinking a beer and gazing out over the water. There was a storm in the distance, lightning flicking from its dark underside along with a wash of blue rain. Occasional thunder rolled across the sea and beneath our feet. I introduced Monica and there were enthusiastic greetings all around; the Conchs of Hell and Dammit were nothing if not hospitable.

Crystal gave Monica a close once-over as she invited the girl to sit beside her. I sat nearby, hoping to listen in on their conversation, but Stacy was at my side, wanting to talk about the July Art Festival coming up in a few weeks.

"It's all organized," I told her, once she paused and let me break in. "The people park at the empty lot next to the Mermaid, they shuttle in on the truck and trailer Henry built,"—Henry, an artist and welder from Little Bucket, had built seats onto an open trailer to ferry guests across Little Bucket Key to Hell and Dammit, where we really had no space for parking more than a few cars—"and then we'll have the studios open and the grills going to sell lunch. The band plays at three, the festival ends at five, and everyone is back to Key West in time for Fourth of July fireworks."

Stacy pursed her lips. "We need this one to go well," she said.

"We need them all to go well," I answered. "It *will* go well."

"I hope so," she muttered, looking away.

"Hey." I tapped her on the thigh. "Why are you being so crazy about this? What don't I know?"

Stacy sighed. "It's probably nothing."

I gave her a look.

"Fine. Pacey Johnson's boys are going to be here and they're heavily in with the Monroe County Zoning Board."

"Pacey Johnson? Should I know that name?"

"Johnson Land Development? Yeah, I think you should."

I stared at her. "But we already stopped the zoning changes," I said finally. "That part is *done*. We're in maintenance mode now. Just keeping public interest up."

"Well, we gotta keep it *high*," Stacy informed me. "All the way up. Because this is Florida, baby girl. Keeping the vultures out is *never* done."

Just like that, the weight of the island's many needs descended on my shoulders again. I reached for a beer and Crystal intercepted me, handing me a dripping bottle from the cooler. She smiled, and I realized she'd swiped lipstick on before coming over this evening. I glanced at Marchant, busy at the grill, then back at her.

She gave me a coral-pink smile.

"Thanks, Crystal," I said. "How great is Monica?"

Monica beamed at me. "Thank you so much for bringing me out here, Katie. I'll owe you forever."

I hoped she knew what a big statement that could turn out to be.

Eventually, the conversation turned to boats, as it always did in the Keys. Monica let it slip that we'd gone to Islamorada to look at sailboats, and Marchant blinked at the two of us in pure astonishment. "You went looking for boats for *me*?"

"Well, yes," I said, feeling uncomfortable about it. "But I guess you'd like to pick out the boats yourself." That was probably half the fun of the entire idea to him: doing some boat shopping.

"That's so kind." Marchant shook his head, evidently overwhelmed that we'd spend a day off working on his dream. "So very, very kind."

Crystal stirred impatiently. "But a mite foolish," she declared. "Thinking you'd get any kind of deal off a salesman. I know where you should be looking."

"You do?" Marchant looked at her. "Where? Who?"

"You goin' senile, Marchant? Skip Fletcher, that's who!"

"Ah," Marchant smiled. "Of course. Skip. Good ole Cap'n Skip."

"Who is Cap'n Skip?" I asked patiently. I was used to their circular conversations. Sitting across from me, Monica looked bemused.

"The Coast Guard man," Marchant explained. "Based out of Cudjoe Key. He knows all the boats around here."

"Oh, like who is thinking of selling, that kind of thing?"

Stacy chuckled. "Like, where the boats are stashed, more like."

"What?"

Marchant's smile twinkled. "He's always impounding boats."

"But don't those belong to the government?"

"The ones that he does through work, sure. The ones that he takes on the down-low, no. Those are for him."

It turned out that our local "Coast Guard man", working through some loophole in maritime law which may or may not exist outside of his assertion that it did, had a brisk side business restoring abandoned boats he'd found. If he found and reported the boats while he was on duty, they went to the government's slips. But if he missed them while on duty and just found them while he was out sailing on his own? Apparently, that was his own business.

"How is this not illegal?" I asked Marchant dubiously.

"All depends on who's involved, doesn't it?" he said cheerfully. "It's only illegal if busybody folks want to make it illegal. And I don't think none of us do."

He was right there. I couldn't think of a single person in these islands who would get the Coast Guard or any other government authority mixed up in their lives or anyone else's. Conchs took care of themselves; if you asked nicely for help, they'd take care of you, too. But they sure wouldn't go running to the cops just because they thought their neighbor might have gotten a boat through less-than-legal means. Worrying about the feds was a job for rum-runners and coke dealers, not a man fishing the flats or sailing on a fresh day.

Or a woman, you know.

Crystal was already dialing up Cap'n Skip, inviting him over for grouper and beer. Monica and I stared at each other in mutual astonishment, while beside me, Stacy fished in her purse until she pulled out a single-sized bottle of champagne and popped the cork, swigging from the miniature bottle like a rock star. She always did prefer bubbles to beer.

I knew what kind of picture we must make to an outsider: the richly dressed Black woman enjoying a personal bottle of Moet; the leathery middle-aged Conch woman with her gray-streaked braid and her sixth bottle of Corona in one hand, her grimy iPhone in the other, talking to a Coast Guard officer about his stashed boat inventory; the white-haired, wild-eyed old salt at the grill, flipping over foil packets of fish while he chattered about bringing a love of the sea to tourists; and me, of course, frizzy-haired and sunburned and probably turning into one of them faster than I could even see it in myself. I saw all this and I wondered what I looked like to Lou, who was still able to flit in and out of this island life without trouble. Would I eventually be too far gone for him? Too locked into the patterns and problems of the island he visited, but never stayed at for long?

For a moment I felt that rising panic again, that Hell and Dammit Cay had trapped me with its sweet nature and endless need, and I'd never live the bright life I'd longed for. I'd just traded one seaside community for another.

Then, almost by magic, my phone lit with a text. I snatched it up and read the words hungrily.

Surprise gig tonight at Blue Dolphin, you in? Going on at ten. Stay with me tonight. Miss you. Say yes.

My fingers flew, three letters made breathless by my deep need to escape. *Yes.*

Monica saw my face and tilted her head, questioning.

I knew I should tell her, invite her—hell, even use her for an easy ride into Key West. But I didn't want to. We'd spent all day together, I told myself. It was normal to need some time away. Natural to not want to bring her to a gig with my boyfriend. Totally understandable to lie and say, "I'm heading back home, just realized I've got an early ride tomorrow. It was so fun having you, though."

"Oh," Monica said, surprised. "Okay. Well, um, see you in a few days, right?"

"Definitely. Text me."

Marchant brought over plates heaped with blackened fish, steaming into the humid night. "Take a few over with you and eat before you turn in," he urged me. "We'll feed Monica here. Don't worry about your friend."

"Thanks, Marchant," I said, taking a paper plate from him. "Goodnight, everyone. Bye, Monica."

Chapter Ten

IT STARTED RAINING as I crossed the bridge from Stock Island to Key West, and as I sat at the stop-light at Roosevelt Blvd, the windshield wipers scraping, I saw tourists scrambling to pull up soft-tops and hunching over on their rented mopeds, unprepared for the ferocity of the Keys' tropical downpours. Most of them turned right, the easy way to the hotels on the north side of the island and the parking garages close to Old Town. I turned left, passing through the staid, almost mainland-like neighborhoods on the southeast side of the island and the giant fiberglass conch shell outside the high school before the road narrowed and the tropical foliage closed in around smaller, older houses.

I found a parking spot on a quiet street near the cemetery. The rain tapered off to a slow drizzle, and as I stepped around the puddles in the road, a passenger jet flew over, so close I could see the treads on the tires. It was a strange thing to see over the queen palms and the nineteenth-century cottages, but that was modern Key West for you.

Lou was waiting on the porch of the same house where I'd seen him a few days ago. The fluffy cat was sitting next to him. I felt my heart lift from my chest right into my throat at the sight of him; I'd been so busy and angry I hadn't had time to miss him. But now I felt it all, a choking longing that sent me dashing up the stairs and into his arms, even though I'd hoped for a more dignified entrance. His arms went around me and my cheek, pressed against his chest, thrummed to the quick rhythm of his heart.

I sighed, letting go of everything but this: Hell and Dammit Cay, the artists, the circling developers, stolen boats, even Monica all slipped away. For a moment, it was just Lou and me.

The way it should be.

Then the cat rubbed against my bare ankle, startling me, and I jumped. Lou thought something bad was happening to me and lurched backwards, dragging me with him, and I kicked the cat as I scrambled to keep my footing on the slippery porch. The cat yowled with outrage and scampered down the pathway, disappearing onto the cracked sidewalk.

"Oh, damn," Lou said. "I wasn't even supposed to let Muffin out at night."

"Muffin?" I asked, and then I started laughing—hysterically, maybe, but I was due one small breakdown.

"Kev's cat," he muttered, running down the steps. "Muffin! Muffin, come back here."

"Kev?" I repeated, but Lou was already in front of the next house, then the next, with Muffin apparently leading him on. I sighed and went inside to put down my overnight bag. I'd never understood cats, and I wouldn't be any help to him.

Lou was evidently staying in the tiny front bedroom, judging by the clothes tossed on the bed, so I added my backpack to the scrum and then poked around a little more. I'd only seen the hallway and the kitchen the last time I'd been here. There wasn't much more. Across from Lou's bedroom was a second bedroom, this one far more lived-in and smelling mustily of pot, which must be Kev's room. Then there was a small, damp bathroom which hadn't been updated since the 1950s, and a living room just big enough for a sofa, a lounger, and a TV on an old table. This was very much a boy's house. I began to revise any ideas I had about staying with Lou more than tonight.

I came out of the living room just as Lou burst back into the hall with the cat in his arms, meowing lustily. "Beep-beep," he said, hustling towards me. "Muffin needs wet food to keep her busy, and then we can run for it."

I jumped out of his way and watched him push canned food on the cat with the urgency of a dealer who knows the cops are on their way. Then he took my hand and rushed me back up the hall. We were out on the street before I knew what happened.

"Wanna get some food before we hit the club?" he asked.

"Where's your gear?"

"Kev took it over already."

"Okay," I agreed. "But you gotta tell me who Kev is."

The last time I'd had a meal with Lou in Key West, he'd taken me for Cuban food and refused to tell me a thing. This time, he took me to a quiet restaurant down Amelia Street, led me onto the half-empty balcony off the second floor dining room, and took a bottle of wine from his backpack.

"This place is BYOB?" I asked skeptically, looking around for someone determined to set us on the correct path. We hadn't even waited for a seater or a server to tell us where to sit. It felt a bit like we'd snuck in to use their table and cutlery for free.

"I know the owner," Lou said, pouring wine into the glasses already set on the table. A server came over, her expression thundery as the weather, but she loosened up when she saw Lou's face.

"I'll bring you some menus," she promised, disappearing back into the indoor dining room, which was full of loud tourists.

"Who is the owner?"

"Kev," Lou said, grinning. "See? And last time, you thought he was my *dealer.*"

"I made an educated guess, based on the state of that house," I retorted, embarrassed.

"That house is worth half a million dollars," Lou told me. "Even unrestored. Drink your wine. It's very good."

I took a sip. It *was* good. "Fine, you can pick out wine and your friend has a very pretty restaurant, even if the house looks like hell. So, a gig tonight? How did this happen?"

Lou winked. "Rivers."

"Rivers? *My* Rivers?" That came out wrong. "I mean—"

"Your Rivers," Lou replied, giving me a little head shake. "Inasmuch as anyone can own a record company executive."

"Please, he runs one little label. He's hardly a mogul."

"Menus," the server chirped, returning. "Kev says to get the bisque."

"Then you know what to do," Lou told her. She nodded and went back to the dining room, her black flats flashing on the creaking wooden floor. "So I ran into Rivers at the jazz club last night."

"Nice to know you're getting out and enjoying yourself while I'm working on the island," I said.

"You're welcome here anytime..."

"For the last time, I have a *job*," I snapped. Already, the warm and fuzzy feeling I'd gotten at being back in his arms was being overtaken by irritation. Was this what love was like, once you got to know someone's faults? You just alternated between elation and disappointment? "Forget it. Tell me your story."

Lou dipped his head and continued. "Rivers and I had a few beers, and he said he owned the Blue Dolphin now, that club above the biker bar a few blocks down Duval, and then today he calls me up and asks do I want to do a gig. He had openings. I guess there's usually just a DJ. So anyway, I said yes, how about tonight, and he laughed and was like 'yeah I guess I better book you while I can, before you run off again,' and I was like yeah." Lou paused for a sip of wine. He swirled his glass for a moment, then went on. "I could do a gig without you, but that's not what I'm about anymore. I don't want to be the lonely indie guy doing Silvery Star. I want what *we've* got. So, that's why I texted. I'm sorry it was last minute."

I sighed. The disappointment was abating, replaced with the elation. Life was going to be exhausting with Lou, I could tell. Constant swapping of emotions. "It's okay," I told him. "Thank you for asking me. I'm—that's—I'm touched," I faltered. "That you'd rather perform with me than without me."

"It's an old chapter of my life, Silvery Star." Lou took my hand. "I'm still figuring out how to read the new one, but I know you're on every page."

Charmer, I thought, but I was already a goner.

We forgot everything else for a bit, and there was a lot of finger-stroking and giggling, until the server brought us two bowls of a fragrant lobster bisque so velvety-smooth on my tongue that I nearly stood up to march into the kitchen and proclaim my love for Kev, as well. Then there was ciabatta bread dressed with a spiced olive oil and goat cheese, followed by a plate of plump Key West pink shrimp, steaming and encased in their lobster-hard shells. The mood lightened over food and I let Lou tell me about how he'd met Kev in high school up in Big Pine, and how they'd reconnected online a few years back, ending up with this unlikely reunion in Key West.

"He learned to cook in Paris," Lou said, a little in awe of his old friend. "He lives for it."

"Is that why the house is so gross?" I couldn't help myself. "Lou, you two are living in that place like squatters. I'm tempted to drive back to the island tonight and sleep in my own bed, just so I know when the sheets were last washed." To say nothing of that mildewed bathroom.

"Is it that bad?" Lou asked. "I hadn't noticed."

"Liar. No one who lives in your mother's nice, clean house could possibly just switch into that decaying old cottage and not notice how gross it is."

"Did you come here to compliment me all night, or did I just get lucky?" A soft voice startled me into looking up; I saw a red-haired man with a freckled face and a rueful smile next to our table.

"Damn, Kev," Lou said appreciatively. "You have the softest step in the Keys. You could sneak up on Batman."

"It's my one true talent," Kev said. "That and hollandaise sauce. I'm naturally gifted with hollandaise sauce. But you didn't order *anything* with it."

"Bring me a bowl and I'll eat it," Lou suggested. "With a spoon."

"Absolutely not, you animal," Kev told him affectionately. Then he turned back to me. "You weren't supposed to find out about my pigsty house. No women are allowed in there for that exact reason. I'm still trying to live like an adult. And failing."

"You just need bleach," I said. "And a robot vacuum to do your floors while you're at work."

"I'll try it," he promised. "And if you want to clean up anything—"

"No," I said, laughing. "Don't even try it."

Kev gave Lou a sorrowful look. "Well, an attempt was made. I better get back to the kitchen. A big old group from New York just came in downstairs and they're probably going to want everything off-menu."

"He shouldn't allow that," I said as Kev scurried back to work. "The menu is what he's making. Why do extra work because people think they're special?"

"That's what I like about you," Lou told me. "You know no one is worth extra work."

"Well, certainly not just because they *decide* they are," I replied. "And definitely not because of their money."

"That's another thing I like," Lou said. "You don't like people with money."

"Well," I said, "maybe if they weren't so awful all the time, I would."

By the time we'd finished up, the night sky had cleared and a crescent moon hung lazily over the western shore. We couldn't get to the seaside on this part of the island, because of the naval base, so we walked along a backstreet, avoiding Duval until the very last block, until we got to the Southernmost Point. There were a few tourists standing around taking pictures, and a woman selling glow necklaces and rum drinks from a cart on the sidewalk, but it was mostly quiet. We stood a few feet down from the big concrete marker that said *90 miles to Cuba* and watched the foam from the small breakers slapping against the broken seawall. The night smelled of rain and salt and some exuberantly blooming tropical flower. Oh, and a hint of weed from some kids sitting on the fence across from the Southernmost House, their scooters abandoned at their feet and blocking the sidewalk so retirees couldn't come over and tut-tut at them.

"Ah, Key West," Lou said, sniffing the air and grinning.

"Where rebels are born," I joked, nodding at the puffing teens.

"And the good die young. Or at least get put on serious restrictions when they get home."

"Did you come to Key West to smoke weed when you were a teenager?"

Lou laughed. "No. Never. We hung out behind the gym like normal teens. What about you? Where did you sneak out?"

"I never did," I told him. "I was a truly good girl. That's why it hit my mom so hard when I ran off with The Bombers. She never saw it coming."

"She must miss you."

"I'll go back soon," I said. "When I have time."

I wondered when I'd have time.

Lou must have been wondering, too, because there was a long pause before he said, "You have to find someone else to take on the island before we go on tour next year."

A month ago, when we'd been planning our career together, next year had seemed so far away. Six whole months. Now, it felt entirely too close for comfort, and yet the idea of going on tour with Lou was so alien that it also felt like it could never, ever happen. I nodded and said, "But I don't know how that's going to happen. We need someone else to take over the ranch duties, *and* someone to deal with the art festival. And of course, there'll be the hotel..."

I realized Lou didn't know what was happening with Marchant's hotel. He was staring at me, astonished. "Hotel?"

"Oh, god." I looked back out over the dark sea. "How to explain this? You know Marchant has always wanted a sailboat hotel, just a couple of boats moored off the island, right?" Lou nodded. "Well, we are...um...doing it?"

"You're *doing* it? You're starting a hotel—on the *island?*"

"I mean...yes. I don't know how long it will last, or if anyone will come and stay, or really anything. But it's in the planning stages. We've looked at boats. Today, actually."

Lou shook his head, astonished. "I leave for a few days..."

"I guess you have to stick around and keep an eye on me," I suggested. "Quit running off all the time."

"I guess! Jeez." He rubbed his beard, then asked, "Who did you look at boats with?"

"Hmm?" Suddenly, I knew telling him Monica was a big part of this was a huge mistake. The last time we'd talked about her, he'd called her a spy for his father. She was part of the reason he was here. Maybe the *entire* reason.

Lou knew me well enough to see I was stalling. "Who went with you to look at boats? You said *we*."

"I did, didn't I."

Lou shook his head. "Monica, right? You went with Monica."

"She knows how to run a hotel," I argued. "She's the only choice to help me out. She's the right choice. Even if you don't like her."

"It's not that I don't—" Lou stopped himself. "We should get to the club," he said. "Kev'll have dropped off our gear, but he won't have set it up. Come on, it's just up Duval. We can walk it."

And Lou started up the sidewalk, giving me no choice but to scurry after him, scattering the weed-smoking kids like a flock of startled chickens.

Chapter Eleven

WE HAD SO much fun on stage.

So much fun. If I needed a reminder of why I wanted to be a performer, our gig together was the jolt required...and then some.

The Blue Dolphin had a big following in the queer community, and in Key West, that meant every night was busy. I could see why Rivers was eager to get live music going in his new acquisition; the crowd was rambunctious and eager for excitement, and a DJ spinning club tracks could only tap into so much of that energy. What they were looking for was humanity, a show, someone on stage to get them as hyped up as they'd hoped to be when they'd decided to come out on this hot, humid night.

And, I wondered, as I spotted Rivers leaning against one corner of the bar, could tonight be a chance for him to hear what Lou and I were supposedly so busy cooking up? A test run to make sure his investment was operating the way he'd expected? After all, we were an unknown entity as a group.

When Rivers offered us a record deal, he'd done so knowing that Lou was a solo artist and I was a former backup singer. We weren't a band yet; we did one song really well together, and that was my homesick ballad *A Love So True*. A song Justin and The Bombers had stolen from me, until I decided to steal it back. We'd performed it together at the benefit festival back in May, and he'd seen the potential in us, like She & Him with more synths and fewer choices from the American songbook. Should be a slam dunk with a certain crowd, right?

You'd think so. I'd sure think so.

But tonight was his first opportunity to see if his guess had been correct. And Rivers was all businessman, underneath his soft-hearted veneer. He could act like a good friend, but any tears that man shed over canceled deals were of the crocodile variety.

Well, Lou and I had a couple of songs and the ability to surprise one another. I hoped that would be enough to renew his faith...and get Lou back on board, too.

More than anything else, though, it felt *good* to be here.

I loved standing in front of people, loved a stage, loved a crowd watching my every move. The club wasn't that big, just one wide room in a Victorian building on Duval Street, but with the rainbow lights dancing around us and the packed crowd shimmying and shouting, ready for our set, I was able to find that old thrill from my early nights with The Bombers. We'd played all sorts of venues, stages of all kinds, but the little clubs had a heart and intimacy to them that was hard to beat.

Tonight, we'd really know if Lou and I had the magic necessary to captivate a crowd hellbent on partying until sunrise. I looked at him, and he looked at me, and then without consultation he launched into the opening chords of our first song we'd written this summer, *Target Acquired*.

And then, we had that entire club in the palms of our hands.

* * *

Forty minutes.

Forty sweaty, glorious, soul-stirring minutes.

I didn't know we had that many songs, but at some point we were just riffing. We played *A Heart So True,* and I was so turned on by the tears on shiny faces, waterproof mascara glistening under the lights, that I launched straight into a cover of *Veronica* by Elvis Costello and everyone started jumping around like they were teenagers again. Lou pounded on his synths like a madman and we took the roof right off that bar.

Forty minutes, and then we looked at each other, exhausted, and I knew the night was over.

Lou put down his guitar, closed his laptop, and signaled to the music engineer to flip the sound system back on. A heavy thudding beat descended on the club, something old from *Sound of Silver* by LCD Soundsystem, and he turned to me, his shirt soggy with sweat, his eyes glittering with excitement. He held out one hand: an invitation to step off the stage and into the tiny, cramped wings where we could escape the crowd.

But I wasn't ready to give up this amazing audience; even now, despite the insistent bass cajoling them to start dancing, they were still watching us. Waiting, hoping for more. I waved and scooped up the laptop instead, darting into one wing of the stage where they couldn't see me. The crowd shouted and stomped, demanding an encore. But of course, we didn't have one. Dammit.

Lou came after me, his guitar in one hand and keyboard in the other. "That was intense!" he shouted, his eyes so wide he might as well have been on something. "I love it!"

He wants more, I thought with satisfaction. Finally, Lou was bitten by the rock n' roll bug. Now all I had to do was drag him back to Hell and Dammit Cay to get the rest of our songs written.

Oh, and find someone else to take over all my duties on the island while we went on an epic world tour. Look, I loved my ponies, but the stadiums awaited, full of screaming fans.

Or the early show at small clubs—I could take either. Sometimes fame isn't instant, fair enough.

But, no, I wasn't going to think about that tonight. This wasn't the time to sit and fret over my responsibilities.

Instead, I was going to revel in my triumph.

I mean, *our* triumph.

Obviously!

We slipped into the tiny green room together and Lou slammed the door shut with a finality which must have cut through the heaving beats coming from the speakers. He gave me one wild look, and I knew what was coming. My heart pounding, I let him take me by the wrists and push me against the wall, his lips capturing mine for a searingly hot kiss. My head was swimming, my body was tingling, and all I wanted in that moment was for Lou to throw me on that sagging green room sofa and—

"Knock-knock!" The voice outside the door was gleeful, but insistent. Rivers knew exactly what he was interrupting.

Lou sighed against my mouth, his fingers tightening around my wrists, then loosening in defeat. With a hot glance that promised there was plenty more where that came from, he whirled around and flung open the green room door.

Rivers stepped inside, smoothing his perfect hair as if he'd been the one about to get frisky behind the stage. "You *killed,* my friends," he informed us happily. "Absolutely *killed.* For a moment there, I thought they were going to storm the stage or burn the place down looking for you. I think we need to work on our encores, eh? You can leave them wanting more, but not volcanic, you know." He sat down on the couch and smiled up at us, a cat who has lapped up every bit of the cream.

"We'll work on it," Lou growled. I could still hear the passion in his voice; he was still revved up, ready to spend all this wild energy on me. I wished Rivers would get the hell out and give us five minutes of peace, but I knew he wouldn't. He was going to make sure both of us left here still wanting more, too. More of this feeling, more of this insatiable rush left by enchanting a crowd from a small stage eighteen inches above a dance-club floor. Frustrating our raging sex drive was all part of the plan.

"Don't take too long," Rivers warned, stretching out his arms and getting comfortable. "It's what, almost July? I want you in the studio and recording by September first."

"September first?" I exclaimed, instantly tumbling out of my high. Nothing less sexy than deadlines. "But we have until December!"

"To give me a finalized, finished product," Rivers corrected me. "You think your first take is going to the presses? Trust me, sweetheart. You're new to this process, so believe me when I say you're going to record, get a shit-ton of feedback you don't like, and then you're going to head back to your rehearsal space with a lot to think about before you book more time and try again. You're talented, and people love you live, but you're not wunderkinds. You had a great night for sure, but you're not going to recreate this kind of magic in the studio the first time around. Probably not even the second, third, or sixth. You gotta give it time, and to give it time, you gotta start *soon*."

I looked over at Lou, feeling defeat creep in and slowly push out my elation. But Lou seemed unconcerned, and for the first time in weeks, I felt like he might be taking our deadlines seriously. "It's fine, Rivers," he said crisply. "We'll be in touch."

"Feel free to drop in and try new material here," Rivers said, standing. He gave us a satisfied look, and nodded, more to himself than to us. "Yes," he said. "Feel free."

And then he was gone, closing the door behind him. The bass thumped through the walls and beneath my feet, sweaty in my black ballet flats. Lou rubbed his face and sighed. "Do you want to just head back to the house?" he asked. "I could use a drink, and *not* one from that guy's bar."

"Yeah, sure," I agreed, and we carefully stacked our equipment, ready for Kev to pick up tomorrow morning, before closing the green room door behind us.

Back at the cottage, we drank bourbon and played with Muffin, trying to level out after the peaks and lows of the past hours. We chatted a little about prospective songs, tunes we'd been playing with before Lou had stopped working, and I felt optimistic that things were turning around. Maybe this night on stage, even with its anti-climactic finish and thinly veiled threat from Rivers, was exactly what he'd needed. What we'd *both* needed. A reminder that we were really, really good together. And the prospect of stardom was just a few months of hard work away.

But there was no thought of the work ahead without being reminded of going home to Hell and Dammit Cay, and then my thoughts just spiraled into the infinite workload and impossible task of finding a replacement me for next year, and I began to feel despondent all over again. I poured myself a little more bourbon, added a couple more ice cubes, and sighed.

Lou looked up from the floor, where he was sitting on the splintering parquet, teasing Muffin with a foil ball. "Why so sad, sunshine?" he asked gently. "We had a good night."

"Just thinking about going back to work," I said. "The Sunday scaries, good any night of the week."

"Don't go back, then," he suggested casually.

"I have to go back, and so do you."

To my surprise, he didn't argue that point. Then he said, "You know, we have to work out this thing with Monica and my dad."

"Work out, how?"

"Well," Lou said, tickling Muffin's toes until the cat flexed his claws in warning, "we need my dad to stay away, and we need to know Monica isn't reporting back to him everything going on around the islands."

I sighed, disappointed in him. "Seriously, Monica is not a spy, and you're going to have to accept that your dad might be within five miles of Hell and Dammit and it won't kill you. Come *on,* Lou. I know he sucks, but that's *your* home and he doesn't live there. And Crystal isn't about to invite him back. What about Marchant?"

"What *about* Marchant?" Lou shook his head and moved on. "Look, she was never really mad at my dad, not for herself. She didn't want to marry him, and when he left, she was okay with raising me alone. I'd rely on my mom for anything, except maybe for staying away from my dad."

"So, what, you think she'd get back together with your dad and he'd move to Hell and Dammit and try to pick up where he left off? Invite you out for games of catch?"

Lou's gaze met mine. His expression was pained as he admitted, "That's exactly what I'm afraid of, Katie. And frankly, I think my mom needs to understand it's him or me."

This is how he tells me, I realized. *He's not coming back.*

And for once, I wasn't sure I could blame him. Would I go back, with the specter of the father who abandoned me, waiting to step in and seduce my mother one more time?

I couldn't answer that question. Not without being in that position. And I was so, so thankful I wasn't.

But we still had a future of our own to contend with.

"So, what are we going to do?" I asked at last. "About the record, I mean. If you're not coming back to work with me."

"Come here," he urged me. "Stay with me and we'll do it here, in Key West. It'll be fun. Take some time away and we'll live here and —"

"I can't live here," I said quickly. "The horses, remember? And the art festival. And the *bathroom*."

"The bathroom, I can clean. My mom took care of the horses just fine before you showed up. And the art festival is all set; you don't have to be there every single day between now and July Fourth. Certainly not afterward. Come on, Katie." Lou shifted and put his hand on my thigh, his fingers warm and encouraging. Definitely an argument to stay with him. "Artists come to Key West for a reason, you know. Yeah, it's full of tourists and drunk assholes on motorcycles, but there's still all kinds of wild stuff going on here. The vibe is totally right for making music. And the club is right here, so we can test tracks, lyrics—"

"Stop," I insisted, using everything I had in me to push him away. "I can't make a decision like this now. It isn't fair. Your mom is the one who took me in when I had nothing and no one, Lou. I can't just abandon her. And there's Marchant to think about, too. The hotel is in motion. What would that do to him if I just stopped working on it? I made commitments. I'm not breaking them."

"Katie, you're going about this all wrong." His voice was smooth, confident. Convincing. The con man who sold swampland, a hundred years after the Florida land boom bubbled up and burst. "We're artists. We can't do things like everyone else. We have to follow the muse. Follow the creativity. The vibe, the beat, hell, whatever you want to call it. You can't say no when it comes for you, because you don't know when it's coming back. Maybe never."

Luckily, I knew him too well to fall instantly under his salesman's spell. A lesser woman would have swooned for it. Me, I got mad.

"What's your point?" I demanded. "Are you saying we're better than everyone else because we can string words together and slam out a few notes to match?"

"I'm saying that if you want this, you have to give it everything," Lou said, undeterred. "You never know when it's your last chance."

I slumped in my chair, sighing. The worst part was that I thought he was right. I *agreed* with him. I could see why he felt like Key West was the place, and why Hell and Dammit might not have been the end of the road for me. Instead, maybe Mile Marker Zero was, just like it had been for so many other artists. The way we'd performed tonight, the way we'd felt...like we were standing on the cliff, and all we had to do was take one more step and we'd free-fall into the sea, loving every moment we weren't bound to the earth.

But the people we would hurt to get that feeling...

"I can't," I decided, standing up. Muffin darted beneath the sofa. "I can set things in motion, I can try to find help, I can do a lot of things to work towards this, but I can't just walk away tonight."

Lou's gaze dropped to the floor. "I think you're making a mistake."

I shook my head, heading into the bedroom to grab my bag. "God, I might be, Lou. You know? But it's the only choice I've got."

Chapter Twelve

TWO DAYS AFTER I drove back to Hell and Dammit Cay in the wee hours, my eyes swollen with crying and my heart aching with misgiving, I took Monica out for a trail ride through the jungle, and showed her the beach on Little Bucket Key.

She loved it. Who wouldn't?

"I feel like I live in a dream world," she laughed, rubbing Ruby's waterfall of red mane. "Coming here was the best thing that ever happened to me."

I gave Reggie a pat. "Yeah," I agreed. "Me, too."

We let the horses stand in the shallow water and looked across the blue-green flats towards Hell and Dammit Cay. Marchant's house stood tall on its stilts in the distance. His sailboat, moored at the dock, rocked gently on waves cast from a passing fishing boat.

"So, the sailboats go right there." Monica nodded at the dock. "Anchored, or docked?"

"I think it depends on the person," I suggested, although I wasn't really sure. One more thing we hadn't nailed down yet. "Some people will be too nervous to stay away from the dock, right?"

"I'd think so. And what will they do?"

"Ride," I said. "Snorkel. They can come over here and sunbathe, splash in the water. There's the little beach behind the barn, too. The one we just added. But this one is prettier." Somehow, natural was always best, even if we'd done our best to create a realistic beach of our own with a few truckloads of sand.

"You don't own this beach, though," Monica said. Ruby turned in a circle, her hooves splashing the water. "Isn't *this* trespassing?"

"Oh, no, that's not an issue. Beaches in Florida are all public. It's like, our best law. If they come over by boat, there's no issue. Or we can ride them over, since we're able to use the jungle trail. We do have permission for that."

"Hmm." Monica nodded. "Well, in that case, yeah. I think it could be great. As long as we keep it small."

I liked it when she said *we*. If I had to do all this on my own, I'd go crazy. "Wanna come with me this afternoon? Marchant has Cap'n Skip coming over to get us, and we're going to look at some of his boats."

I hadn't yet met their Coast Guard buddy, since I'd gone to Key West to be with Lou instead of sticking around the night he came over for dinner. But apparently the hotel idea had gone over well with him, and he was supposed to be drawing up a map of his favorite boats, which he seemed to have stashed all over the out-islands. Marchant told me this with a wink, his twinkling blue eyes answering all my unspoken questions.

Nope, nothing shady about what we were getting up to at all. But this was the Keys, not the mainland. Conchs did things their own way...and sometimes, you just had to go with the local vibe. And there was always an off-chance Skip actually had the titles to these boats, right?

But I didn't say any of this to Monica. She might not understand. She was new here…she'd come around.

"Boat shopping," Monica said cheerfully. "Sure! But first, we get to give these babies their baths, right?" She patted Ruby affectionately.

Monica, it turned out, was absolutely dying to give a horse a bubble bath. I didn't know where this obsession came from, but it was an easy wish to fulfill. "Sure," I agreed. "Baths for all. But you should know, you'll be ten times as dirty as the horse was when the bath is over. There's some kind of dirt transference principle at work. Scientists haven't named it yet."

"That's fine," Monica laughed. "I can just hose myself off when we're done."

And she did, which was why Cap'n Skip's eyes were nearly popping out of his skull when his boat came thrumming up to Hell and Dammit Cay on our side of the island. We had the horses tied on the narrow, scrubby strip of land between the barn and the beach, and we'd just finished their baths. Monica had turned the hose on herself and was spraying off all the sand and assorted dirty patches that had accumulated on her tank top, shorts, and bare skin while she'd been bathing Ruby. She looked very much like she was prepping for the wet t-shirt contest of a lifetime.

I heard the boat approaching and braced myself for wolf whistles from some gross passersby, but when the middle-aged man at the wheel turned off the engine and called hello across the few feet of clear water separating the island from the channel, I realized it was our ride to look at potential hotel boats.

"Stop that," I hissed, as she trained the hose over her neck, closing her eyes against the cold water. "We have company. A business associate."

Monica opened her eyes. They widened briefly as she took in Cap'n Skip's admiring gaze, then she laughed and tossed the hose aside. "I'm so embarrassed!" she shouted. "Can't believe you saw that!"

Skip laughed appreciatively. The sunburned old lech. I was annoyed, but I could also see his side of things. Monica wasn't exactly hiding away her, um, assets. And at least she was *clean*. I was dirt and sand from head to toe.

"Go up to the house and put on something dry," I suggested, hoping she'd thought to bring a change of clothes. "I'll put away the horses."

With the show over, Skip motored the boat on, heading for the opposite side of the island and Marchant's dock. I shook my head as I walked Ruby and Reggie around the barn, a lead-rope in each hand. The horses tugged on me, eager to get back to their paddocks for a good roll in the sand. I barely managed to get Reggie's halter off before his knees were buckling and he was heading face-first for the deep gray sand just inside the gate. He groaned contentedly as he dug his neck and spine into the dirt, coating his wet hide with a thick layer of sand and crushed shell.

Ruby looked on impassively, waiting while I latched the gate.

"I know you're just waiting to do the same thing," I told her. "So quit acting so regal."

But Ruby couldn't help her patronizing attitude. She was the queen bee of Sea Horse Ranch. And I loved her for it. Even with all her disdainful stares at Reggie, she had her legs in the air before I had *her* paddock gate latched, too.

I wished I could be so happy covered with dirt.

I'd hung up the halters and was heading for the house, intent on changing and maybe wiping some of the dirt off my face and arms, when Monica came outside. She leaned over the porch rail, holding something small and black in her hand. It took me a moment to realize what it was.

Then my heart started thudding wildly in my chest. What was she doing with my lyric book?

"Hey," I choked, taking the stairs two at a time. "Hey—um—why—"

"Is this yours?" Monica waved the book at me as I stumbled onto the porch. "Did you *write* this stuff?"

She'd had five minutes alone. How on earth had she found the time to rummage through my room and find my lyric notebook, *and* start reading the contents? Where had I even left it? Surely it was in my bedside table drawer—

"It was laying open on the bathroom counter," Monica said. "I just looked down and started reading and *wow*, I couldn't stop!"

It was a clear invasion of privacy, but I wasn't immune to compliments. Especially when they validated the work I'd done this morning.

I'd been scribbling away before I'd even gotten out of bed, carrying my book around with me as the ideas flowed like a high tide over Duval Street, my pen going a mile a minute in my right hand while I brushed my teeth with my left hand. It was one of those days when I woke up with a whole series of lines and rhymes ready to go in my brain, and I had no choice but to jot them down before they had a chance to dissipate into the morning sunlight.

"Seriously," Monica went on. "These are quality. Poems? Songs? I wasn't sure. I like this part here," —she began flicking through the book— "about jealous water, jade with envy? That's really pretty."

I hadn't been sure about those lines. They'd been beautiful as I wrote them, but when I looked back, they felt a little pretentious for a pop song. Hearing Monica paraphrase them, out here in the glaring midmorning light, didn't really help. I had a sudden desire to hide the book under my bed.

"Thanks," I told her, reaching for it. "But I don't usually share my stuff before it's finished."

She relinquished the notebook reluctantly. "Sorry, I didn't know."

"It's okay, really." And it was; I wasn't angry at all. Just... uncomfortable. "I mean, I did leave it out," I went on, taking all the blame. "And you liked what you saw? How much did you read?"

"Just what was open," she assured me "I hope it wasn't too—"

"Personal?" I finished for her, thinking of the lines I'd written right after my eyes snapped open and I reached for the book by my bed. What had it been about? A little bit about betrayal, a lot about love. Of course. Maybe I'd been channeling my feelings about Justin and the way he'd dumped me for another singer on our small nightclub circuit, or maybe my subconscious was already working through the conflicted way Lou made me feel with his coming and going, his ups and his downs. But if I couldn't identify it yet, that meant Monica wouldn't be able to, either. My secrets were safe. I managed a smile and started to walk past her, heading inside.

"It's about Lou, right?"

I turned and stared at her. "How did you—I mean, no, that would be crazy. Can you imagine if I got up in front of him and sang all that —about him?" I forced a laugh to show her just how nuts that would be.

Monica laughed too. "What makes you think he'd realize it was about him?"

This was an excellent point. "You know, you're right. They're not very perceptive, are they?"

Monica smiled and pushed back her cloud of wavy hair. "Hey, I get it! Men are the ultimate pains in the ass."

I couldn't help but grin. "You got that right."

"So, some angsty lyrics, I just assumed they're about the jerk-slash-love in your life." Monica gave me a one-shoulder shrug. "It could be

Lou, or any other dude on the planet. Anyway, I feel privileged to know someone so talented with words. I hope you'll invite me to your next gig."

"I will," I promised, suddenly feeling bad I hadn't taken her to the Blue Dolphin. "I would have before, only I didn't know what to expect. With Lou, I mean. He's kind of...temperamental."

"Yeah, I don't doubt it." Monica laughed. "Go change! I want to see these stolen boats hidden in the mangroves."

Chapter Thirteen

With Crystal, Marchant, Monica, and myself all packed into Cap'n Skip's boat, we made a tight fit, but it was fine. I waved to the horses as we motored away, but they didn't look up from their hay. Typical horses. I was learning that horses valued food above all other things—even housing, or the ability to get out of the rain. Definitely above friendship.

Monica noticed my slightly disgruntled expression as the boat picked up speed and we left Hell and Dammit Cay behind. She giggled at me. "You're so funny, watching those horses like they're your very bad kids."

"Honestly, that's what they feel like," I said truthfully. "I've never been around horses much before, but these guys have kind of taken over my life."

"That's what horses do," Crystal said, overhearing me. "Why do you think I've moved heaven and earth to keep six horses on a remote island like that? Anyone with half a brain would tell you it's a terrible idea."

Cap'n Skip touched her arm and repeated something Marchant had just told him, and her attention strayed from Monica and me.

Monica's gaze stayed on Crystal's back for a moment. "Why's it a terrible idea to have the horses?" she asked.

"Oh, logistics," I said. "Getting grain and hay down here is a real pain. Luckily, we can get deliveries from the same company that ships supplies out for the Key West Mounted Posse. But the real worry, too, is always hurricanes."

Monica's eyes widened slightly as she looked back at me. "Hurricanes?"

"Yeah, you know." I gestured at the sky. "Big spinny thunderstorms, lot of wind, Jim Cantore stands on the beach and scares everyone away?"

"I know about hurricanes, obviously." Monica gripped a handle next to her seat as Cap'n Skip laughingly put his boat through its paces for Marchant and Crystal's entertainment. She looked the slightest bit uncomfortable. "But I never thought about the horses and hurricanes. What if there's a storm surge? Or damage to the barn roof?"

I shrugged, turning away. The questions made me uncomfortable, because I didn't know the answers. Crystal had said something about only have six horses because it was the most she could evacuate; the old six-horse trailer sitting on the far side of the house wasn't in the best shape, but it could ferry the horses to occasional church carnival or local festival for pony rides and photo ops. We'd last used it to take horses to the art and music festival we'd put on with Rivers to support the island. "I'm sure Crystal has a plan," I said finally, my eyes on the turquoise sea. "Remember, she's in charge of the horses. I just do the work."

"Do you really think she has a plan?" Monica persisted. "Shouldn't you find out what it is, like, before it's a problem?"

"I'm *sure* she has a plan. Trust me. Crystal loves the horses. Nothing is going to happen to them. And why are we even talking about this? It's hurricane season. We shouldn't be tempting fate by even *mentioning* it on a pretty day like today." And I gave the sunny horizon a meaningful glance.

"At least not when we're out on the water," Monica agreed.

"Or all the time. Pretty sure the best thing we can do is keep our mouths shut until December first."

Monica mimed zipping her mouth shut, like we were both six-year-olds, and I laughed. Obviously, we'd have to have conversations about hurricanes at some point in the next six months. Hurricane season was half the year, and here it wasn't just a scary specter in the evening news or on the weather report. It was part of life. At some point this summer or autumn, there would be a hurricane scare, maybe even an actual threat...maybe even two or three. It had happened before.

But there was something perverse and a bit dangerous about bringing up hurricanes on a gorgeous June day, when the sky was impossibly blue, the clouds were fluffy puffs of cotton, and we were out on the big bathtub of the Gulf, slipping across crystalline waters nearly as warm as the surrounding air. For one thing, I had enough trouble to deal with; no need to borrow tomorrow's problems by bringing up the things which might go wrong. And for another, who knew who or what was listening up there, or down below, the gods of the air and the sea? I had that seafarer streak in me, from the pirates of yesteryear; that streak had a touch of the superstitious, as well. I didn't believe a bored Poseidon might get to stirring up the seas with his trident, but at the same time, I couldn't truthfully say I *didn't* believe it, either.

Anyway, I knew there was no telling what might happen in this hurricane season or any other, so there was no point in dwelling on it or I'd just go crazy. December first was a long way away; almost as far away as the December thirtieth deadline for our record. Why did one seem like forever lay between us, and one feel like it was rushing at me like a freight train?

Suddenly, Cap'n Skip throttled back the boat, and it slowed to a growling, surly crawl as we slipped across pale green seagrass flats. Long fish lolled in the waving beds of grass, their slim dorsal fins breaking the surface and dimpling the smooth surface of the water. An egret lifted out of the water in the distance, long white neck telescoping into a neat fold as wide wings beat the air. The bird flew ahead of us and landed on the dangling arm of a red mangrove, sending long-billed iris scattered from its gnarled roots.

"First stop," Cap'n Skip declared. "Moonshine Key."

It was called Moonshine Key for fairly obvious reasons, Cap'n Skip explained, steering the long boat carefully between two grasping arms of the mangrove. Apparently a tiny harbor, hardly big enough to bear the name, lurked within this barely-there island. The long-legged mangroves wrapped themselves around the little heap of sand and dead coral that formed its base, creating an impenetrable jungle with their tangled fingers of root and branch, which in turn protected the inlet.

"Just long enough for this old bird," he said, patting the wheel affectionately. "And it was perfect for the little motorboats they was usin' during Prohibition times, which is where it got its name."

Slowly, carefully, he steered the boat around a curve in the drooping mangroves...and then the inlet opened up, a tiny lagoon of clear water, with a graceful, if rather battered, sailboat sitting in the middle. The proud little ship had a green-painted hull and a few elegant embellishments of brass and dark wood along her portholes and deck.

"Oh, boy," Marchant muttered to himself. "Look at her. Thirty foot and pretty as the morning."

Crystal gave him a pat on the arm.

"Now this fine lady," Skip began, cutting the engine and letting his boat drift into the lagoon, "I found up to no good out near the Dry Tortugas."

Marchant glanced at him. "That's Martinez's jurisdiction."

"And a whole lot of other fine colleagues of mine," Skip agreed, nodding. "But I was out doin' a little sight-seein' of my own and spotted this lovely lady with some owners who were beneath her." He glanced back at Monica and me, theatrically waggling his thick eyebrows. "They was diving for lobster where there ain't no lobster, if ya follow me."

Crystal took pity on our questioning gazes. "Someone drops the drugs in lobster pots and someone else picks it up," she explained. "Old tradition."

Tradition seemed like an odd word to use, but we *were* in the Keys, after all.

"Precisely," Skip agreed, nodding. "Anyway, I convinced the custodians of this fine vessel that she would be in much better hands if they followed my precise coordinates and then headed very swiftly to parts distant, and they agreed with me. So, here she is. Abandoned, and the property of the United States government."

Marchant's eyes were practically popping out of his head. He looked like Cap'n Skip when he saw Monica hosing herself down. "I know the United States government don't want this pretty boat going to rot out here."

"They surely do not," Skip intoned pompously. "I hear they'll sell you this ship for a song."

Marchant looked like he'd just been presented with a banana split and an entire can of whipped cream. "Ship number one," he said. "Here we go!"

Monica edged close to me as Marchant and Skip stepped onto the deck of the impounded ship. "This is exciting," she whispered, her mouth close enough to my ear for me to feel the warmth of her breath. "Isn't it? We're out here with a Coast Guard captain on the wrong side of the law and your neighbor is going to buy a boat to turn into a hotel—the Keys, I mean, it's crazy what goes on here! I love it."

"I do, too," I confessed. "Sometimes it stresses me out, because I feel like I'm the only sane person here, but I'm not sure I could trade my life here for anywhere else."

She gave my thigh an excited little squeeze. "Oh, me neither. And trust me, I'm here to see you through all the hotel logistics. I know before I said it was a non-starter, but you've come so far, and that boat..." she nodded at the sailboat in question. "It's really cute. I could imagine spending the night on it, waking up with the island a couple dozen feet away...sounds magical, honestly."

"So, you're saying you think it might work?" My heart lifted. I hadn't even realized how worried I'd been, freaking out that all this work we'd put into Marchant's dream might still all be for nothing. I couldn't bear to think of him disappointed—not now, not so late into his twilight years.

"Oh, it's definitely going to work!" Monica's smile was ear to ear. "I'm so, so in!"

Chapter Fourteen

THREE SAILBOATS BOBBED on the water now, lending a new dimension to the view when I strode out onto the porch each morning and looked around the island. Each one needed TLC, brass polish, and some fresh upholstery, but Marchant wasn't afraid of hard work—despite his age, which worried me and apparently no one else—and Crystal revealed a previously hidden talent with the needle. As the heat and long days of July settled over the island, I started to get used to the hum of distant power tools and the swearing of a woman who has just poked herself with a straight pin *again*.

While I cleaned stalls and groomed horses, I thought about the nitty-gritty of the hotel business, the licenses and the fittings and the marketing. Monica took them off my plate with grace and kindness, and I fell even more in love with her. I started to think of her as my best friend. It was freeing, and delightful, and more moving than I'd expected, to have a best friend again for the first time since high school.

And thank goodness for her because the things which should be moving like a well-oiled machine were catching and twisting and breaking constantly. On the morning before the Fourth of July Art Festival, Stacy stumbled on her staircase and twisted her ankle. She came back from the doctor in Key West with crutches, a brace, and a seriously sour attitude towards life. And she wasn't the only artist in trouble.

Daphne, who was usually so steady and a true rock amongst the swaying personalities of Little Bucket's artist colony, was having some sort of writing epiphany and hadn't bothered to put together a single tile mosaic or mixed-media collage in the past month. Since her work had been a huge draw at the art and music festival, getting profiled closely by several travel blogs and featuring in innumerable Instagram posts, I expected her studio space to be quite a draw. But now, she was telling me she didn't have a thing to exhibit.

When I suggested she dig around her attic for work that hadn't sold before, she was *very* offended.

Peter, the woodworker from Little Bucket, refused to set up his studio space for the festival because he was unhappy with his work and didn't want anyone to see it. He was threatening to start a bonfire out of all his latest pieces instead. *That* would draw a crowd, he told me darkly.

"This is not a bonfire of statues kind of crowd we're expecting," I informed him. "We are talking grandmas and grandpas who want driftwood sculptures, maybe a tiki god."

"I'll burn the tiki gods and we'll call it an offering to the storm lords," Peter suggested, looking alarmingly pleased with himself.

"Please do not do that, Peter. I am begging you."

He shrugged, which I did not find reassuring, and said he would look over his work again.

And then there was George, a watercolor painter who lived for his tropical garden. He was still upset that Queen Tom had made off with his new traveller palm and planted it amongst the garden paths we'd landscaped between the little studios. So he decided to do an entire gallery display of traveller palms in various states of dismay, being carted away from their rightful homes to parts unknown, and eventually dying in grisly watercolor drama.

"George, who is going to buy a series of watercolors featuring unhappy and dying palm trees?" I asked him, standing in the doorway of his studio as he arranged the paintings in the shape of a giant cross on the wall.

"Darling, they'll buy what we tell them to buy," he assured me, pushing his long gray hair over his shoulder. "And this tells a *story*. The story of my betrayal by a six-foot-five man with stunningly beautiful arms and a very high forehead who took away my prize traveller palm and left me bereft."

"The traveller palm is five feet away," I pointed out, annoyed that this drama was still playing out, more than a month after Queen Tom put his landscaping skills to work on the studio gardens. "Think of it like it's in your *second* front yard."

"I don't think you appreciate the enormity of what has happened to me and my palm," George sighed. "Leave me in peace."

I left him, because at least he'd shown up with work, even if it was terrible. And George was probably right, some people *would* buy his bizarre traveller palm paintings, if only because he was standing right there, fixing them with his crazy blue eyes and making them feel as if buying a painting was the only way to escape safely.

Crystal waylaid me as I was walking towards the house, muttering about crazy artists. "Everything okay, honey?"

I looked into her faded eyes, like washed-out versions of her son's big gem-colored ones. She was so sweet and good, the perfect second mother for a girl who already had a pretty good one waiting for her back home. "Just worn out with our artist friends," I told her.

Crystal smiled understandingly. "Now you know why we value Stacy so much," she said with a chuckle. "The least temperamental artist you'll ever meet."

And yet Stacy was sitting upstairs with gin in her tea and a chip on her shoulder, as if the staircase incident had been a personal affront from the island and possibly me in particular. But maybe that wasn't about being artistic; she just had a sore ankle and no one to complain to but me. "I think you better take her dinner tonight," I suggested. "She shouldn't be going up and down those stairs for a few days."

"We will," Crystal agreed, with a glance in the direction of Marchant's house.

I wondered when the *I* had so easily morphed into *we*. But not for long. I had my own *we* to worry about. Changing the subject, I asked, "You mind if I take the truck into Key West tonight? I need to work with Lou on some stuff."

"Of course not, that's fine." Crystal looked back at me, her eyes focusing again as if she'd just wandered away and come back in the space of a few seconds. "Lou's not coming to the festival, is he?"

I stared at her, shocked by the negative phrasing. "You don't want him to come?" I asked after a moment.

"It's not that—" Crystal's gaze shifted away, darting around the island. "His father is coming," she admitted at last. "If we could just keep that part quiet, things would be easier."

This was not the bombshell I needed.

"Oh, no, Crystal. Why? Why does he have to come here at all? Let alone on a festival day when I'm going to be busy and could really use Lou's help." I said this as if I had any assurance at all Lou was planning to come help me. The truth was, he hadn't mentioned it and neither had I. We were both taking things one session at a time. I understood that with Lou, sometimes, being in the moment was the only speed he could handle.

Crystal pursed her lips for a moment, then replied, a trifle testily, "You know, Lou isn't the only one who lives on this island. I can't be tiptoeing around for fear of upsetting him *forever.*"

I sighed. She was right, but...was she? I felt like this was a problem with many possible answers. But Crystal had chosen one, so— "Okay, you invited him. This is what you want, huh?"

"I've always liked Arnie," she announced, without a trace of apology. "And I'd like to see him again. He called me the other day —"

"The *other day?*"

"And he said he'd be in Cutlass Key the weekend of the Fourth, and I said to come on out and see what we've done with the place. I'm not inviting him to live here," Crystal added, defensiveness creeping into her expression. "I just asked an old friend if he'd enjoy seeing what I've been up to after twenty years. And after all—" she swung her arm around, indicating all the work we'd done. "Wouldn't you be proud of it all, and anxious to show this off to an old friend from your past? Show them what you'd done with your life?

I'd never really known that Crystal thought of her ex this way: an *old friend,* someone with whom she'd simply parted ways and lost track of. But maybe there was something else to it, as well, the more pure and simple break-up message of: *"Look what I've done without you around to hold me back."*

Crystal had told me before she wasn't cut out for marriage, or maybe she'd said it more like marriage wasn't cut out for her. Either way it was phrased, she was right. Crystal was a proud and ragged island cat, walking her wild lone, waving her wild tail. Every impression I'd gotten of Arnie was that he was a fast-talking charmer —and I could definitely see the family resemblance in his smooth son, who could charm the birds from the trees if he wanted to—so Crystal might have been taken in briefly, but not long enough to consider vows, a ring, the word *forever.*

And I suspected that was a lucky escape on her part.

But I didn't know! I shouldn't be putting Arnie into boxes when I hadn't even met the guy yet. Ugh, that word *yet*—it was a steady reminder that I was going to have to meet Lou's father, and be nice to him, and risk being charmed by him as well...and that Lou was absolutely going to be upset about it.

My loyalty was going to be called into questions by both sides. See, this is why Monica's friendship was so refreshing. She wasn't pulling me in different directions. She just wanted to hang out on the island and be my buddy.

Crystal put a hand on my elbow, bringing me back to the present. "You have fun, babe. The week is going to be quiet outside of festival prep. We've got no rides booked until the fifth, anyway, so the horses can sit outside and chill. Let them relax, you relax. Go see Lou tonight, and tomorrow we'll finish setting up and then boom, the Fourth will come and go so fast we hardly'll know what happened. Okay?" She gave me a hopeful smile. "Now, I'm gonna walk over and see what Marchant's up to."

A lot of banging told me that Marchant was up to something in one of his new boats. As usual. He was rarely found anywhere else these days.

"Tell him to get out of that saloon and to take a break with you," I suggested. "I think he's been skipping lunch lately."

A fond smile crossed Crystal's lined face. "That man," she said, and then she headed off across the scruffy grass covering the center of the island, her flip flops snapping with every step.

I watched her go for a moment, envying her sureness of step and purpose, wondering if it came with age or personality or some combination of both, in which case I'd only ever be able to acquire half of it. Then I headed for the house. Time to shower, shake off the cares of my island, and head into Key West in search of the next set of problems the universe felt ready to dump on my shoulders.

Chapter Fifteen

A CLOUD WAS pushing over Cutlass Key when I pulled into the lot outside the Slutty Mermaid, rumbling to itself and sending out gusts of wind that scattered sand in tiny whirlwinds around me. I'd left earlier than I'd expected and I was hoping there might be some of this morning's gooey, soft cinnamon rolls left in the Mermaid fridge. A little taste of home for my exile in Key West. And even if they didn't begin the hard work of luring him home, at least I'd get to enjoy them, too.

Inside, not much was going on. Even in the Keys, it was a little early for the session drinkers to be in their places. Still, the constant game of pool was in motion at the far end of the building, lit by a dusty glow from high windows which hadn't been cleaned of salt in years. Two men in sandals and NASCAR hats leaned over the game, muttering to one another. Closer to the bar, a gray-haired woman sat in a booth and played Candy Crush on her phone, occasionally sipping from a highball glass. Johnny Cash was singing from the fuzzy speakers hanging from the ceiling, adding an extra and interesting layer of doom to the dark bar.

Monica was sitting on the customer's side of the bar, reading a magazine and slowly sipping from a bottle of Corona. She glanced around as I came in and her face lit up. She exclaimed, "Girl, I didn't expect to see you today! What's up?"

"Heading to Key West," I explained, slipping onto the stool next to her. "And I'm here hoping for some sweet treats to charm my chronically depressed boyfriend into cheering up."

"Oh, I have a couple left! You're lucky; I was saving them for—I was saving them," she amended, "but you can have them."

I cocked my head; that wasn't a very smooth cover. "Who were you saving them for?"

"No one," Monica lied, turning her head so that her gorgeous curls covered her face.

"Monica! Do you have a little island crush?" I was delighted. "Because cinnamon rolls are the key to everyone's heart, I don't care who you are. Man, woman, non-binary—"

"No," she said again, laughing now. "Oh, heavens no. They're for Arnie, silly."

"Arnie?" My head swiveled, looking for some strange man lurking in a dark corner of the bar. "He's here? I thought he was coming over the weekend."

"He's back in the area already, and he's coming here later," she said. "Relax, you don't have to meet him. He said he'd be here around six."

"And then what?" I asked, feeling panicky. What if he decided to visit the island early? I wasn't ready for this guy to really show up. I didn't have a *plan*. Everyone on Hell and Dammit Cay was going to react differently to Arnie, and it would be up to me to figure out how to keep feathers unruffled, temperatures from rising—

"And then he's taking me to get some food at Conch Mama's," Monica said patiently, naming a popular locals' restaurant two islands up U.S. 1, a glorified shack where fresh fish was cooked on a propane grill out back and a great blue heron named Earl arrived on the waterside patio every day at four o'clock, ready for the early bird special. "Relax! He hasn't come to burn down the Mermaid or meet with Hilton executives. He's just visiting, like a normal human would."

But a normal human didn't have the ability to put my small world into a totally out-of-control spin. Everything about Arnie's arrival in the islands gave me a bad feeling. I took a breath and tried to slow down my words so I wouldn't sound freaked out when I told her, "I should get moving if I'm going to hit Key West before school traffic starts."

Just an excuse, of course. There was always traffic in Old Town, anyway. But if I accidentally met this guy right before I went to see Lou, there'd be no way I could hide my discomfort. He'd be on to me in a second. Perceptive boyfriends may sound great on paper, but when you're actually dealing with them, it's a real pain.

Monica seemed to understand what was driving me. "Of course," she replied, pushing back her bar stool and standing up. "Let me grab you those cinnamon rolls. I don't want to send you down to Lou's place empty-handed. Arnie can have one tomorrow."

Because he'll still be here tomorrow, I thought miserably. Driving to Key West this afternoon won't save me from knowing he's up here on Cutlass Key, just waiting to drop in and throw everyone out of whack.

But there was nothing I could do about it right now. Deep breaths, I told myself. Stop freaking out.

I watched Monica waltz into the kitchen, the light streaming into the bar as the door opened, then cut off immediately as it swung back into place. Then I pulled out my phone, checked the time. Just after three thirty. Not that I knew when Arnie was planning to arrive, so it wasn't like I was racing the clock or anything. I just knew that the later it got, the more likely it was he'd show up—

The front door opened. I watched the reflection of it in the mirror over the bottles, saw the man standing in the doorway, with all the gleaming light of summer behind him. I took a breath, but it seemed to catch in my throat.

Then, there was a sharp crack of nearby thunder, and the sunlight was dashed out as the cloud I'd seen earlier finally advanced over Cutlass Key.

But despite the roar of the impending thunderstorm, the man didn't race inside for shelter. He remained standing there in the doorway, taking it all in. And I took him in, still watching him in the mirror. Broad shoulders, strong build. A dark beard cut with gray.

I didn't have to turn around to know who was behind me—that was Lou's father, sure as the rain was about to fall.

I closed my eyes for a moment, praying for some kind of intervention, but when I opened them again, it was to find him setting his canvas bag on the bar, a few stools away from me, putting a respectful distance between himself and the only other customer the way that bar etiquette required. At least he wasn't a creep who settled down right next to me. I flattened my hands on the bar-top, wishing I had a drink to distract me, but of course, I had to get on the road. Now. Fast. Should I even wait for the cinnamon rolls at this point? Or should I just turn and walk away?

It would be a weird move, of course. He'd stare after me, wonder who I was and why I'd stomped out the second he'd come in. And it wasn't like this was the only moment we'd meet. He'd see me again by this weekend and he'd wonder why I'd been so rude at the Mermaid. No, I couldn't make that kind of first impression. Crystal wouldn't like it, if nothing else.

The rain arrived and drummed down on the Mermaid's flat roof with a sudden roar, like an army beginning its artillery assault. Thunder crackled and rolled around us. The guys playing pool reset the balls and broke them again with a sharp snap. And still, Monica didn't come back out of the kitchen. How long could it take to wrap up two cinnamon rolls?

"Quite a storm," Arnie said.

I didn't look at him. "Mm-hmm," I agreed. I took out my phone and looked at my weather app. One little blob of a storm over Cutlass Key. It wasn't even cloudy at Hell and Dammit Cay. Typical Florida.

"Glad I beat it," he said, settling himself onto a bar stool. "Been driving all day. Left Naples this morning real early."

"Oh," I said. "Okay."

"It's always a real disappointment when the bridge from Naples isn't open and I gotta go all the way around by U.S. 1."

I managed to hold back a snort of laugher, but just barely. The "bridge from Naples" was an old trick Floridians had been playing on new residents and tourists for decades. I didn't know how many gullible people followed their new neighbors' advice and actually drove to Naples looking for the exit to the bridge to Key West, but my guess was that it was not zero.

I rubbed the bridge of my nose to give my hands something to do and nodded in response.

He tried again. "You live around here?"

I looked at him then. Really saw him, for the first time, not in a mirror, not out of the corner of my eye. He was a thoughtlessly dressed, no-shits-given retiree, one of a million or three in Florida at any given moment, wearing a Guy Harvey t-shirt with a hole in one armpit, plus khaki shorts and sandals. He looked like he belonged here, like he hadn't taken much care of himself, like a waterlogged Florida native.

But he was also handsome, in a rumpled, put-away-wet kind of way. His hair was going more salt than pepper, completely white above his ears. He had deep lines around his eyes, etched into bronzed skin to give him a permanent squint, and I didn't have enough light to know for sure, but I'd bet they were the same stormy blue as Lou's.

I thought: *Of course I live around here, how else would I know to come in?* And then I remembered my trail ride clients from earlier in the summer, who had waltzed right in to pee and buy Mexican Cokes like they belonged here, and I felt a little proud that I might look so brazen and bold. "Yeah," I told him. "I live around here."

His smile, which looked habitual, broadened. "Well, how about that! Someone new in the neighborhood. And they said it couldn't be done. You live here on Cutlass? Or one of the out-islands?"

"Out-island," I croaked, desperate for Monica to save me before I had to give myself away.

"Which one—" he asked, but there she was, coming out of the kitchen with a to-go container and a rueful expression.

"You would not *believe* the trouble I had finding—oh." She stopped, a smile lighting her face. "Arnie!"

He stood up, the stool sliding backwards sharply. "Monica!"

The two of them met halfway between the bar and the kitchen door and hugged like a pair of long-lost twins, Monica carefully holding the to-go container out with one hand. Arnie clapped her on the back with so much force I was afraid she'd accidentally throw up, like a baby after a bottle, but all she did was screw up her face in a grimace and go, "Not so hard, Arnie!"

He let go and stood back. "You look fantastic."

"Stop," she said, still smiling.

They gazed at each other with a worshipful fascination.

I ran my tongue around my molars, touching each one in succession, while I tried to figure out what the hell was going on here.

"See?" Lou said. "There's something going on with those two. I knew it."

I shoved a cinnamon roll his way. He was only getting one because of good behavior; while he'd been living here at the Old Town house without me, he'd put together the arrangements for three songs which we could layer with lyrics I'd written in my head during horse chores. We'd already set down some preliminary work on one of them, and I had a good feeling about it. So, I'd called for a break and got the cinnamon rolls out of the truck. Lou's eyes lit up when he saw them.

But after a bite or two, he got moody again.

"Do you think they're sleeping together?" he asked, chewing grimly.

"What?" I stared at him, aghast. "Okay, I realize you weren't there to see this, but no. My god. He's *way* too old for her, number one. And there wasn't any sexual vibe there. They just seemed like really close friends. Much closer than the story she fed me about him being her cousin's uncle's friend or whatever it was." It had been something like that, right? Either way, no point in keeping the story straight when it was clearly not factual.

"So what could it be?" Lou took another bite, still looking like the cinnamon roll was a chore that tasked him. If he was going to keep eating that treat like it was a burden, I was going to take it away from him. "I mean, it's kind of odd that they'd be so close, right? Unless he saved her from a burning car crash or something. And I feel like she'd have led with that."

I didn't want to say the most obvious thing that popped into my head. I would have said it to anyone else. But Arnie *was* Lou's father.

And that hug *had* been pretty familiar.

But I wasn't about to just suggest Lou had a previously unknown half-sister working in the bar on Cutlass Key. Some grenades you simply cannot throw.

So I shrugged and kept my opinions to myself. "They must be more closely related than that, and they have some reason for keeping it quiet," I suggested, carefully working around my one and only hypothesis on tippy-toes.

"Like they're cousins?" Lou asked. "Not friend of a friend of a cousin or whatever."

"Right, exactly. Like that. Cousins."

"And why wouldn't they just say so?" His gaze grew speculative. "You know what it is? He must be breaking the law in some way and doesn't want her implicated. Typical."

"Maybe, he's on the run from the mob, and doesn't want her getting mixed up in it, too."

"Like, they could kidnap her and hold her as bait, so he comes to their lair," Lou said, getting into the spirit of things.

"That's probably it," I agreed, thankful for the distraction. "I mean, this is Florida. Nothing is too ridiculous in Florida. And that goes double for the Keys."

"I hope he's not connected to any of those boats," Lou mused. "It would be a shame if they got impounded to be used as evidence in a trial. Marchant would be devastated."

"Oh, good point. I think we better stay *far* away from this one. Don't want to accidentally tip off the law."

"You know me," Lou laughed. "The law's best friend." He leaned back in his flimsy chair and the thing nearly fell over.

I rolled my eyes, so relieved we'd started steering away from the forbidden subject of Arnie that I was able to start eating my own cinnamon roll. Lou had dabbled in land speculation—as Marchant pointed out, what Floridian with waterfront property nearby *hadn't?* —and while I was pretty sure he'd never outright broken the law, he hadn't exactly been overly honest on some of his deals. But all that was behind him now. He was focused on music now.

Just like I was, occasionally. "You ready to pick back up with our work?" I asked, wiping my fingers on a paper towel. "The more we do tonight, the less we have to do tomorrow before I head back to work on the festival. In other words, make me happy by letting me sleep in tomorrow."

"Oh, I'll make you happy tonight," Lou chuckled, giving me a tap under the chin, which made me laugh. "And we'll finish these songs, too."

I was so happy he was willing to drop the subject of his father, I let him distract me from our work for a little while after that.

What? I missed having him at home.

Chapter Sixteen

A TAPPING ON the windows woke me up early on the Fourth of July. I rubbed my face groggily, then got up and put my feet on the floor.

The cold, damp feeling of the ceramic tiles on my bare skin gave it away immediately.

"It's...raining?"

Going to the sliding-glass door with a sinking feeling in my stomach, I pulled back the vertical blinds and looked at the stony gray sky outside. Rain pooled on the boards of the deck. Not only was it raining, but this didn't look like the usual fast-moving summer shower. This was more like an all-day, northern-style rain event.

"I can't believe it," I said to the clouds. "You really went and betrayed me. After all I've done for you."

The island below was slurping up the rain with pleasure. The plant life was a verdant, gorgeous green, adding an extra touch of tropical exoticness to our surroundings...but, rain tapping into the puddles was not what tourists were going to want to see. They came to Florida for warm sunshine, even in July when it was so hot that they'd spend more time complaining and jostling for a spot in air-conditioned rooms than actually outside soaking up the light and heat. No one came to Florida for the rain.

And with this rain falling, our turnout was going to get hit, hard. I thought of the parking lot tram we'd worked so hard to build and get road-worthy. I thought of the artists sitting in empty studios all day.

My skin grew clammy.

Or maybe that was just the humidity seeping through the old window frames.

I went into the kitchen. Crystal was out there, poking the old coffeemaker, obviously hoping that would make it brew faster. We needed a new one, I thought absently. This half-hour's wait for caffeine was getting insane. Aloud, I said, "Was there rain in the forecast?"

"There's always rain in the forecast," Crystal said idly. "When you live on a tropical island, anyway."

"But like, a *lot*." I took out my phone and studied the weather forecast. "I'm pretty sure no one was saying ninety percent chance of rain yesterday. Am I being gaslit by the National Weather Service?"

"Whatever else happens to you in life," Crystal told me, tapping the coffeemaker with one finger, "do not believe there is a vast government conspiracy aimed at you. *Especially* if it involves the weather."

"Known a lot of conspiracy theorists?"

Crystal groaned in response. I took that as a yes.

Whether it was a conspiracy or just the fickle nature of island weather, the rain settled in to stay and there was nothing we could do but grin and bear it. Thankfully, the studios were built out of former bungalows meant for overnight stays, and the seals were weatherproof. The same couldn't be said for the open sides of our parking lot tram. I scoured the island for something we could use as ponchos or raincoats to lend to the potential festival guests, at least to get them to and from Hell and Dammit Cay without getting drenched. Marchant rose to the occasion with a huge roll of plastic sheeting, which he rigged along the sides of the tram. It flopped in the breeze, but it could be held down by passengers. And hopefully it would add something to the day—an adventurous spirit, of sorts.

"Everyone expects things to be a little rough and ready out here," Marchant declared, looking at his handiwork. "If they wanted the Met and fancy coffee, they'd go to New York City."

"Where they'd also get wet in the rain," a deep, humorous voice muttered, and I whirled around, hands to my mouth.

"Lou!" I hissed, barely keeping my voice down. Lou was lurking behind one of the pillars beneath Crystal's house, clearly trying to keep his presence a secret. I ran over and took his hands. "What are you doing here?"

"You thought I'd miss your big day?"

"I mean, it's hardly *my* big day," I muttered, blushing. Maybe I'd made too big a deal out of this festival. "I'm just organizing things. The artists are the ones having a big day, really."

Lou's lips brushed against mine. "Don't sell yourself short," he murmured. "You're doing the work they can't...or won't. Remember, they sat over there in their houses for years. No one had any idea what they were up to inside their walled gardens. You're the one who brought everyone out here to create something special."

I nodded. "I did," I agreed. "With help."

"And you've got my help today." He grinned, his eyes gleaming merrily in the half-light under the house. "As soon as I surprise my mom. *That's* why I'm hiding. But after that, I'm yours. Make me do whatever you need."

"Even with—" I didn't want to bring him up, but how could we ignore the absentee father in the room? "Even with *him* here?"

Lou glanced around, his expression thundery. "Wait, is he here now?"

"No, but...he'll come. You know he will. Since he was in the Mermaid this week, I assume he's around the islands for the whole holiday, at least." I didn't actually know how long Arnie was staying in the Keys. Maybe...I gulped at the thought...maybe he was *staying*. Maybe this was a permanent move back to Cutlass Key.

Or worse, what if he was thinking of wiggling his way into Crystal's affections and scoring an invitation to live here on Hell and Dammit?

The idea was enough to make my head spin with anxiety. Arnie had the potential to upset everything.

Lou seemed to be thinking the same thing. His jaw was set and hard. I imagined I could hear his teeth grinding. Then he shook his head, like a horse shaking off a fly. "It's fine," he said. "He's no one to me. Another stranger at the festival. It's nothing to worry about."

I squeezed his hands one more time before letting go. I could hear Marchant calling me; it was time to take the tram up and see if anyone had shown up yet. I imagined a small crowd of wet, bedraggled tourists staring at our *Art Festival Parking Shuttle* sign and wondering where we were at. "I have to get started," I told him. "Don't scare your mother too bad, okay?"

Lou agreed to make his surprise a gentle one, with no jump-scares, and I left him there under the house. I tugged down the brim of my hat as I walked back into the steady rain. Marchant gave me a leg-up into the truck and I paused for a moment, studying the road ahead, the studios behind, the great unknown of the day to come. Rainwater spilled down my back as a palm tree swayed in a gust of wind, its laden fronds creating a cool waterfall.

And just as I started the engine, I heard a shout, and then Crystal yelling, "Lou! Dammit, you scared me!"

Lou's laughter spilled across the island.

I took off for Cutlass Key with a smile on my face.

I saw him standing there before I'd even stopped the truck.

My heart sank. Somehow, I thought he'd just drive out; Arnie seemed like the type to ignore rules, to believe that the everyday guidelines for polite life just didn't apply to him. If we put up a sign which said *Local Traffic Only,* he'd assume he was a local, because he knew where the road led.

But then again, maybe he'd never been to Hell and Dammit Cay. Crystal had only moved there, what, less than ten years ago? I couldn't remember the timeline exactly, but she hadn't raised Lou there. It had been her father's fishing camp. She came from farther up the Keys, and so did Arnie.

At least, that's what I seemed to recall. I really needed to hear some of her stories when we weren't all getting pleasantly tipsy on Marchant's porch. Then I might retain some of the details.

I turned off the truck and Arnie stepped away from the small cluster of tourists waiting for us, his face bright and handsome in the gray morning. "Well, if it isn't our own limo driver!" he exclaimed, walking up to the truck cab. "Nice to see you again, Miss—"

He stopped then, and I realized I'd never told him my name. Or even that I lived on Hell and Dammit Cay. At the Mermaid, I'd kept my answers short, and then Monica had come out of the kitchen and distracted him. I hadn't even *existed* once she'd come back into the bar. So we'd never been introduced.

I wondered once again what was going on between those two.

But there wasn't time to speculate; thunder rumbled overhead and the nervous tourists started racing for the tram. It was one of those random, rainy-day rumbles, the ones that don't seem to have lightning attached to them or even indicate they're any particular distance away, just a deep growl as if the clouds were bored and had to let loose with something a bit stronger than rain, but nothing as serious as a lightning bolt. I might not have even noticed it, but for the out-of-towners, it was a threat directly from the heavens, and they wanted the relative safety of the parking tram immediately.

The truck lurched a little as they piled into the seats, and Arnie gave me a sideways look before he went back and joined the crowd. I was relieved; for a moment, I'd been sure he was going to ask to sit in the cab beside me.

The tram sat twenty, and it was nearly full—a good start to the morning. Especially considering the rain.

Marchant settled into the passenger seat, satisfied everyone was settled safely in their seats. "You can drive us, boss," he said, placing a sheaf of papers on the console between us.

It was the first time I'd noticed the papers—I'd been distracted back at the island, I guess. "What's all that?"

"Oh," he said, smiling shyly. "These are just flyers for the hotel."

"They're *flyers*—" I picked up the top one and flipped it over. My jaw dropped. Marchant had been busy over the past few days. "Sea Horse Lodge?" I asked, reading the header. "You named the hotel?"

"I had to, on account of all those forms Monica made me fill out for the government what-not," Marchant explained. "I was talking to Crystal, and she liked the name, so I just used it. You like it?"

I considered the flyer. *Sea Horse Lodge: An authentic Keys experience like nowhere else!!!!*

I liked it. Especially the exclamation points. It was so very Marchant. Absolutely nothing slick or professional about it, just joy and enthusiasm.

"Yes," I told him. "I love it."

"That's good," he said. "Because I gave every one of them a flyer and they all seem real excited about it."

I bit back a sigh, adding another worry to my mental tally. We were still probably months away from getting both the boats ready and the government paperwork taken care of. I hoped Marchant didn't get over-eager and do something crazy, like start taking reservations *today*. With my luck, he'd write them all down in a note he folded up and stuck in his wallet, and in a month's time I'd have a horde of eager tourists descending on the island, ready to stay in their newly refurbished sailboat and demanding to know why I wasn't ready and waiting for them.

That last part, especially. Because of course I knew I'd be concierge and hostess for these families Marchant was going to introduce to the world of sailboats and the Keys. It would be one more job to add to my daily routine on the island.

I looked over at him as the truck rattled up the shell road across Little Bucket Key. Marchant gazed forward, his eyes bright, his expression hopeful. I couldn't help a little smile crossing my lips as well. I'd do anything for these crazy islanders of mine. Even if they made me insane every day of the damned week and twice on Sunday.

Roger and Rogerina were at their posts as we sailed across the short bridge between the islands, and I slowed down to make sure the tourists could get a good look at our iguana mascots, one on each side of the rocks lining the bridge—a bit like the stone lions in St. Augustine, really. Easily just as stately as those masonry cats, for sure. Not surprisingly, the tourists were enchanted.

Just you wait, I thought, pulling up alongside the horse paddocks.

The ponies of Sea Horse Ranch were wet and muddy—any grooming would have been completely pointless in this weather— but to the tourists, they were the most beautiful creatures in the world. And honestly, they weren't entirely wrong. With the dark clouds overhead and the green palm trees swaying in the rain, the horses looked remote and unknowable as they watched the tram park next to their paddocks, their long manes dripping water and their black eyelashes forming a soft black veil around their curious eyes. They looked like wild things again, as their ancestors had been. There was actual jostling to get off the tram and hustle to the fences to start taking photos.

Crystal and Lou walked up, brims of their Sea Horse Ranch caps pulled down against the rain. Crystal's eyes sought out Arnie immediately, as if the old friends were connected by an invisible thread. He saw her and his face brightened into that gorgeous smile again.

Lou took a step back, turning his head as if he didn't want to see their happiness. He started back towards the house, but I caught up with him and slipped a hand into his.

"Don't worry about it," I murmured. "Just let them catch up and do their thing, okay?"

His fingers pressed against mine, bone against bone. I tried to absorb his unhappiness as best I could.

"He didn't see me," Lou growled, his voice barely audible above the rain pattering on our hats and shoulders. "Some things never change."

"He doesn't know you," I attempted, but it was a foolish argument, because Arnie had *chosen* not to know Lou, and we both knew there was no fixing that. Suddenly I felt a rush of angry frustration, that Crystal could be so naïve and unthoughtful as to let this man come to the island. She wanted Lou here. She'd been so happy when he'd come back from Chicago, so why was she letting Arnie chase him away? Did she really think he could just forgive being left without a father? What son could accept that and move on?

"Let's just go into the tack room for a minute," Lou urged me, tugging at my hand. "I just need a second without all these people around."

It was my job to lead all these people up to the studios and introduce the artists, but I felt rebellious now—what *wasn't* my job, anyway? I followed Lou up the soggy path between the paddocks, puddles splashing beneath my rubber boots, and into the damp coolness of the tack room.

He sat down on a pile of fat saddle pads and gazed up at me. "This is so completely awkward," he said. "I wish I hadn't come."

"But Lou, this is *your* island," I told him forcefully. "You shouldn't feel like you have to run away from him. If it's really bad, just…just go upstairs, go into your room and work on some music. I'll handle things down here."

"You deserve my help, at least," he grumbled. "I came here to support you."

"And I appreciate that, but—" I stopped myself from saying he was just making more trouble for me by adding one more thing to worry about to my plate. "But I wouldn't want you running into him before you're ready," I finished lamely.

"He didn't even see me," Lou said, as if we were on another subject altogether. "Did you notice that? I was standing right next to Mom, and he looked at her, but never saw me. For god's sake, I'm nearly two feet taller than she is! How did he miss me?"

Two feet taller and you look just like him, I thought sadly. "He knows your mom," I suggested, knowing that led to the inevitable conclusion, *He could have known me, too.*

Lou shifted to one side. "Could you just—would you mind—just sitting with me for a second? Just a second."

His face was vulnerable, and there was no way I could deny him. The world could wait. I squeezed next to Lou on the saddle pads and put my arm around him, feeling the tension in his shoulders, the stiffness in his neck. "I'm sorry," I whispered. "For all of it. It isn't fair."

And Lou, who must have felt about five years old and newly abandoned in that moment, slumped against me and wiped his eyes.

It took him a little while to recover himself, and I didn't begrudge him a second. I just held him tight, bracing my left leg a little to keep from sliding off the teetering pile of saddle pads, and waited it out. Finally, he lifted his head and looked at me. His eyes were so close, I felt like I could drown in them. Like I could slip under all his sorrows and never find my way back to the surface. Was it the weight of Lou's unhappiness? Or was it the weight of all these hopes and dreams, the island I carried on my shoulders day in and day out? I didn't know the answer, only that it was a lot.

"Thanks," he murmured eventually. "I think I can go out there now."

"Are you sure? Go upstairs, seriously, if you don't want to see him."

Lou's mouth twisted in a sardonic smile. "What makes you think he'll even see me? Maybe I'll just fade into the background, one more tourist splashing around in the rain."

I didn't think that was possible, but I decided to let him believe that. "Then let's head out," I told him. "I have to do another tram run. I'm sure some people will be ready to leave already, with the weather like this."

But we found no one wanted to go yet, because the rain had actually stopped. There was even a cool breeze, making the day uncharacteristically comfortable for July, and the gray clouds still roiled overhead, casting a pleasant shade over the island. On every shore, the water glowed with an unearthly luminescence, its turquoise shades somehow picking up the rays of the sun through the overcast skies. The greenery of the island seemed like a brooch cast atop a box of jewels, each one more shimmering than the last. Most of the visitors just seemed dazzled by their surroundings, wandering around staring and pointing more than they were taking photos.

Or buying artwork. I left Lou by the paddocks and ran over to the studios, jumping over puddles along the way, and popped my head into each bungalow. "You should be out and welcoming," I told the artists, one by one. "Talk to each other and look like you're having fun. Get them over here or the sales will be a bust!"

A few people laughed at me, but as I picked my way back to the truck to start up the tram's second run, I noticed they were following my directions and emerging from the studios. And as they did so, the tourists noticed the activity and started heading in their direction. *That's the way it's done,* I thought. I hopped up into the truck cab, satisfied with the way my morning was starting out, and I was just about to pull out when I saw Crystal and Arnie disappearing into the house.

My eyes met Lou's across the paddocks, and he shook his head at me slightly.

He'd seen it too.

I sighed and put the truck into gear. I had to get through this day somehow, and so did Lou. On our own, unfortunately.

Chapter Seventeen

THE LAST TRAM run came at five thirty, and I watched the final tourists head for their cars with a weary feeling of satisfaction. The day had stayed cloudy, and while the strikingly beautiful glow just after the rain hadn't stuck around, the cool breeze had. This would go down in history in one of the coolest and most comfortable July days in Floridian history. I almost wanted a sweater.

The cool weather had added up to an incredibly successful day, with lots of large packages wrapped in brown paper taking up spots on the return runs of the parking tram, and a few extra drop-offs at the artists' main studios when patrons decided to have big items shipped home.

Peter sold his biggest tiki god, standing nearly ten feet tall, and no one had any idea how it was going to get shipped to its new home in Wisconsin, but the buyers had been emphatic and swore they'd pay any price. George sold enough of his sad traveller palm series to reduce the display from a cross to a minus symbol, which I told him was more than he deserved. Even Daphne managed to make some money, despite her complaints that she didn't have any new work since she'd spent the past month writing, and Stacy had hobbled down from her eyrie to oversee a near-total sellout of her gorgeous horse mosaics and paintings.

If it hadn't been for Arnie showing up and spending half the day in the house with Crystal doing heaven knew what, the day might have been considered perfect.

As it was, I turned off the truck and walked across the gravel lot to the door of the Slutty Mermaid. I wasn't ready to go back, not with him there. I'd left Lou safe in the barn, doing horse chores, and told him to stay put until I came back. I felt like I'd earned a few minutes of respite from my responsibilities on the island.

The Mermaid was humming with unusual traffic inside; I realized some of the tourists had found their way inside despite the forbidding exterior. The booths were full, along with half the bar; brown-wrapped packages gave away the way they'd spent their money earlier today. Monica looked at me from behind the bar, her expression changing from wariness to pleasure as she realized I wasn't one more newbie.

"Girl!" she exclaimed. "It has been *crazy* in here today! I'm almost out of triple sec. Can you believe it? These maniacs want to come in here and drink like they're at the sunset celebration. Speaking of which, I hope they all get up and head down there soon." She laughed and began to pour me a beer from the tap without bothering to ask for my order. "So this is all you're doing today, right? This is the last of them?"

"Jeez, I'm so sorry," I apologized, slipping onto a bar stool a good five spots down from the nearest art festival patron. I really didn't want to answer any more questions about Hell and Dammit or the Keys in general today. I'd spent most of the day as something between an unpaid travel agent and an information terminal as it was. "I had no idea they'd come in here and start working you to death, Monica."

"Oh, it's fine with me, really," she assured me, slipping the glass across the bar. "This is still nothing compared to the kind of crowds I dealt with in South Beach. Working the old muscles a little. And I'm guessing it means you guys had a really successful day! I see all the packages and most of them are painting-shaped, right?"

"Yeah, they are," I agreed. "Those little canvases that fit into suitcases went like hotcakes. The bigger stuff, that has to be shipped, but it moved pretty well, too. I think everyone's going to be really happy with their sales."

"And that's what you guys are going for, right? Big sales."

"Well, it helps. I want the artists to feel invested in the island, so they keep showing their work and tourists really start to see us as a place to come for art. That keeps away the big bad bulldozers, at least...I hope it does."

"You and me both," Monica said. "That place is too special to be ruined."

"It came really close." I took a sip of the beer, found it extremely relaxing, and took another, longer one. When I came up for air, I noticed Monica was blushing and turning away, busying herself with empty glasses. I looked around to see what had her hot and bothered, and found Lou was settling onto a stool next to me.

"Where did you come from?" I asked, pleased to see him. "The horses didn't keep you occupied nearly as long as I'd hoped."

"I hitched a ride with Queen Tom," Lou said. "He's heading into Key West tonight."

"Good grief, why? It's going to be insane on a holiday."

"Some people like insane," Lou replied mildly. "Monica? A beer?"

She hustled getting him a beer to match mine, her cheeks still pink. I figured she was remembering the first and last time they'd met, when she'd accidentally said Lou's father owned the Mermaid and sent him storming to Key West. Hard to believe that was only a couple of weeks ago; these long summer days could make weeks pass like months.

Lou accepted his beer with a pleasant smile, picked it up, and drained it in one power gulp. We stared at him.

"Um, Lou?" I asked, as he set it down on the bar. "Is everything okay?"

"Oh, everything is great," he said, smothering a burp with his hand. "Monica? Another? Thank you."

She took the glass, watching him warily. Her eyes flicked to mine. *You better ask him again.*

"Lou, babe, what's going on? What did I miss?"

Lou turned to me with an owlish gaze, blinking slowly. "Nothing too crazy," he told me after a moment's pause. "Just Arnie, moving into the house with Crystal. And you," he added, as I gasped in shock. "But definitely not with me."

He took the new glass from Monica and drank about half of it down.

"Oh, my god." I got up and looked around, as if Crystal would materialize in the doorway. But of course, she wouldn't. She never came to the Mermaid in the evening, preferring to spend the sunset hours with Marchant on his deck. And now Arnie would be there, too, so she'd be entertaining him. I remembered suddenly that he'd gone in on the tram this morning, so he'd need a ride back out.

Except that he was apparently planning to stay.

How could I not have seen this coming? He'd probably lost whatever half-legal gig he was running up in Naples, needed a place to crash, and thought, *huh, wonder what's going on with Crystal Linney?* Then magically, his bar—which we all seemed to think had run itself for the past however many years—acquires a bartender, a young woman from off-island who supposedly didn't really know him...but their interactions certainly indicated otherwise.

Lou was right, I thought, my toes curling in my rubber boots. Monica was Arnie's spy. His advance scout. She'd been sent here to report back on Crystal and the situation here in the islands.

I looked up at her, half expecting to see her smirking and jotting notes into a tiny book, but just then Monica was called away by a patron down the bar. She looked grateful for the interruption, her wavy hair bouncing on her shoulders as she scuttled to help the person waving her down.

Beside me, Lou was putting the finishing blows on his emptying pint glass. He sighed as he set it down. "Can you give me a ride back down to Key West?" he asked.

"On July Fourth?" I shook my head. "You're out of your mind. Stay up here tonight. I'll sneak you into my room. He won't come in there, even if he's staying at the house. And maybe he isn't—maybe Crystal's driving him back to wherever he's staying up here, right now. I mean, there's no guest room, and there's no way he's—I mean —"

Did I really want to finish that sentence? I did not.

Lou chuckled mirthlessly. "You know, you've got the guest room. So if you weren't living in there, Arnie would *have* to take that room. For appearances."

"Lou, I don't think it's possible that Arnie is moving back to, um, to *be with* your mom. He might be staying, but it's not like...it's not like that."

"Why do you say that?"

"Because of Marchant," I replied. "I think they have something."

"Oh, Marchant." Lou scoffed. "No, they're just friends."

"Maybe they've been just friends for years," I said, "but I'm looking at them with fresher eyes than you, and I think they're edging towards something more."

Lou laughed into his beer glass. "I just thought of something," he said. "What if Marchant makes him the first guest at Sea Horse Lodge? Tonight?"

"He can't," I said. "Those boats aren't ready."

"That's what would make it really funny," Lou chuckled.

Ugh. I couldn't sit here and make guesses. "Come on," I told him, picking up my keys. "Let's go back and see what's really going on."

"No," Lou hiccuped. "Not going."

"Yes you are," I said, and I hooked one hand under his armpit, lifting hard. He had the choice of standing up or resisting me and causing a scene in front of all these tourists who were supposed to go home and evangelize our art festivals; fortunately, he was still sober enough to choose to stand up. I slipped my hand down to his, gripped it, and tugged him away from the bar.

At the door, I realized I hadn't paid Monica for our drinks, but I decided not to worry about it. Arnie was the cause of our problems. He could surely see us a few free beers.

Chapter Eighteen

BACK AT THE island, things seemed relatively unchanged. The studios were tidied and closed up. The extra trash cans we'd set out were emptied, hosed out, lined up neatly, and ready to go back into storage under the fourth house—the one which had never been finished.

I looked over the tidy island with pleasure. They'd done work without me! I wasn't absolutely one hundred percent necessary!

And then I noticed something I'd never seen before.

There were lights upstairs in the fourth house.

Moving lights, which meant flashlights. It wasn't yet sunset, but the gray evening was dimmer than usual, so without electricity hooked up, a person would want a little extra brightness to explore an empty house. I thought about bugs and mold and gave a little shudder.

Lou noticed my involuntary movement, and his gaze followed mine. I felt him stiffen.

"What the hell?" he growled roughly. "No one should be up there except my mom, and she—why would *she* be up there? Now?"

I couldn't answer him.

But Stacy could. She came limping over from her locked-up studio, a key jingling in one hand, pressed against the crutches she was so angry about. She nodded towards the house as she approached.

"You see that?" she asked. "See them up there?"

"Them?" I repeated.

Her regal face gave away nothing. But I suspected disapproval. It was in her rigid bearing, her taut lips. She said, coolly, *"He* went up there about half-hour ago with Crystal. They've been poking around ever since."

"You have *got* to be kidding me," Lou exclaimed. I heard the ragged anger at the edges of his words. "With *him?"*

"I wish I was." Stacy shook her head, lips pursed while she considered the infamy of it all. "But he's been hanging around her skirts all day long, and every time I wished she'd tell him to back off, she just smiled and crooked her finger and he came right on after her. I think she's enjoying the attention."

I realized Stacy and Lou were going to embark on a little character assassination they'd come to regret—I *assumed* they'd come to regret —if I didn't step in. I held up my hands and said, as mildly as I could considering the heated atmosphere, "Now guys, we don't know the whole story here."

"Well, who's going to go and get it?" Stacy demanded.

"Yeah," Lou said. "You want me to go up there and break up their party?"

They both fastened their gazes on me, waiting for me to take the reins. As ever.

I sighed and shrugged. "I am, obviously."

"If you push him down the stairs," Lou said, "we won't tell anyone."

"And we'll help you hide the body," Stacy added.

She sounded serious.

I reflected on how little I knew about Stacy as I walked away from the bloodthirsty little duo. An artist from Miami who found respite and purpose in creating whimsical representations of the Sea Horse Ranch horses, who hated going back to the mainland, who had taken a proprietary interest in Crystal, Marchant, and the island at large until I showed up...then passed it all on to me.

Yes, I had to believe that Stacy would know how and where to hide a body, and she'd do it with panache. No wonder she hated the crutches so much; they were cramping her usual flair.

And preventing her from quietly, easily climbing stairs.

Well, she had an excuse today, I thought.

"But one of these days," I muttered, "I'm going to let you guys figure out your *own* problems."

One of these days. Hah! Yeah, right.

I tried for a silent approach, but it wasn't easy. The stairs to the fourth house creaked with age and neglect and the constant assault of humid salt air. Still, I didn't worry I was going to go crashing through them. The houses had been built strong, to last. You wouldn't want to build a house in a hurricane zone any other way. As I reached the last step, I noticed the spectacular view from this house's deck: an unobstructed vista of the great northern sweep of the mingling gulf and bay waters. Just below and off-shore, a dark blue channel cut through the jade-green flats, and I could see the long, dark body of a tarpon swimming off in search of its dinner.

I loved the view from Crystal's house, but this must be the best one on the island.

I lingered on the porch for a few moments, admiring the sea and weighing my options, and so I lost any advantage of surprise. Crystal happened to look through the open sliding-glass door and beckoned for me to come inside. I realized that I couldn't exactly leap in and accuse her of hanky-panky with Arnie when I was being warmly invited to join them. But that was for the best. Better to come in as a friend and see the lay of the land.

Inside, the unfinished house wasn't quite as scary as I'd always imagined it would be. The floors and walls were a little cobwebby, and there were small piles of old shavings scattered around, but nothing too bad. It wasn't exactly the haunted house I'd expected. In fact, some parts were surprisingly familiar-looking, like the kitchen fittings—the same cabinets and taps that I saw every day in Crystal's house. It looked like the kitchen was as far as the building had gotten before things stalled. There were no doors, just empty doorways, and the floors were bare plywood.

Crystal was sweeping the flashlight's beam around the walls, checking for damp, or maybe spiders. "Ever been up here?" she asked cheerfully.

"No, never," I said. "I'm not big on abandoned buildings."

"Oh, it's not really abandoned," Arnie called from the other side of the kitchen. "Just paused. It could be finished at any point. Little clean-up, finish the floors...wham, perfectly good house. I'd probably put in new impact-resistant windows, though," he added thoughtfully. "In case of a big storm."

Crystal nodded eagerly. I got the feeling they'd been talking about domestic things like window installation for a while.

Jeez. Talk about making himself right at home. "What—um— what's the plan now?"

"Arnie's thinking it's time to finish this place," Crystal said, sounding chipper. "I agree with him. It's about time we turned this into a proper house. What are we doing, letting this place sit abandoned right next to all our houses? And then inviting tourists to come out here? It ain't right."

I didn't dare inquire who she thought should live in it. Carefully, I asked, "And where's Arnie going to stay while he's finishing it?"

Arnie turned off his flashlight, evidently wrapping up his tour of inspection. "I'll just stay at Marchant's house," he replied, surprising me. "He has a spare room and I'm only a little allergic to cats. A few Benadryl and I'll be the best houseguest he's ever had. I even clean the bathroom."

I eyed Arnie suspiciously. "Does Marchant know about this?"

Crystal and Arnie burst into peals of delighted laughter. "Does Marchant know—" Crystal repeated, wiping at her eyes. "Oh, you *are* Lou's girlfriend, god love you! So distrustful. He's taught you well. Don't worry about a thing, my dear. Marchant knows about it. Everything is out in the open. We aren't doing anything in secret."

"Except for telling Lou," I pointed out, but Crystal shook her head.

"Of course we told Lou," she replied, surprised. "But the boy ran out and left before we could tell him *where* and *why* Arnie was sticking around! If he assumes the worst of me, well, sometimes I can't get up the energy to feel bad about it, Katie dear."

And as much as I hated to side against Lou, I could certainly see her point on this one.

I wanted to ask more questions, like who the house was being finished for, and if we could expect Arnie to be a full-time resident of Hell and Dammit Cay from here on out. But I felt like I might be pushing boundaries if I did. Bad enough that I was acting all sulky and suspicious like Lou; this still wasn't *my* island, and I didn't really have the right to start questioning Crystal on her motives and decisions.

So I just went back downstairs, a few steps ahead of them, while they laughed and told halves of jokes, evidently sharing a million private reminiscences while I was just trying to stay out of their way. I found Lou lurking by the barn and I dragged him around the back, where there was no one to overhear us but gentle surf and the horses in their stalls, slowly eating their hay, unaware or uncaring or both that the people of their island were capable of such constant upheaval.

He stared out to sea after I told him.

I sat beside him and gazed out, too. We were looking the wrong way for the sunset, but when the sun finally sank beneath the lowest layer of clouds and a brilliant golden light shot across the water, we were able to watch the palm trees on the closest shore of Little Bucket glow as if they'd turned to molten lava, while the little frizzles of white foam on the beach turned orange. Our shadows fell on the sand we'd bought and had trucked here, our artificial beach for photo ops. I let him be quiet for as long as I could.

"I have too much on my hands to run, as it is; I can't handle an island war between the two of you," I said eventually. "You might as well go back to Key West, I guess."

Lou rubbed his hands over his face. "I really wanted to stay," he complained, sighing.

"Well, are you going to?" I looked at him, the strong lines of his profile, the dark shadow of his beard catching the golden light like stardust. "Now that he's staying here, will you?"

A long pause. "No." A deep breath. "I'm not there yet."

"Okay," I said. I took his hand. "Okay."

I had to believe, at this point, that it was better this way. I could stay here and get through my mountains of work, and he could sit in Kev's house and pick out new arrangements for our songs, and we'd reconvene every few days and make it work.

I would miss him. But for now, I could accept it. He had things to get used to. Things I didn't think he should have to bear, but maybe all of us had to face these traumas at some point. Maybe our chickens always, always came home to roost.

"I'll take you back after the fireworks are over," I said.

"I have my car," he reminded me. "I don't need a ride."

I nodded slowly, feeling slighted, even though that was a little irrational.

"But," he said, "I sure would like to take the horses out with you."

He saddled Bart; I took Ruby. There was no way I was getting on Reggie, whose sensitive ears picked up distant thunder like an AM radio station finding its way across the country in the middle of the night. We rode out through the darkness with our knees and feet brushing together, our horses pressing close for comfort. On the moonless strand of beach, we let them splash in the water and absorbed the vast starry sky over our heads. To the west, the golden glow of Key West throbbed steadily.

I didn't want to look at it. Tonight, at least, I was tired of this town that kept swallowing up Lou, which had spat me out but kept drawing me back again for more nibbles at its fun-loving heart. Key West was a haven for runaways. Well, I wanted to run away, too, but I knew I never could. Not without hurting people—people who trusted me, people who needed me.

I wished I could disassociate like Lou, but at the back of my mind, I knew it wasn't an attribute he was proud of, not something he wanted. It came from a past he shouldn't have to have lived, from the idea that he wasn't good enough, that he couldn't keep his father in his life because he didn't deserve one. Anyone could tell Lou now that Arnie's decisions were *Arnie's* problems, not Lou's, but he couldn't listen and believe it, not when his entire childhood had been based on the lies he told himself. And of course, whatever

Crystal's game was now, it wasn't helping her son deal with his abandonment issues.

So I did what I could. I told him I loved him. And that I understood why he had to leave.

We looked at each other in the starlight and we couldn't see one another's faces, but we knew how the other person felt.

And it wasn't easy.

Chapter Nineteen

Marchant and I were surrounded by brass fittings from a sailboat's dilapidated saloon, up to our gloved elbows in metal polish and half-drunk on fumes, when I heard Crystal shouting my name.

Marchant looked at me and I gave him a tired glance in return. "What does she want?" I muttered.

"Sounds like the house is on fire," Marchant remarked.

"Good grief, Marchant! What a thing to say!" I straightened up slowly; my back was sore from bending over the brass. We'd pulled everything tarnished out of the saloon and spread it across the grass near the shore. Marchant was afraid that if we did the work inside the boat's cramped quarters, we'd pass out from the fumes before we were half-finished.

And getting the job finished was paramount right now. Marchant had done exactly what I'd hoped he wouldn't do—he'd taken his first hotel bookings from tourists attending the art festival. I'd barely had a chance to recover from the exhaustion of the day when he'd shown up on the porch with his good news. Two bookings for the second weekend in October.

"Columbus Day weekend," he explained. "Great time to visit. And I could charge a little extra for it being a holiday and all."

I'd gazed at him blearily and tried to think of a way to say that he shouldn't have charged his *first* bookings anything at all. I'd hoped we could fit in a soft opening, with just a couple of invited guests to stay and test things out. Make sure the beds were comfortable, the heads were up to the challenge, the nights out on the water weren't too scary for sailing newbies. Monica had said that was the way to go, that all hotels began with a dry run. I expected her to dissuade Marchant from taking paying guests as soon as mid-October.

Instead, Monica accepted the news with a chipper attitude, saying that now we had a deadline to work towards and that would make everything that much easier. "Now I'll put everything we have left into a spreadsheet and assign due dates," she mused cheerfully.

I gave her a wary look. "You're *excited* about a spreadsheet?"

"You could do with a few spreadsheets yourself," Monica informed me mildly. "You're always doing all the things and running yourself ragged. Imagine if you had a planner to keep track of it all."

I'd never learned to be organized. I'd also never been so busy before. Hard to believe just a few months ago I was spending most of my time staring out the window of a smelly van full of guys and musical equipment, traveling back and forth across the country in search of an elusive living. "Maybe it's something to try," I allowed, but that was as far as the conversation went. At least for the time being. When would I have time to get organized? Everything was rushing at me so quickly.

I was grateful to Monica for handling the paperwork side of things, so I went with her optimistic outlook. Inside, though, I was quailing at the amount of hard labor yet to put into these boats. Paint and polish were tough things to apply in the middle of a

Florida summer, when every moment was alternating between glaring sunlight and tropical downpours.

I had to admit to myself that there were a lot of things I'd rather be doing with my July. Most of them involved being inside, or underwater. Ripping out the furnishings on a dank, dark sailboat and updating them with fresh fittings while the pitiless sun burned overhead and reflected off the water's surface was probably at the bottom of my list.

But Marchant was happy.

And that was what this was all about, right? Making Marchant's dreams come true. I hoped when I was old and gray and whimsically irrational, some nice young thing might do the same for me.

He waved to me with his polishing cloth as I slipped my flip flops back on and ran across the grass. Crystal met me on the road, her eyes wild and her hair falling around her face. She looked like she'd been napping on the sofa again. Crystal was having a much more restful July than me. Something about having Arnie on the island, hammering away at the fourth house, seemed to settle her. Or maybe it was just the effect of the sunlight shimmering down on us, filling her to bursting with Vitamin D and good vibes.

But right now, her vibes looked annoyed.

"What's wrong?" I gasped, skidding to a halt beside her.

"There's a client coming," she informed me. "Did you forget?"

"Oh…" I racked my brain until a little shard of memory poked out. "Yes, I sure did. I'm so sorry. Are they here?" I looked around, but there weren't any new cars or people wandering around.

"They called from Cutlass to double-check directions. That's when I looked out and saw you with Marchant, instead of getting horses ready. You've got three riders coming. You need help getting them ready?"

I glanced over at the horses, who were dozing in their paddocks, tails swishing lazily against the occasional fly. They weren't exactly clean. We'd been getting rain every day, and they'd found plenty of puddles to splash in this morning. "Ugh, I think I do," I admitted. "Sorry."

"It's fine," she said. Crystal was already wearing a pair of rubber barn clogs. She set off for the barn while I ran upstairs to get on jeans and riding boots. I tried not to take out my paying clients in shorts and bare feet. It set a bad example.

I was just tugging on my boots when Arnie appeared in the living room, looking around with a concerned expression. "Everything okay? I saw Crystal running downstairs."

"It's fine, yeah," I told him, not surprised he'd come wandering into the house without knocking. I was used to him popping up now. For the first few days of his stay here, it had been confusing having a new face on the island. Especially one which bore such a striking resemblance to Lou's. I didn't really want to like him, or even talk to him. But, just as Crystal had promised, Arnie was a nice guy. Unassuming. Friendly. Always ready to help with just about anything going on, from getting supper ready to picking up palm fronds after a heavy storm.

He swung the hammer he was carrying. "Anything I can help you with?"

I grinned. "Only if you can tack up horses."

"Oh, well, it's your lucky day!"

I stared at him. "You can tack up horses?"

"Oh, sure. I was in the circus for a while."

Of course he was. I didn't even blink. Arnie was that kind of guy. And the Keys were that kind of place.

* * *

Arnie made himself useful for the entire trail ride. He even rode in the back, with Crystal, while I guided. The clients, a trio of middle-aged women in the Keys on a girl's trip, were delighted with his twinkling smile and roguish good looks. He was basically the kind of trail guide Lou would be, if Lou weren't always glowering into the jungle and thinking about song bridges.

I tried not to remember that Arnie was the reason Lou was that way. But it stuck in the back of my head, as he joshed and kidded with the riders, that all of this sparkling personality had been wasted on other people for almost thirty years, when it could have been lavished on his son.

Hell, even the horses liked him. He rode with an easy seat and gentle hands, and when Reggie threatened to spook at unseen storms in the distance, his voice seemed to calm my horse better than I could.

"That's a good boy," he told Reggie affectionately as we stood the horses on the beach, swiping his neck with one big paw. "You're a good fellow, aren't you?"

"So, what did you do in the circus?" I asked him, watching closely as Crystal took the riders into the water for their splashing session. I was basically the lifeguard on this ride, standing back to make sure no one got into trouble.

"Oh, this and that," Arnie replied absently, his gaze on Crystal as she neck-reined her horse through the water. "I guess I did whatever needed doing, helped whoever needed helped. It's a big family, the circus. Everyone taking care of each other. Really nice atmosphere."

Again, I thought about the family he'd chosen *not* to take care of. I bit the inside of my cheek and didn't reply.

Arnie seemed to sense my tension. Well, that didn't make him amazingly perceptive; it was probably coming off me in waves. He nudged his horse a little closer, letting him touch noses with Reggie. "I actually joined the circus after Crystal and I broke up," he volunteered, lowering his voice. "That was a hard time."

I couldn't help but look at him with disbelief. "Didn't you have anything to do with that, uh, *hard time?*" I asked snippily. "Why didn't you stay and take care of Lou?"

Instead of getting upset, Arnie chuckled, as if I had missed some important joke. "Well, honey," he said cheerfully, "I appreciate you asking that. The truth is, Crystal wouldn't keep me around. And I guess I didn't deserve her. She didn't have time for a man like me around the house, and she told me so. Said I could settle down and work a job and bring home a check or I could get out. And..."

"And?" I prompted.

"And I couldn't do it," he admitted, his endless smile finally fading —although only for a moment. "So I got out. She was right about that part. I wasn't any help to her. More a hindrance."

Months ago, Crystal had told me that Lou's father was no good. I'd assumed that meant he'd just taken off and left. But, I reflected now, it could just as easily have meant she'd tested him, found him wanting, and sent him on his way. It was all in the way I'd interpreted her words.

And wouldn't that be exactly the way Crystal would handle things? She wasn't a woman who let things *happen* to her. She was a woman who got things done. She made lemons into lemonade and old fish camps into tourist attractions like nothing else in the Keys. And she'd raised Lou alone because she'd decided that was the only way she could manage it.

"I came back once or twice but she never was open to talking to me," Arnie went on, his eyes still on Crystal as her horse splashed in the water. "But I thought maybe this year would be different. I've been keeping an eye on my interests down here all this time, y'know.

Just waiting to see if she'd take me back."

"Has she?" I blurted. "Taken you back?"

"No," Arnie said. "But she let me back in. That's more than enough for me. I can make her life a little better, start making things up to her."

"Where have you been, Arnie?" I asked, aware it was none of my business and not caring in the least. He still hadn't mentioned Lou, and what he owed his son.

"Just wandering, for a long time," he said, glancing at me with a rueful smile. "I get these itchy feet. It's hard for me to settle down. That's mostly why I joined the circus for a while, that and I always wanted to know what it felt like to belong to something."

I nodded, looking down at Reggie's mane. I ran my fingers through the thick strands of horsehair, trying to make sense of my feelings. *Itchy feet.* It wasn't a phrase I wanted to hear, not from Lou's father or from anyone else. I didn't want to feel connected to him, didn't want to think we had something in common.

Didn't want to believe that without the binding glue of these people on our island, I would be just like him, back out on the road, looking for something undefinable that was always just over the horizon.

You already belong, I told myself, my inner voice fierce as a football coach. *You found your family and the place you belong.*

And this place was as much as circus as the Ringling Brothers— most days, anyway.

"Time for a canter!" Crystal called, waving to us. "These girls want to feel the wind in their hair!"

I raised my eyebrows. "I thought these were new riders?" I said to Arnie.

"Well, if they fall, it's only sand," he replied amiably, shrugging. He started to turn his horse towards the beach.

"Arnie?" I called.

He looked back at me, eyes questioning.

"Arnie, if you stay, Lou's not coming back."

He nodded slowly. Then he said, "I might have a plan to help you with that."

"You can't," I told him. "It's bad. And I want him here. I don't—" I took a breath, aware what I was saying went beyond the bounds of my position on the island. "I don't want you to be the one that keeps Lou away from his home. I think you should leave. I'm sorry, but—"

"Listen," Arnie interrupted. "You might know I've been a contractor..."

"Add that to the list," I said dryly. "Contractor, circus, dive shop operator, owner of local bar..."

"Well, yes." His chuckle rasped in his throat. "I'm a little bit of a Jack of all trades. But it's true about being a contractor. And I can fix that house up for you. I *am* fixing up that house for you. It's not for me, honey."

I didn't know what to say. For *me?* Surely he meant—

"It's not my house," I said. "It's Crystal's. It was her father's."

He nodded. "And Crystal wants you and Lou to have it."

I stared at him.

"I'll finish up and then I'll get out of your hair," he said. "Find someplace on Cutlass, maybe, where I can be there. Just in case he changes his mind about me. But he don't have to. I know that."

It was my turn to nod. Arnie gave me one more smile and circled his horse back towards the turquoise water.

I watched him ride away for a moment, too stunned to follow. My head tried to click through the reasons, figure out what his angle was. Maybe he just wanted Lou and I out of Crystal's house, so he had more room to romance her. Or maybe it was really to make up for everything he'd never given Lou.

I didn't know. But I made a decision in that moment and vowed to stick to it.

I would stop judging Arnie Morehead. It wasn't my place to do it. It was up to Lou, and to Crystal, to forgive him and decide on the terms of their relationship. I couldn't do that for any of them, and it was inappropriate for me to even try.

"Guys, come on!" Crystal was turning her horse in circles, the water splashing around her feet. "Let's go!"

"Arnie," I called.

He looked over his shoulder.

"I don't know if he's coming back," I said.

"He'll come back," Arnie promised. "And he'll have a home and a recording studio when he does."

Chapter Twenty

TALK ABOUT INSIDE information. I carried that promise with me for the rest of the day, while we hosed off the horses and turned them back out, while I went over to Marchant's to finish polishing what was left of the brass, and while I drove to Key West to have dinner with Lou and work on our music. And hopefully, I thought, I'd manage to keep my mouth shut about Arnie's little project.

It was going to be tough, though.

In Key West, July vacations and cruise ship tourists were colliding in the tropical heat. The roads were busy and Old Town was throbbing—with bass lines pouring from bars and clubs, with motorcycles and mopeds racing in and out of traffic, with shouting street performers and drunken *everyone*.

There was respite from the sound and crowds behind the lush garden of the little shotgun cottage. The cat was curled on the porch steps, green eyes unblinking as I walked past and slipped through the storm door. Lou was waiting for me with warm arms and a hot kiss. I settled in for the evening happily; there was no reason to go back onto those crowded streets.

Kev had left us a gorgeous dinner in the fridge: a velvety crab bisque studded with golden, summer-sweet corn, a paella of yellow rice, fat local pink shrimp, and slivers of octopus; a soft, fresh loaf of Cuban bread. We took the feast into the tiny backyard, which Lou had been clearing, taking out a bit of jungle every day. His work had revealed a concrete patio with a shimmering tile mosaic around the edges, a garden walk edged with chipped conch shells, and a depression we suspected had once been a koi pond. Palm trees in the neighboring yards shaded the yard, and the cat came to join us, stalking lizards beneath the bougainvillea bushes lining the fence. It was almost quiet. I could hear a distant beat pulsing from Duval Street, and a few houses down, a parrot was repeating, "Thank you, have a nice day," in a clipped British accent.

"I'm starting to see how this place could be worth half a million bucks," I joked as we dipped spoons into our soup. "The parrot alone edges it up in my book."

Lou grinned and shook his head. "That bird keeps me on my toes. Yesterday it was saying, 'Mind the gap, mind the gap,' while I was up on the roof pulling down those vines." He pointed at a pile of wilted foliage near the garden gate, waiting to be bagged up for trash day. "I can't decide if it was actually born in a shop next to a tube station or if the owner just has a crazy sense of humor."

"It's Key West, so probably the latter," I laughed. My regular visits were showing me the local side of Key West, and I was developing a fondness for this eccentric city, despite the proliferation of socks-and-sandals tourists. The characters who lived here were every bit as unique and free-spirited as the ones I met in the out-islands... possibly even more so. But I still preferred the tropical isolation of Hell and Dammit Cay to the noise and constant energy of Key West; to say nothing of the family I'd found there. "This place is growing on me," I admitted. "But only in small doses."

"It can be a lot," he agreed. "The weekends are loud. And when there's a cruise ship in port, the whole place is overwhelmed. Like tonight. I guess you're not spending the night here, is what you're saying."

"No, I'll stay." I put down my spoon and my fingers found his. We smiled at each other for a moment, and I thought about everything I wasn't telling him. What a massive secret to keep. But it would be worth it.

"After all," I added coyly, "We have a *lot* of work to do."

"You and work!" Lou snorted. "I don't think you want my body. You want my brain."

"Disgusting of me," I agreed mockingly. "I am a slut for hot brains full of melancholy songs."

"I guess I'll have to take my ripped bod out to the clubs to find someone who really cares," he went on, mournful as Huckleberry Hound.

"Make sure you cut a shirt off as a crop-top," I suggested. "Girls love that. And guys, too. You'll be fighting them off you."

"I have some scissors in the kitchen. Good thought."

"Maybe wear cut-offs? Eyeliner is always good, too."

"Would you stop trying to whore me out?" Lou begged, laughing. "My god, woman."

"I just want you to enjoy your time in Key West," I said demurely, dipping back into my soup. "Because as long as you're here, the food is amazing. I don't get fed like this back on the island."

"Ah, but Kev doesn't have Dammit Salt," Lou reminded me. He tore off a chunk of Cuban bread, smeared it with butter, and pushed it my way. "Think how good that would be with this nice, soft bread right now. The spice, the way it tingles on your tongue..."

He was right. Marchant's signature seasoning would be amazing on this bread. The way it was on just about everything else. "We're actually going to incorporate that into the hotel," I said. "A special dinner, cooked by Marchant, as part of the stay."

Lou leaned back in his chair, the wicker seat creaking. "I can't believe that's going forward. You said he already has bookings?"

"Yeah. Monica convinced him to do these weekend packages, so we don't always have strangers running around. Two nights, breakfast supplies on the boat, one dinner with us, and one elsewhere...maybe the Mermaid, we haven't worked out those details yet."

Lou's expression clouded the moment I said *Monica.* "So she's really involved with this, huh?"

"I couldn't do it without her. Not with everything else going on. And anyway, none of us have hotel experience. We'd be flying blind. We're really lucky she showed up."

He looked as if he had another word in mind besides *lucky,* but he kept it inside, stuffing his mouth with bread instead. I sighed and set my attention back on my soup.

"It's not a coincidence that she showed up," Lou said eventually, unable to let it go. As usual.

"Of course it's not," I agreed. "She's obviously connected with Arnie, more than they wanted to let on. But I don't think it's a conspiracy, either. Everyone in the Keys has their secrets. Why should they be any different?"

Lou surveyed me, his eyes troubled. "Because it involves all of us," he said finally. "Because it involves *you.* And I don't want anything to happen to you or anyone else."

"Happen? Do you think Arnie is going to use the island for something illegal?" I recalled the kind, fun-loving man back at Hell and Dammit Cay, finishing the interior of an abandoned house to give his long-lost son somewhere stable to live. It wasn't the same person that Lou saw when he thought about his father, I knew. But that was going to change soon. I just had to wait out the construction. I told Lou, "Honestly, I don't think he's up to anything criminal. He doesn't strike me as that type."

Lou shook his head. "This is Florida, Katie. The word *criminal* is pretty fluid here."

He wasn't wrong. I thought about the boats Marchant had bought, and Cap'n Skip's interesting way of interpreting the law he was sworn to uphold. Something about Florida, and especially the Keys, just invited behavior that...well, it wasn't always normal, let's put it like that. Maybe it was the heat, or the humidity, or the way people would visit and shake their heads and say, "It's nice for a vacation, but I don't know how you live here." Or maybe it was the giant spiders who took up residence in the most inconvenient of places. I didn't know.

Maybe it was just an attempt to take care of our own in a place boiling over with venom and thorns, where traps were festooned with bright flowers and refreshing waters might be harboring the toothy descendants of dinosaurs.

I was about to say something deep and thoughtful about the whole idea when my phone began buzzing. Distracted, I pulled it from my purse. "Huh," I said, surprised. "It's your mother."

Lou raised his eyebrows and waited for me to answer the phone.

I put the phone to my ear and asked, "Crystal? What's going on?"

"We have a problem that requires our attention," Crystal said flatly. "Have you seen the latest weather report?"

Chapter Twenty-One

LOU WASN'T TOO upset about the weather forecast. Certainly not as freaked out as I was once Crystal was done with me.

"It's a tropical depression," he said, shrugging. "And it's miles away. Thousands of miles, actually. We'll worry about it when it's an actual problem."

"But we can't start prepping too soon," I fussed, picking at my paella disconsolately. The bloom had definitely gone out of the supper. "Crystal says the horses will have to be shipped out if there's a hurricane threatening. And the forecasters are all saying there could be a hurricane watch by *tomorrow*."

His brow furrowed. "That seems really soon for something that's literally non-existent."

"That's how it works now. With the models and the supercomputers and all that doing the forecasting. They tell you ahead of time and then everyone panics and buys all the gas. It happens in Louisiana like, three or four times a year."

"How often are they right about it hitting?"

I shrugged, annoyed. "I don't have the stats in front of me, Lou. But it doesn't even matter what our opinions are, because the horses belong to your mother and she gets to say what happens with them, not us."

"So what are you saying?"

Our eyes met across the table. "I'm saying that tomorrow we have to come up with a plan to get the horses off the island. And I don't know how I'm going to manage that." Not on top of everything else. To say nothing of where *we* would go if we had to evacuate. The island houses were on high piers; we could stay through a storm surge...up to a certain point. High winds and tornadoes were another story, though. Not to mention the potential of a long period without electricity or everyday services, like a nearby grocery store. What if we didn't have running water for weeks? There were so many bad things to imagine. I could spend all evening coming up with them and there would still be more.

Lou sighed and went back to his meal, spearing a shrimp on his fork. "Tell you what, sunshine. Let's go out for a drink after dinner and you can see how the Keys really responds to the news saying there's a tropical depression somewhere in the Caribbean."

I shrugged again. Like I'd said before, it wasn't about how *I* reacted. This was entirely up to his mother.

And I knew she wasn't going to play any games with the safety of her horses.

After we finished up, Lou ushered me out into the humid streets. The sunset celebration was in full force down at Mallory Square, and the streets of Old Town were crowded, pedestrians flooding into the roads and car horns honking. Music blared from open bar windows and the gardens of stately Victorian homes that had been transformed into restaurants. There was a median age of about fifty-five; the music trended towards classic rock with a heavy helping of Jimmy Buffett.

If Lou was trying to prove Key West didn't care about some hypothetical hurricane, the island was certainly happy to help him. I watched stilt walkers careen through a crowd on a side-street, their skimpy costumes dripping with feathers and jewels; I saw a man juggling coconuts while a fat snake writhed around his neck; I observed two young women get into a slap-fight while a pack of frat boys chanted encouragement, pumping the fists that weren't holding frozen drinks. Sullen teenagers dragged behind their parents as far as they could manage, taking in the lewd t-shirts and bongs in the Duval Street souvenir shop windows with wide, appreciative eyes.

We threaded through the calamitous weekend festivities until I couldn't take anymore. Then Lou sensed my unease and his hand went to my back, guiding me towards a white Victorian on a corner at the far end of Duval. I recognized it immediately: Southernmost Jazz, where the live music was coming from a groovy quartet, the bartenders served drinks mixed by hand and not poured from a swirling machine, and Rivers McLean was sitting at a table near the stage, drinking an old fashioned and tapping his hand along with the beat.

Lou stiffened when he saw Rivers, but I plowed forward, eager to let him know that we were finally getting the work done on our album. Rivers glanced up as my shadow fell over his table, and his face lit up with a smile. "Katie LeBlanc!" he announced as the band took five. "Fancy meeting you here."

He gestured to the open chairs, and I slipped into the one next to him, leaning over to speak as the house music came up. "This is the only place in Key West that isn't playing either Jimmy Buffett or Bob Seger," I said, laughing. "Don't be surprised if you see more of me in the future."

"Spending more time on the big island?" he asked, signaling to a bartender to bring us a round. "What's gotten you off your sandbar?"

"This guy," I told him, nudging Lou, who had taken the chair next to me and was managing not to look like a total grump for once. "It was his idea, anyway. We're doing our work here. More energy in the air," I ad-libbed, trying to think like I was a bullshitting pop star being interviewed for a magazine.

Rivers caught the nonsense and guffawed. He took a quick drink, finishing his cocktail as the bartender hustled over with three more on a tray. You didn't have to wait for service when you owned the place. "I hope you can work on the mainland," he said. "Seen the weather forecast?"

Lou groaned, while I blinked quickly, trying to get my bearings. "I have, but I don't know—"

"Trust me on this," Rivers said. "Tomorrow night we'll be announcing our closing so that we have time to board up and sandbag. As soon as they call a hurricane watch, they'll ask tourists to start evacuating. U.S. 1's gonna be a parking lot from here to Homestead."

My mouth fell open, too dismayed to make any actual words. Beside me, Lou accepted his old fashioned and took a healthy first sip. More like a gulp, actually.

Rivers was more sanguine, taking a sip of his own drink and nodding at the bartender in thanks. "It's a shame," he continued, "but that's the cost of doing business in the Keys. We're always on the edge of getting sent back to the mainland with our tails between our legs. Not that I always evacuate," he added. "But there's no point in leaving the club open when the tourists are gone, and some of my staff have kids or old parents to worry about. So we all come in and prep for the worst, then hope for the best."

I found my voice at last. "I didn't realize it could happen so quickly," I said. "In Louisiana, my family would usually wait until the day before a storm to board up."

"It's different down here at the end of the highway," Rivers reminded me. "One way in, one way out. And a whole lot of people trying to get out makes quite a traffic jam. You can't start too soon."

Suddenly, I knew we weren't going to get any work done tonight. The music was going to have to wait, as foreign as that concept was to me. I knew Rivers wasn't going to hand us any extensions, but we were caught up, weren't we? Or close enough? "I think we'll be heading out," I told him. "Sorry to just drop in and dip like this—"

"Finish your drink," Rivers advised, putting his hand on mine. The gesture was fatherly, but I felt Lou tense beside me. Rivers didn't see anything wrong. "Give yourself time to think. You can't do anything tonight."

That was precisely the problem. And not entirely true. I could do something tonight: get myself back to Hell and Dammit Cay and sit down with Crystal, to start making our plans.

If we had to leave tomorrow, I couldn't leave anything to chance.

Chapter Twenty-Two

"I'LL GO WITH you." Lou was walking next to me as I hustled up a side-street, doing everything in my power to avoid the crowds on Duval. Before, they'd merely seemed like vacationers with high spirits. Annoying, for sure, but honestly, whomst among us hadn't gone a little too crazy on a trip mostly centered around booze and sunshine?

Now, with this fresh perspective on the strange weather to come, everyone out there partying on the asphalt and in the clubs just seemed like assholes who couldn't get their act together when there was a storm threatening the islands. I wanted them to go home, pack their bags, and get out. Right this very minute. If I had a bull-horn, I'd start shouting into it. *Partiers of Key West, go check out of your hotels and hit the road!*

Luckily, I didn't have anything like that. And I was distracted by Lou, anyway. I stopped power-walking through Old Town and gazed up at him, conflicted by his offer.

He stood beneath the waving frond of a palm tree, with an orange-lit cloud hanging over us both, and gave me his most serious, frowning expression. "Seriously, you're not going back alone."

"Are you sure?" I asked. "Arnie—"

"He isn't as important as taking care of you, my mom, and the horses," Lou answered flatly. "Obviously, I'm going back. Just give me a few minutes to pack up my things."

"What about Kev? Will he need help with the house?"

"He can bring back some guys from the restaurant," Lou said. "Don't worry about Kev."

I was going to worry about Kev. I was going to worry about everyone on this island. One thing to know about my capacity to worry: it was unlimited. How else would I have made myself the caretaker of so many hopes and dreams on Hell and Dammit Cay, if I wasn't worrying, constantly, about the happiness of the people who lived there?

But I could also accept that some people were capable of taking care of themselves, that my constant concern was not going to be the deciding factor in their safety. I put a hand on Lou's arm, and he squeezed it with his other hand, as reassuring a gesture as I could imagine. "Thank you," I said.

His smile was grim. "I'm just sorry you didn't automatically assume I'd come."

I swallowed. *Chew on that, Katie!*

Maybe he didn't need my protection, after all.

Back at Kev's little house, he packed a bag in a matter of minutes. The bedroom he'd been living in quickly lost all evidence of his stay. If anything, the way he'd lived out of his backpack should have told me how temporary his stay in Key West had always been. He'd been here almost a month, but as we closed the door behind him, the bedroom looked as blank as a motel room. Bleak, even. I thought about him living like this for all these weeks and almost felt bad I hadn't sided with him and moved down as well.

Almost, but not quite, because now I knew not to take sides in this family feud. I didn't have all the information—no one did, I understood that, but once Lou was caught up on Arnie's activity on the island, he'd have more than I did. He'd have his own feelings to sort out. All I could do was guess.

I just hoped the next twenty-four hours brought about an end to his sadness. I wasn't sure how that might happen...but it was better than the alternative. I could easily imagine Lou and Arnie fighting over who took care of Crystal and her possessions, while Marchant and Stacy looked on and the horses paced in their stalls, sure something was about to happen but unable to tell just what.

On the way home, I flipped on the radio and instantly regretted it. But I couldn't turn it off, either. It was like when the news got dire, I had to have more. "The National Hurricane Center will likely issue a hurricane watch for the entire Middle and Lower Keys by tomorrow afternoon," a newscaster said. "And this will be accompanied by calls for evacuation of all non-residents to begin by nine a.m. the next day. So as you make your plans for the weekend, consider that you might well be dealing with excessive traffic, store closures, and even empty gas pumps."

I looked in the rearview mirror, where the lights of Lou's car were trailing my truck. Crystal's truck. I glanced at the gas gauge and made a spontaneous decision, pulling into the last gas station before the lights of Stock Island receded and the darkness of the Lower Keys took over U.S. 1.

"Here?" Lou asked, getting out of his car as I pulled the gas tank lid off. "Murray has notoriously expensive gas." He hooked a thumb over his shoulder, pointing out the sign indicating we were about to pay nearly fifty cents more per gallon than we would have back on

Key West. "And he's probably already raised the price, in anticipation of the state law against price gouging. It goes into effect as soon as the government issues a state of emergency, so if they really call for an evacuation—"

"There's nowhere else to fill up between here and Big Pine," I interrupted, sliding my credit card into the reader. I could hardly afford to fill up this thirsty old truck, but something internal was driving me—an inner voice, or an inner terror, I wasn't sure which. "I don't want to get caught in traffic with no gas and six horses trying to get to safety," I told Lou. "Can you imagine? We'd have to walk them the rest of the way to the mainland."

"Someone would top off our tank before it came to that," Lou said, but he finally seemed to catch some of my urgency, because he went and filled up his own gas tank as well.

Back on the road, with the starlit water and dark mangroves surrounding the truck, I switched the radio to a music station and tried to forget, for just a few minutes, that I was driving back to my island in a panic over a storm which might not happen, which might not even exist. It just felt like such a perfect culmination of everything that had happened to me over the past few months, the ways my life had changed, the way my priorities had shifted from putting myself first, to the happiness of a handful of people I had only just met. Of course, now I had to rush home to try to save them from a phantom storm. Of course, I had to put my goals on hold again.

Why couldn't things just be nice and easy for once?

As I slowed the truck in Cutlass Key, I noticed the full parking lot at the Mermaid. For a moment, I considered stopping off and going in. I'd like to talk to Monica, if she was working. What was she thinking tonight? Where would she ride out a hurricane? Did she plan to leave? Did she have any plans at all? Or was she like one of the partiers down in Key West, ignoring the existential threat of a storm which hadn't been born yet, concentrating on the now—or on nothing at all?

And even more than that, I wanted answers to everything else. About Arnie, about what really brought her to Cutlass Key and the Mermaid. I wanted to know, more than anything, if she was related to Arnie.

And if so, how?

Was it any of my business? I guess some people might say no.

But I had to disagree with those people. I imagined crowds of strangers eager to tell me I was being too nosey, digging into secrets which didn't concern me. And I dismissed them all, because what happened to Lou also happened to me. That was how relationships worked.

So yeah, I thought I could reasonably ask. If I could only find the words.

And the right time.

But if she was working tonight, she'd be busy. Too busy to sit and discuss all the terrors preying on my mind tonight. I turned down the road to the islands from Cutlass Key and let the Mermaid disappear behind me. Lou's headlights followed, shining in my rearview mirror.

Almost home.

Chapter Twenty-Three

THE ONLY THING that could knock fears of a hurricane out of Crystal's head was the sight of her son.

She was sitting on the sofa when we walked into the house, watching the news, fingers tapping a nervous pattern on the side of her head. One look at Lou, and all traces of fear were gone. She leapt up and ran for him, and if she shoved me just a little as she threw her arms around her son, well, that was understandable. Lou just had that effect on women. Or at least he did on me and his mother.

But once the hugs and kisses were exchanged, Crystal was back to business. She plucked a beer out of the fridge for herself, told us to settle in, and returned to her news-watching with grave concentration.

The newscasters, looking gravely at their notes from a shiny studio somewhere in Miami, were talking incessantly about evacuation routes, gas station pricing, the rate at which bread and water were disappearing from grocery store shelves. It was like watching a holiday special, starring all the big favorites of hurricane season. I could easily have been back in Louisiana, just swap out a few major waterways and change the names of some bridges.

But of course, the Keys had one thing no one else did: the Overseas Highway.

And to hear these broadcasters talking, this road was going to be bumper-to-bumper by breakfast time.

Crystal stirred on the sofa during the commercial break. "You kids have fun in Key West?"

Lou assured her we'd had a hootenanny.

"That's good," she said absently. "Nothing but hard work in store tomorrow."

I glanced at Lou and he lifted his eyebrows. Then he headed for my bedroom, beckoning for me to follow.

With the door closed behind us, he scattered various contents of his bag around my bed until he found what he was looking for. He held it up to me and smiled. "You wanted to work?"

I looked at the little plastic thimble in his hand. "A thumb drive?"

"All the good stuff is on here. I didn't want to worry about someone stealing my laptop and losing everything."

I made a skeptical face. "Who would steal your laptop? Kev?"

"Focus," he said. "Do you want to work or not?"

I sat on the bed, cross-legged, and rubbed my face with my hands. "Obviously, but now I feel totally distracted by all this storm talk."

"Well, then let me distract you away from it," Lou suggested. "Deadlines. Rivers. Studio time."

"Stop! What are you doing?"

"Listing all your favorite things. Feel like working yet?"

"Let's go," I said, reaching for his laptop.

And it worked for a while. We sank into the music and all our ideas seemed to flow into each other. We'd been on the same page even though we'd been on different islands. The knowledge made my heart full. We were going to figure this out in the end. And we'd get our record made and Rivers would book a tour for us and—

And then what?

Well, I didn't know. But while I was working with Lou, not knowing the future didn't seem so bad.

We fell asleep sometime in the early hours of the morning. I woke up curled around Lou, who in turn was sort of wrapped around his laptop. We made a cute trio, I thought wryly, picking myself up. The sun was rising, golden light creeping beneath my blinds and picking out motes of dust swirling in the air. I wondered why dust was always on the move. Where was it going?

Quietly, careful not to wake him, I slipped through the verticals and slid open the door. The decking was cool beneath my feet, and there was a gentle surf breaking on the beach. The sound it made was more sizzle than roar, bubbles popping as the water ebbed backwards to meet the next lapping wave. A few straggling fingers of seaweed drifted on the surface, pulled endlessly between the flow of the channel beyond the island, and the golden sand at its edges.

I watched the seaweed for a few minutes, wondering if the island or the channel would finally win out. But neither side seemed to be winning. The clump of seaweed just hung there, shoved back and forth.

I didn't want to compare myself to a drifting patch of sargassum, but sometimes the metaphors just presented themselves.

And if I was seaweed floating on the tides, who was the island and who was the channel?

"Now you're talking ridiculous," I told myself, turning back to the door.

Lou was standing there, peeking at me through the blinds. He smiled. "Talking to yourself?"

"Always a good conversation," I returned, shrugging. "And I work alone a lot, so...it can get to be a habit."

"Everything's going to be okay, you know."

It was so unlike him that I had to laugh. "What, specifically, do you think is going to be okay?"

He shrugged. "This whole storm thing. It's going to blow over." A wink. "Pun intended."

"Oh, you think so?"

"Turn on the TV. I'll bet it's heading for Mexico or something now."

"I'll take you up on that," I promised. "And what about the rest?"

"The rest?" Lou repeated, looking evasive.

"What about Arnie? Is that going to be okay, Lou? Are *you* going to be okay?"

He frowned, and I felt bad; it was too early for this nonsense. He'd barely slept. I shouldn't have brought it up. Should have just left things light and silly—

"I think whatever happens, happens for a reason," he said finally.

I blinked at him, stunned. That wasn't usually Lou's philosophy. In fact, now that I thought about it, I wasn't sure he *had* a philosophy. Other than following the path of least resistance, which, quite frankly, was not something I could really fault him for. "So," I eventually replied, feeling for my words, "if you run into him, you're not going to leave, right? Don't go back to Key West, Lou, not now. I'm asking you to stay."

I knew it was a big ask. He'd come late in the night, high off the excitement of working on our music. But this was early morning, and nothing from the night before was ever quite as charming once the sun was shining.

"I'm not going back," he assured me, and then he opened his arms. "C'mere, worry girl," he said tenderly.

I stepped into his embrace and wrapped my arms around him. He smelled like saltwater and the faint fragrance of my sheets. He smelled comforting.

He smelled like home.

If I was a clump of lonely seaweed floating between the beach and the channel, then Lou was the grasping tide, pulling me home with him, tugging me back out to sea with him. More powerful than the horses, than the islanders, than the overwhelming sense of responsibility for the happiness of everyone around me, Lou pulsed with the careless gravity of the moon.

Chapter Twenty-Four

I WAS CLEANING stalls when Monica came driving over the bridge, her Jeep sparkling in the sunlight. She pulled up alongside the horse paddocks and came walking between them with a swing in her step, her happy shimmy made more obvious by the tiny denim shorts she was wearing.

"Good morning, Daisy Mae," I greeted her, leaning on my manure fork. "You look very edible today."

She laughed. "You're so weird, Katie. I'm going up to Bahia Honda to meet some friends, that's all. I wondered if you wanted to come."

"To Bahia Honda? I wish I could." The beach at Bahia Honda State Park was lusciously tropical, with a plantation of coconut palms leaning over electric teal waters. It looked more like Hawaii or the Caribbean than the scruffy Keys. But the day ahead was packed with storm prep plans. Lou's prediction that the potential hurricane, as the forecasters were calling it, would pass towards Mexico had turned out to be wrong. Regretfully, I said, "We have to get things ready in case there's a storm. Did you not have anything to prep at the Mermaid?"

186

She shrugged, the fringe on her shirt swinging. "I mean, fill sandbags and that kind of thing. Nothing that can't be done the day before. I'm not going to get all worked up about a storm that doesn't really exist yet. In Miami, we call that panicking," she added, ribbing me gently.

"But it *does* exist," I countered. "It's upgrading to a tropical storm this morning. Everyone says so."

"When I have to worry about it, I'll worry about it," Monica promised. "In the meantime, I have the day off, and some girls from Miami are in the Keys for the week, so I'm going to the beach." She looked around speculatively. "Question, for you, friend...is that *Lou's* car next to Crystal's truck?"

We both looked at Lou's beat-up little car, as if it had just materialized there while we'd been talking. I didn't want to tell her Lou was on the island. But it wasn't really a secret I could keep. Even if she was gone all day today, she'd be back by evening...and Arnie would probably tell her. "Yes," I admitted. "He's not big on mornings, though. He got up early and went back to bed."

"But I thought he didn't want to run into Arnie?" Monica asked. "Isn't that why he's been in Key West? Arnie's here this morning, isn't he?"

A crashing sound and a shout, loud enough to startle the horses out of their morning naps, was the fortuitous answer to her question.

"He's here," I replied, grimacing. "Working on the house. Sounds like maybe he found another weak spot in the floor, though."

"Too funny," Monica said, her eyes still lingering on Lou's car. "What's he planning on doing with that house?"

I was surprised Arnie hadn't told her that it was supposed to be for Lou—and me. Well, I was surprised for a moment. Then I began to wonder if it was just a line he'd invented to keep me quiet and happy while he was busy barging in on our lives here. Maybe Arnie really did want the house for himself, and he was just planning to insinuate himself into it—I could hear his explanation now: "Marchant needs his space, and I'm still working on this place, it would be so much easier if I just stayed in the house..."

I pursed my lips. I really had to stop coming up with worst-case scenarios all the time. There was no reason to think Arnie was crashing our little party.

"Well, if he's not coming down..." Monica dithered, looking disappointed.

Why did she want to see him so badly? If she'd been sent here to get the goods on us, the way Lou suspected, surely her duties had been fulfilled.

"He's probably not coming down," I told her. "Go have fun! The roads out will probably start getting busy later, so you'd better do it now. Before things get crazy."

Monica laughed. "Oh, Katie. Such a worrier. Things aren't going to get crazy. This'll blow over."

Spoken like a true mainlander, I thought grimly, as Monica took one last look towards the house and then jumped back into the Jeep. Spoken like someone who hadn't lived at sea level for her entire life, watching the water rise in the swamps. I hoped she had fun at the beach. I wished I could take the day to see Bahia Honda's pretty palm grove. I was already getting that metallic taste of foreboding in my mouth, that anxious sense of dread which made me count the beautiful places in my world and wonder if they'd still be with us in a week's time.

I supposed Crystal's nerves were rubbing off on me. She was up in the house making calls right now, looking for a safe spot to take the horses.

Marchant was nervous, too. I could see him over on his dock, fussing over his boats. I wondered what his plan for them was—if he was just going to anchor them and hope for the best, or if there was some more sophisticated plot. I tried to think what my dad and uncles did with their boats before hurricanes, but I'd never paid the watercraft that much attention. I was usually the one on yard and porch duty, bringing in everything that could blow away.

"Oh, well," I said to myself. "Just get these stalls cleaned, and let them figure it out..."

Then I heard a distant hum which quickly revealed itself to be a roaring boat engine. What the—? I discarded the manure fork again and headed out to see what all the commotion could be.

I joined Marchant on his dock just as Cap'n Skip pulled up in his personal cruiser. He was off-duty today, wearing shorts and a Guy Harvey t-shirt. He wore a hat pulled over his gray curls, so like Marchant's. The two of them could have been separated at birth. "What's he doing here?" I asked Marchant.

"Not sure," Marchant replied. "But I ain't mad to see him."

"Ahoy and good morning!" Skip called over the growling engines. He was waving enthusiastically, as if we might not have noticed his arrival. "Thought you might want a hand with these boats of yours!"

Marchant's smile lit up his weary face. "Boy, you got that right!" he shouted back. "What do you propose? I been wondering if a loose anchor ain't the way to go."

"Nah," Skip said, wagging his head. "Hurricane hole. I know just the place."

"Shoulda known you would!"

Shoulda known, I thought, eyeing Cap'n Skip warily. Call me crazy, but was he *really* the most trustworthy man we knew? Someone Marchant should hand over his boats to? I mean, he was a Coast Guard man, for sure, but his grasp of the law seemed kind of clumsy...

"Listen here," Skip was saying, "I ain't about to let anything happen to your boats when you're so close to your little motel opening up. Friends take care of friends."

They gave each other gleaming bromance smiles, and I told myself it was time to stop being so judgemental. Who was acting all mainlander now, Katie?

"Is there room for all three?" Marchant asked. "Or are we splitting them up?"

"All three," Skip assured him. "Got some skippers for this parade? We can go under motor, so there's no sailing skill required," he added, looking meaningfully at me.

Was it so obvious I didn't know a topsail from a jib? I mean, he was right. I couldn't sail at all, and I was a novice with an outboard engine.

Jeez, I was kind of halfway on everything here, wasn't I? A horse novice, a boat novice, a backup singer taking my first stab at lead vocals...

"Is Arnie around?" Marchant asked, bringing me back to the present. "I could use him to take one of the boats."

"Oh, we're doing this now?" I looked around, as if he'd pop up out of thin air. "I can go and get him."

"Or you can get Lou," Marchant added, and I winced at the idea that those two could be interchangeable.

Chapter Twenty-Five

ARNIE WAS HAMMERING away at a new-looking hole in the living room floor when I arrived at the top of the stairs. I could see him through the open door, forehead creased as he pounded in nails. Crystal had mentioned he'd found a few rotten spots that needed patched; I wondered if the discovery had been during a purposeful inspection or due to an unlucky step.

I paused for a moment before going in, admiring the view of the sea and the mangrove islands in the distance. The way this house sat on the northeast corner of the island gave it such a perfect view of the emptiness of Florida Bay, and just now, the changeable colors of the water glowed with a rich royal blue under the morning sunlight. A flock of dazzling white birds flew across the water, ibis looking for a new spot to settle. I watched their determined flight, marveling at how large the flock was—there must have been dozens and dozens of them.

And after a minute or two, something about their flight rang an alarm bell in my head.

They were going north.

I nodded to myself. Of course they were.

Birds heading north: getting out of the islands that might be over-washed with saltwater, heading for the tall cypress trees and windbreaks on the mainland. Birds knew these things better than any other animal on earth.

That storm wasn't going to Mexico, no matter what Lou said. It was coming here. The fresh realization jolted me into action. There was no time to skulk around on patios, admiring the view.

"Arnie," I called, walking into the half-finished living room. It smelled of paint and wood shavings, a marked improvement from the damp smell of a few weeks before. "We need you to help get Marchant's boats to a hurricane hole."

He looked up with a grimace. "Right now?"

"Yup, right now."

"But there's no need to do anything now," Arnie complained. "What is everyone so worried about?"

I studied him for a moment. I wasn't in the mood to argue this *again,* not with Lou, and definitely not with his father. And anyway, the birds were flying north. That was all the convincing I needed.

"Are you going to help or not?" I asked at last. "Because we all have a lot to do. If you're not going to help, then—"

"I'll help, I'll help. Jeez." Arnie got up, groaning a little as he straightened his back. "You can be very demanding," he told me, grinning. "Does my son know that about you?"

"Don't try to charm me," I told him. "I have enough to worry about right now."

I left him trying to figure out what that meant while I went down the stairs. I had to tell Crystal we were going.

Lou was in the kitchen drinking coffee when I came in. He glanced at me, eyebrows raised. "What's going on?"

"Taking the boats to a hurricane hole," I said. "Apparently I'm a driver."

Crystal nodded. "Glad that's getting taken care of."

I wondered if she'd been the one to call Cap'n Skip, but there was no time to ask; she went marching into her room and shut the door. "What's up with her?" I asked Lou.

"She's still making calls to people she knows in South Florida," he said. "Looking for somewhere to take the horses."

"Surely the fairgrounds or something will open up?"

"Maybe," he said, shrugging. "Maybe not. I don't know how those things work. Anyway, let me get my shoes and I'll come with you."

"Arnie's coming," I told him. "You don't have to."

Lou wasn't deterred. "We all have to pull together in this. Marchant's boats are more important than my feelings."

I didn't know what had changed his tune about the hurricane prep; maybe he'd seen the birds flying north, too. I decided not to bother asking for an explanation. Getting Lou on my side was good enough...and anyway, I had no desire to skipper one of those boats alone, even if it was just a ten-minute motor across wide open waters. There was too much riding on Marchant's little fleet for me to feel comfortable at the wheel all alone.

Arnie waved to Lou as he walked down the dock, like they were casual friends who hadn't seen each other in a while. I braced myself for some kind of reaction, but Lou just grunted and nodded. He clambered into the nearest boat and held out a hand to help me aboard. I took it gratefully and then went below decks, busying myself with securing all the bits and pieces of restoration work we'd been doing, while I left Lou to untying the lines and getting the engine started.

This boat hadn't been our first priority, and it showed. There were still mildewed window hangings to take out, and the cabinets in the saloon were in desperate need of stripping and refinishing. Sometimes I wondered how we'd get it all done in time for the first guests in October, or even at all, but Marchant just happily plugged away, working alone when I was involved with the horses or the studios just as cheerfully as he worked with me when I could spend time here. If nothing else, I thought, planning out his hotel and putting in this work was giving him a hobby, a purpose he'd sorely needed. It was no good for men to sit around thinking about the past. They needed to keep their hands busy.

That was probably why Arnie hadn't been much trouble since he'd arrived, too. He was busy working on the house, too busy to hang around Crystal constantly the way I'd feared he might. He seemed content to work all day, sit with Marchant and the rest of us on the porch at night, then turn in early before starting the whole thing at sunrise the next day.

Definitely not what I'd expected.

Lou tapped on the hatch. "We're setting off now. You okay?"

"All set," I called, stashing the rest of my tools in a cabinet and securing the door. Everything in here should be good if the boat got to bobbing on rough seas once the storm was here. If the storm came.

Better safe than sorry. Did the birds think like that, too? Or did they only leave when they knew it was necessary?

The motor started up, rattling harshly, and I had to give up thinking. Probably for the best. I climbed back up to the deck and sat with Lou at the back, watching as our little parade of boats got underway.

The hurricane hole was a slightly larger version of Moonshine Key, with a hook-shaped canal leading into a small, round harbor. The mangroves grew thickly around the water's edge, and there wasn't anywhere to step ashore, but I saw abandoned fish bones and some cans on the roots. "Campers?" I asked Lou as he switched off the engine, waiting for his turn to navigate the boat into the tight little harbor.

"Raccoons," he said with a grin, pointing into the thick branches, and after a moment, I saw their glinting eyes watching us from amongst the glossy mangrove leaves.

"If raccoons get into the saloon of the *Crystal* and tear up the new upholstery, I am going to lose my shit," I informed him.

"Well, hopefully they won't. Lock the hatch and hope for the best."

That felt like all I was doing lately. Hoping, hoping, hoping. But now all I could picture was a crew of tiny trash pandas riding out the hurricane in the gleaming new fittings of the one boat we'd actually made some headway on. The *Crystal* was almost complete. I watched Marchant guide her gently into position.

"Will the boats really be okay here?"

"Should be," Lou said. "Not a huge windbreak from these mangroves, I know, but the way the canal is shaped will stop the water from getting too rough in here and that's what really counts. We don't want them pitching back and forth on big rollers. Skip's waving us in now. Sit down so you don't fall."

I plopped myself down on the deck and watched Lou maneuver the boat beside the *Crystal* with enviable confidence.

We all clambered across the decks and onto Skip's boat after the sailboats were secured. I sat down next to Lou, wishing there was some shade. The sun was climbing towards noon, and the reflection off the water was intensifying the July heat. "I'm almost tempted to swim back," I murmured to Lou, and he laughed.

Crystal sat across from us, and Arnie settled next to her. She said something to him that was drowned out by the motor as Skip launched us towards home at a hundred knots per hour (at least, that's what it felt like) and beside me, Lou stiffened. I sighed. I certainly hoped we didn't end up having to ride out a hurricane together. These were two men I was simply not prepared to stick into the same room for twenty-four hours...not yet.

"I wish we could stick the horses in a hurricane hole," Crystal murmured, watching the little island recede onto the horizon. "Never shoulda brought horses to Hell and Dammit. Shoulda known better."

Lou reached over and squeezed her hand. He didn't see Arnie make a move to do the same thing on her other side, and I was grateful for that. I watched Arnie settle his hands back in his lap, arranging them nonchalantly, and dropped my gaze before he noticed my gaze. I had my eye on him...but he didn't need to know it.

Chapter Twenty-Six

ARNIE DROVE HIMSELF back to Cutlass Key after Skip returned us to our island, saying something about lunch with a friend at the Mermaid. Marchant looked mournfully at his empty dock until Crystal insisted he come back to the house for lunch. I went over and knocked on Stacy's door, hoping she'd come eat with us, but she was deep in work on a mosaic and waved me away impatiently. I didn't even get to ask her if she was planning to prep for the storm. When Stacy was in an artistic mood, there was no talking to her.

Lou, Crystal, and I were eating lunch in Crystal's kitchen when the weather radio and all our phones let out ear-splitting shrieks at the same time. I dropped my sandwich, shaved turkey scattering across the tiles, and Lou nearly choked on a potato chip. Crystal was the only one of us who had the presence of mind to slap the message button on the weather radio, turning off the alarm and turning on the warning message.

The familiar mechanical voice of the National Weather Service started talking immediately, his message already mid-sentence: "—Watch extending from Jupiter Inlet to Key West, including the

Atlantic and Gulf of Mexico waters. A tropical storm warning is in effect for the Florida Keys from Seven Mile Bridge to the Channel Five Bridge. A hurricane watch means that hurricane conditions are possible within the watch area. A watch is typically issued forty-eight hours before—"

I looked at Lou, my heart racing with a potent blend of adrenaline and terror. "This is it," I said. "This is when the roads fill up, just like Rivers said. The tropical storm warning is for the *Middle Keys,* which will make things even worse for us trying to get out."

Just a guess, but Crystal was nodding slowly, so I had to believe I was right.

"It might not hit here," Lou said, stubborn to the end. "The watch goes all the way past West Palm. That's *far* from here. I mean, wait and see. It probably won't even rain here."

"But we won't know until it's too late," Crystal reminded him, rubbing her face in her hands. "We have to move now. It doesn't pay to sit around and wait and see. We've already moved the boats. Now it's time to move the horses."

"What are you planning to do?" Lou demanded. "Since you've already made up your mind."

"I'm loading them up and leaving," she replied, shrugging. "There's nothing else I *can* do."

"Do—do we have a place to take them?" I ventured.

"Not yet." Crystal drummed her fingers on the table, thinking. "But the mainland is a long drive even without traffic. I guess in the next four hours someone might come through with an evacuation spot for them. Otherwise, I'll just keep going until we're out of harm's way."

Driving blind, leaving the island behind, when there was still prep work to do here. Crystal's proposal frightened me in more ways than one. She would leave me—and Lou, and possibly Arnie?—to do the lion's share of the work here. And, I suppose, to ride out the storm here.

Just because the houses were on stilts didn't mean sitting through a hurricane in them would be *fun*.

I ran over the hurricane checklist that lives in the back of my head, a constant presence thanks to years of living along the Gulf of Mexico. It just sat there gathering dust until the first storm warning of the season. The chores ticked over one by one: Everything loose outdoors had to be brought inside, we had to dig and fill sandbags to place around any buildings with first floors, any hurricane shutters available had to be installed or plywood had to be nailed up—that alone could take hours—we'd need to scrub out the bathtubs and fill them with water we could use for flushing toilets if the power was out, and of course we'd need to fill bottles with tap water for something to drink or cook with. I wondered if Crystal had a stash of old water bottles somewhere, like my mom did.

Lou was not on the same page. He shifted in his chair, listening to the weather radio continue to drone on about estimated minimum central pressure and sustained winds. Then he said, "I think everyone is over-reacting."

Crystal sighed and went into the bedroom, closing the door with a sharp click. I heard drawers opening and closing. Packing for the trip?

Lou watched the closed door for a moment, his jaw tense.

I thought it was interesting that this was the moment he chose to argue with his mother. Not over Arnie, but over prepping for a hurricane. What a silly hill to die on, I thought sadly.

"Your mom is doing what she thinks is best," I told him, meaning it in more ways than one.

"Everyone's getting all worked up over nothing," he insisted.

Stubborn man, I thought. No point in arguing with him. He was probably doing enough arguing with himself.

"I should go down and get started bringing the horses in," I decided, getting up from the table and stretching. "Your mom will need help getting everyone ready."

Lou nodded. "That's fine. Just hang on a second? I was hoping to play you something I was working with this morning, and then we all went off on our boat cruise—"

"It's not a good time." Ordinarily I'd be thrilled, but now he was just trying to stall me.

The look Lou gave me was anything but understanding. "Now I *know* you're freaking out about this storm," he accused. "Come on. Just a couple minutes. And then, I'll help you guys. We'll get everything done and we'll have nothing to do but sit on our hands and wait for this hurricane to go past us and rain all over West Palm Beach. It'll be great."

"Fine," I agreed. "One song. And then you go down and hitch up the trailer for your mother."

In Lou's messy room, with the laptop and keyboard and guitars scattered around like toys, I felt like I was in an overgrown teenager's lair. He was deadly serious as he started fiddling with the instruments and pressing keys on the laptop. He handed me a heavy pair of headphones, the noise-canceling ones he used when he was mixing, and put on a second pair, so shiny and new they still rested in their original box. "Figured we'd need two sets for the production work," he said sheepishly when he caught me eyeballing the glitzy packaging. "It's an investment."

I adjusted the headphones he'd given me and gave him a thumbs-up. "Let's listen," I told him. "Wow me."

And so, Lou wowed me. Completely. The song he'd been playing with overnight took everything we'd done over the past few weeks and crushed them, melodies and all. It was a religious experience from the first few chords. I closed my eyes and gave myself up to his spell.

That was the thing about Lou's particular brand of musical genius: it came out of nowhere, took you by complete surprise. There was a reason he'd become an internet sensation with Silvery Star—the man understood sound and melody with an intuition every bit as powerful as the one which sent that flock of birds flying north towards safer rookeries. *This* was why I put up with all his bullshit when he was refusing to work and making me feel like I was going to be doing this record on my own, I thought, as my head began to nod involuntarily with the beat. This guy could only be stopped by himself.

And he'd do it, cheerfully, given half the chance. I had to be the tough one who made him actually finish things.

When the song finished, I made a spinning motion with my finger: *again*. He smiled and obliged, looking very pleased with himself.

"This is good," I mouthed at him.

"I know," he mouthed back, grinning at the quote from *High Fidelity*.

By the third listen, I had an idea where my words could take the emotion of the track and I'd started humming along; by the fourth I was experimenting with some basic emotional tells for the chorus: phrases like *higher and higher* and *out there* and *just beyond*. They were cliches, but I always felt like cliches were a good place to start. Placeholders for the real thing.

Lou grinned as I let the sound take over, doing my thinking for me. He'd seen me do this once or twice before and he said he liked the look that came over my face when the music was in charge. I'd been a little self-conscious after he'd said that, wondering if I looked vacant or drugged-out or what, but there wasn't time or space in my brain to worry about my face now that the lyrics were coming. I snapped my fingers, and he scrambled for pen and paper so I could start scribbling.

We were on to something now.

Chapter Twenty-Seven

AN HOUR LATER we had a gorgeous track—not all recorded in one swoop, mind you, but moods captured in bite-sized chunks, building blocks that we could turn into a full song later. Lou took off his headphones and stretched; he'd been hunched over the laptop, keying in changes as we came up with them, as the lyrics demanded space to move and grow. "That was inspired," he told me as I took off my own headphones. "Thank god you came in here and listened."

"I'm exhausted now," I moaned, rubbing my forehead where the band of the headphones had slid down and pressed against my skin. "I need a nap and a gallon of coffee to recover from it."

"I can probably provide you with the coffee," Lou said, "but do you really want the nap?"

"Oh, there's no chance. I have to help your mom. She'll be—" I stood up and peeked through the vertical blinds. "The trailer is gone already? It must be on the other side of the house."

I walked out of his room and immediately noticed Crystal's door was still closed. "Weird," I muttered, and went to the porch door. I peered out, expecting to see the truck and trailer hitched up near the paddocks, waiting to receive the horses.

The paddocks were empty, and so was the road. No truck, no trailer, no horses.

I looked back at Crystal's closed door, and, with a sudden impulse, turned the handle and pushed it open. She was asleep on top of her bed, snoring gently. The worry and preparation must have caught up with her...but, who had the horses?

My heart began to flutter against my ribs. Horses didn't just up and leave...they were *taken*.

Still, I managed to keep myself from panicking—just. I crept out of Crystal's room and closed her door. Lou was winding up cords and putting away his instruments. He lifted his head, a questioning look on his face. I whispered, "Lou, someone already took the horses, I think. And your mom is asleep. It wasn't her. Obviously."

"Someone *took* them?" His brows came together. "But who would do that?"

"I don't know—" My mind ran over the possibilities. Not Marchant, not Stacy, who had told me several times she never drove anything larger than her Cadillac.

And that was it. That was the whole list of people who might theoretically take Crystal's truck, trailer, and six little horses. Without it being a crime.

Except...there was one more person who might feel justified in taking the horses. Who might think he was a part of the family.

Or worse, might he have been casing us all along? Waiting for the right moment to make his move?

I blurted without thinking, "Lou, it must have been your dad."

"My dad." Lou said the word without expression.

I realized my mistake immediately. "I mean, Arnie."

"Yeah, I know who you mean," he said bitterly. "The guy everyone loves so much."

"I don't love him," I said plaintively. "I'm on your side here."

"Are you?" Lou sat down and sighed. "You think he took the horses?"

"Who else? Maybe your mom asked him to do it?"

Lou looked at me, his eyes hard. "I certainly *hope* so," he said ominously.

"What are you—what are you thinking?" My voice came out in a nervous squeak.

"What do you *think*? That maybe he saw his chance and took it. That's what I'm thinking. I knew he shouldn't have been left here. I *knew* he shouldn't be trusted. But no, everyone wanted to love good old Arnie, the world's most dependable dad—"

We froze as the house made a gentle creak, and Crystal's door opened.

She was up from her nap. I shook my head warningly at Lou. *We can't argue about him now.* He made a face at me: *No kidding.*

Crystal poked her head around the door a few moments later. "Everything okay in here? I just needed a little nap before I got on the road."

"Crystal," I asked tentatively, "did you, um, happen to—I mean—did you maybe ask Arnie to take the horses out of here? To take the truck and trailer and get started without you?"

Crystal looked amused.

"No, of course not," she said. "I'm going to do it. I just needed a little nap before I got on the road—why? Why do you ask?" Her voice raised a little with every word, and suddenly the humorous expression was fading, replaced with something altogether more worrisome—*realization*. "Did that man really—"

And before she could finish her question, Crystal was turning on her heel, heading for the living room door. She flung back the sliding glass door with vicious energy and strode onto the porch.

"Son of a bitch!" she announced.

That would be Crystal noting her empty paddocks, I thought.

I looked at Lou. "Maybe," I said, "he's just doing us a favor. Maybe he took them to help out. He *has* been helpful. He's done some odd jobs for Marchant while he's busy with the boats, and I know he's done some repairs on the studios, and I think he's done some stuff with Stacy..." I didn't mention the house; Lou still didn't know the house was meant for him, and I was less certain than ever that Arnie wasn't planning on sneaking himself into permanent islander status by taking up residence in the house instead.

But Lou already had his fists balled at his sides, his mind made up, and I knew he wasn't going to believe any do-gooder nonsense about the man he refused to call his father. "He *stole* them," he told me. "This must be why he showed up in the first place. He was waiting for a chance to steal something valuable, and the hurricane just gave him the perfect opportunity. He figures he'll disappear into traffic and chaos, and we won't be able to find him again."

"Lou, that's crazy," I said a moment—or a hundred years—later. "Why would he steal six mustangs? They can't be very valuable."

"Everything has a price," Lou growled. "And actually, broke trail horses are very valuable right now. It costs a lot of money to get horses trained like that. They're potential earners for anyone who wants to run a trail-riding business. And there's a black market for other reasons, too," he added darkly.

That set loose all kinds of fears in my mind. I didn't know exactly what he was alluding to, but I could make several guesses, none of them anything I wanted to consider.

Lou was pulling on his shoes and shoving his wallet into his back pocket. "Can you make sure my equipment goes into waterproof containers?" he asked. "There are some in the closet. I just want to be sure nothing happens if there's a roof leak or something."

"Where are you going?" I squeaked. "You can't *leave*. Not now." Not when there was so much to do. The horses we could leave to the police, I figured. Or else Crystal could go after him, make him see reason, or hopefully find out there was nothing sinister going on here at all. "We have to prep the island," I reminded him. "I can't do everything myself."

"I'm going after him," Lou said. He took my face between his hands and kissed me. "I'm going to make sure nothing happens to those horses. You and Mom can handle things here. You've got Marchant, you've got Stacy. Hell, if she isn't on the run already, you might get help from Monica. Just don't stay if there's a threat of high winds, alright? Be safe. I'll come back as soon as I can."

Stunned, I watched Lou stride out of the room and join his mother on the porch. I heard raised voices, and then he was slamming down the stairs. Crystal came back into the living room, looking dazed.

"He's not answering his phone," she said. "I guess I could call the police, but I don't know. They're all so busy with evacuations and such. And what if it's all a misunderstanding?"

"Seriously, you don't really think he stole them, do you?" I asked breathlessly. "That's just Lou talking because he doesn't like him, right?"

She looked at me for a long moment. "I don't know," she said finally, sounding defeated. "It's hard to tell with someone like Arnie. You always hope he'll be the best version of himself, but you know, that's not always possible. Sometimes men just revert to their old ways. They can't even help themselves. It's just...it's just *men*."

"Their old ways?" I repeated, dazed. I sat down on the sofa, feeling like standing up was just too much extra work for my brain to process at the moment. The brain fog after working on a song was real; adding all of this strain on top of it was almost enough to make me pass out. "What are you saying? Arnie's got a history of horse thieving?"

"Oh, not horse thieving, no," Crystal sighed. "Nothing so specific. But you know how it is. A man dabbles in a little black market selling here, a little speculation there. Never anything too serious. But...he's not always on the right side of the law, I guess you'd say. Like a lot of folks. I did think he'd cleaned up his act, though." She shrugged, looking so helpless I wanted to hug her.

So I did, and she hugged me back, and we sat like that until Marchant came up looking for us, wanting to know where all the cars had gone.

I looked at him with a sudden fright. "That's right," I said. "Crystal, your truck is gone and Lou took his car."

"And my car hasn't started in a blue moon," Marchant said. "And Stacy left about an hour ago, too. Said she was heading to the mainland along with a lot of the others from Little Bucket. Maybe all of them, I don't know. Too many of them houses have ground floors. They can take on water real easy."

I shook my head. "So we're stuck here," I said. "We have no vehicles."

"There's Arnie's car," Crystal said suddenly. "Do you think he left his keys in it?"

We all trooped downstairs and snooped around Arnie's old Jeep. There were no keys inside. A check of his dresser and bedside table in Marchant's guest room yielded the same results. No keys. He must have kept them in his pocket and taken them with him when he left.

I didn't doubt we could get off the island if we really needed to; worst-case scenario, I could call Monica to come and get us, or she'd find someone else at the Mermaid who could ferry us up to Cutlass Key. But once we were there, where would we go? Having no vehicle meant we were effectively trapped on our little collection of islands unless we hitched a ride with someone else heading towards the mainland.

It wasn't a great feeling.

"Relax," Crystal suggested as we gave up the search. "It'll all come out in the wash. I'm sure Lou will get to the bottom of this and come straight home."

"What if Arnie's really stealing them?" I asked fearfully. "What will Lou do about it?" I was afraid the answer would be something physical and dangerous. Did Arnie carry a gun? With everything else going on, I figured the answer was probably yes.

"Lou will tail him and call the police to help," Crystal said firmly. "It's not as if it's a hard case to prove. All they have to do is pull the truck over and ask for the registration. If they know where he is, we're a lot more likely to get help."

"Damn," Marchant said, going through the cabinets. "Wouldn't you know, today's the day I was gonna go up to the Mermaid and pick up a couple bottles? And I sure ain't laying here waiting for a hurricane without a bottle of whiskey to keep me company."

"I'll call Monica," I decided. "See if she can bring us some."

But the phone at the Mermaid just rang. I gave it twenty rings and then I hung up.

"Weird."

Crystal glanced at me. "I guess we could always take the little boat."

So, we climbed into the little inflatable that Marchant kept around for getting to the boats he kept off the dock. And it was a pretty ride, puttering along past Little Bucket and alongside Cutlass Key. I couldn't believe I'd never done it before. Crystal guided the raft with a practiced hand, right up to the dock leading through the mangroves to Cutlass Key. The sign on the dock was a lopsided, hand-printed job that read *Slutty Mermaid Parking Only*. I supposed that was the only sign the bar actually had. They weren't as worried about being raided by tourists from the sea as the road.

The dock led to a path up a slight rise, which in turn took us through some scruffy woods where iguanas lurked on sunny logs. It was almost like stepping out of another world to walk around the front of the Mermaid and see the packed shell parking lot and the bleached asphalt of U.S. 1.

Also, all the cars.

So *many* cars. Rivers' prediction was right. The hurricane watch had spurred mass hysteria amongst the tourists of Key West. They were getting out...or rather, they were inching out.

Crystal looked over the packed roadway with something like satisfaction. "There they go," she said. "Out of our way for a few days."

The Mermaid's parking lot was pretty full, too, but as I headed for the door, I noticed something new: about a dozen bikes leaning against the side of the building. "Bikes?" I asked Crystal. "Where'd these all come from?"

She grinned. "Oh, you're going to see the hardcore regulars now, baby girl. These are the folks that don't drive, or knew the road was gonna be packed and didn't want to be bothered sitting in traffic. Just you wait until you open that door."

I was nervous when I finally tugged the handle.

Noise and heat and the smell of salty, sweaty bodies nearly knocked me over. The interior of the Slutty Mermaid had the vibe of a Viking hall right after a hell of a successful raid. If Vikings listened to full-blast Creedence Clearwater Revival and wore cut-offs and sandals to their celebrations. I almost covered my eyes as I walked in; I'm no prude, but there were some seriously bawdy acts taking place in that bar.

Monica was behind the bar, filling beers and putting them on the counter for whoever wanted them. There did not appear to be a billing system in place. It was more like a beer buffet. And she had some very thirsty islanders.

She grinned when she saw me, pushing sweaty bangs back from her eyes. "Welcome to night one!" she greeted me once I was close enough to hear her.

"Night one of what?"

"The hurricane party! Arnie left strict instructions—" she held up a beer-stained folder— "and I'm following them to the letter. Thank goodness, because I don't think they were going to wait for anyone to take charge...they would have just put the party on whether I was here to run things or not." Her eyes roved around the heaving crowd, and I had to agree with her. This was not a rule-abiding group.

"If this is night one, what is night two?" I asked, hardly daring to guess.

"Not as insane, apparently," Monica said. "There's a breather while everyone preps their boats and their houses. But then, whenever it actually starts raining? Forget it. I don't even have to run things at that point. I just lock up the really expensive liquor, do an inventory of the kegs, and get out. People know to step over the sandbags at the door."

Crystal was laughing next to me, and I realized she was already drinking one of the beers. "God love the Keys," she chortled. "Those damn horses knocked all the fun out of me. I forgot how good a hurricane party could be around here!"

And with that, I realized that the rest of the prep around the island was truly up to me. I watched Crystal wave to some friends and wander off from the bar.

Monica was laughing. "You should stay!" she encouraged me. "You have tomorrow to work on things. There's absolutely no rush... unless you're a tourist."

I wasn't ready to rise to her insult. "Honestly, Monica, this isn't really my crowd," I told her.

"I mean, I get it," she agreed, looking around. "I think everyone here is over the age of fifty."

"And that's if you're being nice."

She began to fill more glasses; the ones she'd set on the bar were disappearing with impressive speed. "Well, I like having you here, anyway. I admit, I kinda thought living in the Keys would be less...I don't know...*old*."

"Nope, I know what you mean," I said. "Everyone here is pretty much older than us. That's why I was pretty excited to meet you, actually."

"You were?" Monica beamed at me and momentarily forgot she was filling a glass. The beer foamed over and spilled over her hand. "Whoops! Listen, I was excited to meet you, too. And Lou. I hope I never came on as weird or anything. I was just really hoping to start a new life, with new friends...you guys were the first ones to show up here that made me think it could really happen."

"I hope I wasn't rude or anything," I exclaimed, my words coming out in little bursts as someone bumped into my back on their way to collect a beer. "I haven't had a lot of great friends over the past year. I guess I'm always thinking someone is being nice to me because I have something they want." *Like Lou,* I thought.

"Like Lou?" Monica laughed, unconsciously saying the part I'd kept to myself. "Hey, I get it. But that moody bastard is all yours. I'm looking for more of a surfer type, actually."

Well, she definitely wasn't going to meet that around here. "More a Key West thing," I suggested, reaching for the closest beer. Well, why not? Just one wasn't going to hurt anything. "Although I'd have thought you'd gotten enough of that up in Miami?"

Monica shrugged, still laughing. "Maybe I'll never get enough of surfers," she said.

"Watch the news," I suggested. "There are always surfers getting on TV when they go out to surf the waves before a hurricane. See where they're at and then hightail it down there."

"That's where I'll find my dream guy," Monica agreed. "Right behind Jim Cantore, hanging ten."

She was distracted by her phone at that moment, and while she was answering a text, I looked around the Slutty Mermaid, taking in the bacchanal. Crystal was in the midst of a circle of laughing, shouting, drinking men and women. They all looked about her age. They all looked like they'd been friends for years and were enjoying the reunion. I decided that she'd have no trouble finding a ride back to Hell and Dammit later...or she could phone me, and I'd come back and get her. "I should get back," I told Monica, leaning over the bar so she'd hear me over the racket. "Tell Crystal to call me if she needs a ride and I'll swing the boat back over here."

"No problem," Monica said. "But it might be a late night. I'll make sure to put her in a car with someone sober. Or it'll be me driving, okay?"

I only just remembered to buy a couple bottles of rum and bourbon off her on the way out.

Chapter Twenty-Eight

WHEN I GOT back to Hell and Dammit, the first change I noticed was Stacy's car was back. The yellow Cadillac was parked by her house, and the doors and windows were open. She always liked to air the place out, even on the hottest summer days, after she'd been to the mainland. She said that there wasn't enough salt in the house when it had been closed up for days. But this time, she'd only been gone for about an hour. I wondered what was up.

Before I could find out, Marchant came down to the dock to greet me and help me haul the booze out of the boat. "Nice finds," he told me approvingly, looking at the labels. "But I think you lost a person on the way."

"It's a total rave at the Mermaid," I informed him. "If you want to go and get wasted with Crystal, I can run you back over there. I think I'm getting the hang of this little boat."

"A Mermaid hurricane party!" Marchant's eyes grew far away. "I haven't been to one of those in years. And I don't even remember the ones that I went to. I think I better sit this one out. Might not be good press if the local hotel operator is found pantless in a palm tree again."

I didn't even ask. "What else do you need done around your house?"

"Nothing," Marchant said, surprising me. "All that we have to do is put down the storm shutters, and we won't do that until it's starting to rain. The joy of a house on stilts," he added. "No sandbagging required."

"So, you're definitely not evacuating?"

"Oh, I don't think that'll be necessary," he said, shaking his grizzled head as he surveyed the island with pleasure. "This island has stood through dozens of storms. Hell, maybe hundreds. The water can wash right over it and as long as we're upstairs tucked in, we'll be just fine."

I hated the idea of water running across the island. The saltwater would ruin the sparse grass, the tropical plantings that Queen Tom had put in, the bougainvillea hedge between Crystal's house and the barn. And if it was fast enough, it could topple the paddock fences and take out the bungalows, too. All the work we'd done, ruined.

"Relax, sunshine," Marchant suggested. "It's insured. We already paid for it to be destroyed and rebuilt. Look at it that way."

"I have to get the art out of the studios," I said.

"Done," he told me. "Stacy had everyone clear them out before they went back to shutter up their houses. Listen to your uncle Marchant and just relax. This is the good part, sweetheart! Let's have our own hurricane party on the deck. I'll fish out some lobster I've been saving and we'll invite Stacy over. Don't know why she came back, but I'm sure she'll tell us all about it."

All my impulses which told me to panic and *work, work, work* were firing at full blast, to the point where my hands felt a little shaky. But, as I looked around the island, I could see there was nothing that needed desperate attention. With the horses gone, the vast worry of the storm was taken off my shoulders.

Now I could just worry about where they were right now, and where they were heading. And who was taking them there. That was *plenty* to worry about. Hurricane, not included.

At Marchant's urging, I climbed the steps to Stacy's house and found the artist herself kneeling in the bathroom, scrubbing out her tub. There was a strong smell of bleach. She'd changed out of her usual loose, flowing blouse and slacks and was dressed more like an everyday Conch, in torn denim shorts and an old t-shirt.

She looked over her shoulder at me as I stood in the doorway. "Well, hello there," she called. "I won't be getting up. Come in, if you don't mind a nose full of chlorine. I could use the company."

"I came to see if you needed any help," I said, hovering in the doorway. Stacy's bathroom was tiled in mosaic patterns, itty-bitty pieces of glass and tile from floor to ceiling. It sparkled like a mirror ball. "And with a supper invitation, obviously. Marchant's making lobster."

"Divine," Stacy decreed. "I'll bring champagne. You must be looking for something to keep your hands busy! I notice the horses are gone. I was sure I saw Crystal's truck and trailer when I was driving down. But I was going a lot faster than traffic heading back to the mainland." She snorted inelegantly. "Tourists. I suppose everyone thought I was going to Miami, but I just went up to Islamorada to deliver some work. Better have it hung and paid for *before* a storm than after! Who took the horses?"

"Arnie did," I said, "and we don't know—"

I stopped. It suddenly seemed crazy that kind-eyed, good-natured Arnie would steal the horses. Were we all just out of our minds with storm nerves? Stacy was going to have a big laugh at how neurotic we were being.

But to my surprise, she took my omission very seriously. "You don't know what?" she demanded, turning around and setting her gloved hands on her knees. "Did Arnie take those horses without permission? Where is he going to? Did he even say?"

I shrugged helplessly. If *Stacy* was freaked out by the situation, it was definitely time to panic.

"That no-good..." Stacy seemed to be at a loss for words. She looked at the ceiling for a moment, maybe searching for answers in the sparkling light fixture. It was made of hundreds of tiny pieces of sea glass, probably by her own hands. "He *probably* meant well enough," Stacy allowed finally. "It could be he's just trying to be helpful. But the problem with Arnie is that he doesn't *always* mean well. Nine times out of ten, he's a gentleman and the tenth time he's selling your birthright for a shot of whiskey. Who went after the horses? Crystal?"

"Lou," I confessed. "He left before we could say anything to stop him."

"My, my." Stacy nodded slowly. "That's going to be quite a scene. A long time coming, if you ask me. I wonder if he's caught up to him yet."

"I don't see how he could, in this traffic. At best, he's just going to be trailing him all the way to the mainland. Unless Arnie has to stop for gas or something, it's just sheer gridlock, isn't it?"

"There are passing lanes out there. And a few back roads on the wider islands. And a forceful personality will get you a long way in a sea of rental cars. I wouldn't put it past Lou to find his way up to the trailer. And then..." She lifted her eyebrows. "I wish that car of his had a dash cam."

I ended up helping Stacy prep her house for the hurricane, and the work was satisfying. Not just because it kept my nervous hands busy, but because she liked to talk while she worked, and Stacy remained the enigma of the island, the one resident who was capable, even desirous, of keeping to herself and maintaining some privacy from her fellows. Stacy could like people but not feel like she owed them her life story, so any peeks behind her velvet curtain were highly coveted. By me, anyway.

We talked about her life, about art and her fidgety sister, who ran the art studio she kept in Miami and hated the Keys as much as Stacy hated the mainland, and the way she'd fallen in love with horses at Hell and Dammit Cay when she was going through a dry period and thought she'd never work again. Now she painted, sculpted, sketched, and molded the horses into all of her work. "They're starting to call me the Sea Horse Artist," she admitted, chuckling. "And it's not even a play on the farm name. Or the hotel," she added. "We're all just sea horses out here, I suppose."

"Maybe Lou and I should give our band name something with sea horse in it," I suggested. "The Sea Horse Serenade."

"Very catchy," Stacy snorted. "If you're performing in a nineteen-fifties music hall."

"Yeah, maybe it's not my best work. But you know, when we do get out there, he's going to be billed as Lou Linney of Silvery Star and I'm just Katie LeBlanc. It would be nice if we had a band name that could capture both of us equally. And probably, Rivers will be mad if we don't show up with one. He's not really one of those micromanagers. He'd rather we do all the work and make his job easy."

"A wise man," Stacy observed.

"He is wise," I agreed. "He knows how to make money without it taking up his entire life. He's not like those big-time music executives who just want to churn out hit-making machines."

"Which is why he offered you two a deal."

"He offered me a single," I said. "I turned it into a record. Maybe that was too much, too soon. But we've made some progress. I think we might even get the recording done on time this fall."

"And then you'll just need a name. See, you're doing fine." Stacy lifted canvas pillows from an outdoor sofa and carried them into the living room. They looked drab next to her luxurious indoor cushions. Stacy's taste in upholstery ran towards satins and velvets. "It'll come to you," she went on. "Things like that always come to you when you least suspect it. I wake up from dreams with whole ideas for an entire series of paintings or mosaics sometimes, and then I have no choice but to sketch it all out before it disappears. You've probably had that happen with words, with song lyrics, right? You know the feeling."

She was right. I did know the feeling. Maybe that was the universe's sign that I was at least on the right track. If I was dreaming up the things I wanted to work on, then I was absolutely doing what I was supposed to be...right? But it brought up the question that haunted me here, when I looked out at the horizon and wished I was back on the road.

"Sometimes I wonder if I'm really supposed to be writing songs," I admitted, saying it out loud for the first time. "Ever since I came here, I've had the opportunity to do more musical work, but just about all my time is taken up with the island's business. And it makes me wonder what my true calling is. I want both...is that crazy?"

"Only crazy people choose," Stacy said firmly. "Who could just settle down with one thing? If you want to be here and do this work in addition to all your dreams, it just means your big heart has found the place where it can do the most good. Sometimes that feels like it can tear you apart with all the responsibility, but would you really want to lock yourself away in a room alone and just write songs all day?"

I thought about Lou, spending most of the summer in exactly this position. It certainly wasn't doing anything for his temper. I wondered if he'd taken off after Arnie so quickly because he'd been aching for a cause, any kind of cause at all, to get him out of his room, out of his head. "No," I admitted. "I know that's supposed to be the dream for someone like me, but it sounds awful."

"You see? Your heart is full of all the people and animals here, and that's what inspires you." Stacy gave me a pat on the back. "That means the work is a little harder...but the product is a lot better. You're in the right place, kiddo. Don't ever think otherwise, okay?"

"Okay," I agreed. "Thank you, Stacy. I feel silly, talking so much about me..."

"It's no problem," she assured me. "Now let's go see about that lobster. I'm starving."

Chapter Twenty-Nine

As SUNSET DREW near, we fell into Marchant's patio chairs, exhausted.

He was already heating the grill and prepping the lobster. Nothing could keep that man down. Nothing. I hoped. I watched him watch Crystal, walking across the island in her flip-flops, and wondered if they were in love or simply the best of friends. Maybe it was all my imagination, falling for Lou, falling for this island, which made me see romance where there was none. Tonight, I really couldn't tell. Everything was all gummed up with too much emotion. All my circuits were misfiring. I looked away, gazing over the golden trail of sunlight on water, as she came up the stairs.

There was no update from Lou; I might have known, since I would expect he'd have called or texted me, at least. My phone was a useless weight in my pocket. If it vibrated with a weather update or some stupid notification I didn't need, I studied the screen and considered hurling it into the water. Stacy watched me, her dark eyes entertained.

"You going to smash that thing or what?" she asked.

I'd been glaring at the phone for having the audacity to tell me my mom's cousin Martha liked my picture of Reggie splashing in the water during one of our beach rides. I shrugged, embarrassed to the core at Stacy's seeing me slip into unhinged territory, and dropped it back into my pocket. It sat against my hip like a stone. "Just hoping for an update," I said, as lightly as I could.

"Boy never was good at callin' his mama," Stacy reflected, the cadence of her speech shifting as she sipped her second glass of champagne.

"How are you going to keep your champagne chilled if there's no power after the storm?" I asked her.

"I have dry ice," she said. "Why do you think I drove up to Islamorada today, in the teeth of all that traffic? I was stocking up on essentials."

We were halfway through dinner when Lou finally called, and his voice was so tired and husky that I took the phone to the other side of Marchant's porch. I was afraid he was going to give me terrible news, and I didn't know how I could possibly receive it in front of everyone else's eyes.

"Everything is fine," Lou said, surprising me, and I let out a gusty breath. "We got the horses to a farm outside Homestead where Arnie knows the owners. They have a cinder-block barn and nice grassy fields. The horses will be in heaven here. They won't even want to come home."

I laughed shakily, too confused by his statement to do anything more than latch onto the last few words. "Well, don't say *that*."

"Sorry. After a few days of too much sun and too many pina coladas, they'll be thrilled to come home. Typical vacation. Is that better?"

"Much better, thanks. I miss them already. And—Arnie—? Where is he? Where are *you*? No one has any idea where you guys have been. Or—any of it."

"Arnie's staying with the folks who own the farm. And right now I'm in a car heading back to you."

"Is it safe?"

"If it's safe enough for you, it's safe enough for me."

"Not me, silly. The horses. They're really safe with him? I mean, Arnie's old friends could still be Arnie's old *friends,* if you know what I mean. Do we trust him now? Is the other stuff all wrapped up?"

"We had a long talk," Lou said. "I'm leaving a lot out right now. I'm tired. But I'll tell you as soon as I'm home."

I went back around to the porch, where Stacy was ready and waiting with a fresh glass of champagne. She passed it to me, asking, "Good news, darling?"

"Lou's on his way home," I announced, and I gulped back half the champagne. The bubbles pricked the back of my nose and made me feel like sneezing.

Crystal whooped with pleasure. "That's my boy! Horses all set?"

"With someone in Homestead, apparently. Arnie knows them. Lou said they were safe and happy and we should trust them."

"Homestead! I wonder if that's the Rodriguez couple. Artemis and Diego. They're great people. I just didn't have their numbers. Trust Arnie to know how to reach them." Crystal looked satisfied, and I supposed that was a good enough sign.

Still, I sidled up to her as soon as Stacy and Marchant were on to a new subject. "Crystal, are we definitely one hundred percent sure Arnie's safe to trust the horses with?"

Crystal laughed and waved a bony hand, as if we hadn't been panicking over those horses half the day. "Honey, Arnie's impulsive and he's a fool when it comes to making a simple phone call, but I don't think he's a horse thief. And would Lou really have left them with that man if he didn't believe him?"

"I guess not," I admitted. These people, I thought. Like wind vanes, just flinging themselves back and forth, as changeable as the weather.

But they were the people I'd chosen.

I decided to let myself relax and enjoy this little hurricane party. After all, tomorrow would be more hard work. And Lou would be back...he was hard work all on his own.

We woke up to a breezy, sunny morning. I stepped onto the deck first thing and noticed a change in the air. But it wasn't what I expected.

"Lou," I called through the open door, "It's *dry* out here."

From beneath the sheets, Lou answered with a groan.

Understandable. He'd gotten back pretty late last night, worn out and grumpy after his day of chasing horses up and down U.S. 1. He hadn't wanted to talk about it...but something had gone down between him and his father. I just hoped it was positive. I didn't think he needed to forgive Arnie to the point where they were friends, or anything like that. But I did think he needed to find a way to accept Arnie's presence in his life.

Maybe it wasn't fair, but it was the way things were.

The house, I thought, looking at the empty house next door. That could make the difference. If Arnie ever finished it. The house still seemed a long way from completion...the new holes in the floor he'd been patching were not a very promising development.

"I'm not getting up, if that's what you're waiting for," Lou said from beneath the sheets.

I waved a hand at him and shut the door, padding around to the living room side of the house. Crystal was standing on the deck here, looking south. She glanced at me and smiled. "Good morning, sunshine."

"Good morning. You look pretty chipper. Did something change in the night?"

"The forecast," Crystal said happily. "East." She pushed her phone to me and I looked at the forecast cone. The Lower Keys weren't even in the big scary cone of uncertainty anymore. There was simply no more hurricane threat.

"Wait a minute! How?"

"Models,' Crystal mused. "Supercomputers. Rainbows. I don't know and I don't care. We ain't getting this hurricane and that's all that matters."

"But Homestead and Miami are still in the cone," I reminded her. "The horses—"

"We'll have no problems getting them back," she said breezily. "Don't you know, no one evacuates *to* the Keys. There won't be any traffic coming home. We'll have our kiddos back before bedtime."

It made all the work we'd done pretty pointless, but Crystal wasn't bothered by that.

"A dry run," she called it. "I'm glad we did it. Always good to know what plans will be like if the real thing comes. And of course we got a lot cleaned up." She nodded to the island below us. "The place looks real spic and span. I reckon the next art festival weekend will knock us back on our asses, but until then we can just pretend we live like this every day, okay? No more random buoys or lawn chairs left lyin' around. It's nice."

It was nice. I would miss the several years of my life that stress had surely burned away, but that was Old Lady Katie's problem. I'd deal with her later. In the meantime, I looked around our tidy farm. I had to admit she was right...the place looked pretty great.

Still, I found it hard to believe everything could simply carry on as normal. Especially with the paddocks empty. I wondered what to do with my morning, now that I didn't have chores. I decided I should go back to bed, but once I got there, I stared at the sunlight and shadows on the ceiling for a long time while Lou snored gently beside me.

I was glad he could sleep, but for me, things still felt too weird. Hurricanes made everything topsy-turvy. Life was upturned for two days, then it went straight back to normal. Nothing to see here, folks, just carry on...

But it wasn't that simple. I sighed. Some work would have been nice, for once.

Wasn't that always the way? You wanted a break, you thought about a break, you *craved* a break, and then when you got one, all you wanted to do was your work?

Maybe Lou would want to work this afternoon, when he finally got out of bed. I thought about the song we'd worked on before everything had gone crazy yesterday. It was good then; hopefully it was still good today. Good enough to power the rest of the unwritten album? Maybe so. We could listen to it a few times, feed off that energy, and make something new in a similar vein. I liked albums that told stories, where songs flowed in and out of one another, and so far we seemed to be heading in that direction.

Lou murmured in his sleep and I glanced over at him, feeling a surge of foolish happiness at being in bed with him this late on a weekday morning, and then closed my eyes and snuggled up against him.

I couldn't—shouldn't—be alone on this journey. I needed work and loved ones, to keep the fires burning. I realized that even through the heart-pounding stress of the hurricane prep, I'd been thriving.

That was really something to think about. Especially the next time I got itchy feet.

And of course, the cure to those itchy feet was to go on tour with Lou...something we'd get to do, if we just put together a hit record.

I liked our chances.

I fell asleep.

Chapter Thirty

THREE MONTHS LATER

The song finally finished with a flourish, instead of a clunking collapse. I took a breath, coming back to the real world. "I think that worked," I said tentatively.

We'd been trying to get this song's ending right for hours. I'd been starting to believe it was going to have to fade out on the album, but of course we couldn't recreate that in a live setting.

And yet, we were so close to being done. We'd been working nearly every day for months now. It had been a hard slog, with the fall tourist season starting up in early October, and the prospect of Sea Horse Lodge opening right after. Now we were just hours from the opening celebration. I needed to get outside and check on prep for the event.

But I couldn't leave this room until this song was finished.

I just couldn't.

"Lou?" I asked. "What do you think?"

"It worked," Lou agreed, looking pensively at his laptop.

I waited for his pronouncement.

"We're ready," he said at last. He lifted his gaze to mine, and suddenly a bright smile burst through the clouds. "Let's book the time."

I wrapped my arms around him and hugged him fiercely. "I can't believe this is really happening! We have the songs! We're making a record!"

He laughed and hugged me back. "I can't believe it, either," he admitted. "When you first suggested that we take the deal and up it to a full album, I kinda thought you were crazy. I mean, it took me a year to come up with the Silvery Star tracks and that was just messing around with a friend. This always felt a lot more serious."

"Well, I'm way more than a friend," I joked.

"Yeah, and you smell better, too. Well, most of the time."

"Hey, horses smell good."

"Outside," Lou suggested. "It's a fine smell outside. But when we go to the studio, you really should consider showering first."

I hit him with a pillow and considered the case closed.

Then I called the studio space Rivers owned in Key West and tried to book a couple of weeks. Two weeks would be enough, right? I crossed my fingers as the receptionist answered, hoping she'd know exactly who I was and how important my time was. Surely Rivers had talked about us—

"Sorry," the receptionist said. "There is a high-profile client using the space through the end of November. We won't be able to book anything before December."

"December! But this is only October. You're saying someone has the studio booked out for the next, what, six weeks?"

From across the room, Lou looked at me in shock. I shook my head at him. *It's fine.* But I already knew it wasn't.

"That's right," she agreed pleasantly, as if we were discussing a sunny forecast. "Sorry about that. They're rehearsing for a tour and decided to do it here."

"But Rivers needs our tracks before the end of the year and this is the studio included in our contract," I explained. "Surely there's a way for us to use it for a week or two while they're in and out. I'm guessing they'll take a few days off here and there."

"They booked the whole place," she replied mercilessly. "Don't want any gawkers. Like I said, this is a high-profile client."

"I don't care if it's The *Beatles!*" I exclaimed, suddenly fed up. We'd gotten this far, against all the odds, and now we had to take this momentum and pour it into producing the best possible record. I wasn't about to default on our contract because the space Rivers had promised us wasn't available anymore—and I wasn't going to rush this work by trying to slide it in during the holiday rush, either. There was just no way I could manage the ranch, help Marchant with the lodge, deal with the December influx of tourists, *and* put out an incredible record.

I took a breath and tried one more time, while the receptionist made impatient noises and clacked at her keyboard, trying to get me off the line.

"We're on deadline *from* Rivers and this is his studio and we *need* —"

"Lady," the receptionist spat. "We. Are. Full."

And she hung up.

I looked at Lou in shock.

"What happened?" he asked.

"They won't give us any time before December. Some big-ass band decided to spend their rehearsal time in Key West before they go on tour."

"Oh, no. Who? Did she say who it was? Is it Aerosmith? I heard they like it here."

"Did you hear me scream, *'Oh my god, Aerosmith'*? Because that's what I would have done, even though I'm so freaking furious I could die. Trust me, you would know if she'd told me it was Aerosmith. No, she kept her little secret." I tossed my phone on the bed, frustrated beyond belief. "Now, what are we going to do?"

"Relax," Lou advised. "We'll figure something out."

But his face was worried, and I knew he was at a loss, too. Recording studios didn't grow on trees, especially in the Keys. Down here, there was often only one of everything...and we were being edged out by people from off-island.

I *hated* it when that happened.

"Look, we have to go down and get ready for the lodge opening party," Lou said, tossing me a clean shirt. "We will talk about this later. Or tomorrow. It doesn't have to be settled today."

"I know," I agreed, pulling the shirt over my head. I sucked in a breath and let it out again, wishing I'd taken some time in my life to get good at yoga. I needed that kind of zen today. "Today is Marchant's day."

I'd never let my personal problems get in the way of Marchant's triumph.

The Sea Horse Lodge opening celebration was not quite as raucous as the Slutty Mermaid's Night One Hurricane Party, but it was pretty close. Especially since the Keys hadn't had another hurricane scare since the storm that sent Arnie to Homestead with the horses, Lou in hot pursuit. That storm had hit Palm Beach and spiraled up through north Florida, throwing down a lot of rain and knocking over a decent number of trees. After that, the tropical waters around Florida had gone silent, yielding up the occasional waterspout alongside the daily thunderstorms that skidded across the islands, but nothing more serious.

I'd gotten used to the waterspouts by now. It turned out you could get used to just about anything. I'd heard it before, but this was the first time I realized how true the saying was.

Even Lou seemed to agree—he was getting used to having Arnie around, although the two still didn't go out of their way to spend time together or even speak. But he didn't ignore his father, and Arnie didn't pester him about it. The older man just went to work daily on the house, hammering away inside, although lately, the work had gotten quieter and I'd seen buckets of paint on the porch, which made me think the interior *might* be almost finished.

I wasn't holding my breath, though.

There wasn't time to hold my breath, anyway. I needed all the oxygen I could get, to keep up with the lodge prep, the trail rides, the music, and the occasional day out with Monica. She managed to get me to Bahia Honda before the summer was over, driving us up in her open-top Jeep with Taylor Swift howling over the wind (and Monica howling along—I preferred to keep my voice down in-between practice sessions with Lou). We swam in the turquoise water and took Instagram pics beneath the coconut palms and told each other secrets until I finally asked Monica what her deal *really* was with Arnie.

And Monica, laughing, told me that he was not her father, just a close friend of the family. "I know what you think," she said, wagging a finger in my face. "But it's not true. I'm not Lou's long-lost sister."

I didn't know if I was disappointed or not. Part of me thought it would be cool if Lou had a sibling; the other part knew that Monica's sunny personality and Lou's stormy one were probably not genetically related.

Lou took my hand as we walked across the island. "Ready for the big launch?" he asked.

"I think so," I said. "I guess I have to be!"

Summer was over, winter was on the way, and the Florida Keys were heading into high season. Time to put all this work to the test.

The boats looked beautiful. The *Crystal,* the *Lucky Star,* and the *Sea Horse* bobbed proudly on the turquoise water just off Marchant's dock, with tiny flags fluttering from their masts and plenty of twinkly lights wrapped around the railings, just waiting for nightfall so they could glow for all to enjoy.

"It's a party!" Monica whooped, welcoming us to the event. She and Stacy had done the hard work of setting up tables, tents, and catering. I was left completely out of the party planning for once, and I was both grateful and a little hurt. But Marchant had been insistent on this point: I was supposed to have *fun* at this event, not run it. And I appreciated his thoughtfulness about that. I had done so much work on these boats, physical and technical work I hadn't even realized I was capable of, digging deep into my memories of helping my father with his boats when I was a kid. The results were spectacular; I was pretty sure I did deserve a party!

Sunset was drawing near, and heaps of dark clouds on the western horizon were breaking up, giving us a pretty golden sky for our celebration. Monica poured us both glasses of champagne and led a toast with everyone. "Cheers to the Sea Horse Lodge!" she exclaimed. "Can you believe we got it all done?"

"I can't," I admitted, knocking back a fizzy slug of champagne. The bubbles tickled the back of my nose. I gulped, then added, "It shouldn't even have been possible."

"I didn't think it was," Lou said, earning himself a dirty look from me. "What? It wasn't anything personal. I just couldn't believe it could be done, period."

"But we did it. And all I had to do was file a ton of paperwork and sleep with the guy approving it all down at the county offices." Monica laughed at our astonished faces. "Of course I didn't. You guys are so gullible! Arnie knows the right people. *That* made a huge difference."

Lou lifted an eyebrow. "Arnie greased palms for this?"

"He sure did," Monica said, her smile glinting beneath the twinkle lights. "We're lucky to have that guy around."

She was called away to help some of the hotel guests who would be sleeping on the boats tonight, and Lou and I meandered through the catering tent, picking at the party food. I was spearing a tiny spring roll with a toothpick when Lou said, "I think I have to really talk to him, don't I."

"Your dad?" I asked, glancing over my shoulder for Arnie. I didn't see him, but I knew he'd be around the party somewhere. "You think tonight's the night?"

"Yeah," Lou said. "He's done a lot for everyone here. Well, not for me, but..."

I wanted to tell him he was mistaken, but that wasn't my story. Arnie needed to tell Lou about the house. I'd even harbored a little hope that tonight might be the night. I mean—I looked across the island at the house—it *looked* finished.

The house had a fresh coat of white paint, and the porch had been pressure-washed and sealed. New windows sparkled in the late evening sunlight, and he'd put in the ubiquitous vertical blinds that seemed to be a requirement for all sliding glass doors in the Keys. Every day, I resisted the urge to go up the stairs and try to peek through the windows. I was waiting, along with everyone else on the island, for Arnie to announce the house was done and invite us up for a tour.

And to tell Lou it was all for him.

But now Lou was shaking his head, like he already regretted suggesting they might forgive and forget. "I just wish he hadn't come on so strong. The house and everything…"

"What do you mean, the house?"

"Well, he's obviously planning on moving here, and bringing Monica, I'll bet—"

"Who told you that was happening?" I demanded, suddenly afraid there'd been a change in plans. Monica did often mention how much she'd love to live here, instead of in her rental on Cutlass Key. Was there something she hadn't told me? A scheme to split the fourth house with Arnie? They'd be pretty strange roommates, but…

"Look at that place," Lou said, gesturing towards the house. "It's clearly ready for someone to move in, and who else would he be restoring it for? If I had to bet, I'd say Monica will move in full-time —she's always talking about how much she'd like to move out here— and he'll be around half the time, when he's not out working one of his schemes on the mainland or somewhere else in the Keys. This will be his safe space, for when the heat gets too high, and he has to lie low for a while—"

I shook my head, hating how possible it all sounded. He wouldn't have to work hard to convince me this had been the plan all along. I needed to keep the faith, though. Arnie had told me the house was for Lou. I threw back the rest of my champagne, smothered a hiccup, and said, "I don't think that's it at all, Lou."

"Oh yeah? Well, what else could it be?" He gave me a challenging look, his jaw jutting.

I peered through the crowd of happy people, looking for Arnie. I finally spotted him near the water's edge, talking animatedly to Cap'n Skip. No doubt cooking up some new plot involving creatively impounded boats. Might as well put a pause on *that*. "Why don't you go and ask him," I told Lou. "Right now."

Lou squared his shoulders. "Fine," he said. "I will."

Chapter Thirty-One

WHEN LOU INSISTED Arnie walk over to the bridge to talk in private, I couldn't help sneaking along to listen in. I slipped behind a palm tree while Arnie got ready for the interrogation by swigging from his beer. "What's up, son?" he asked jovially.

I winced at that; he wouldn't normally call Lou anything affectionate. Arnie must be pretty drunk already.

Or he was just feeling very confident.

But Lou skipped over the endearment, going straight for the kill. "When are you planning on moving into that house, Arnie?"

His father laughed, making my heart race. He sounded genuinely surprised by the question—that could only be a good thing for Lou. "Move in?" he asked. "Me? You got me wrong, kid. I'm not looking to be a permanent resident of your little island. This is a...a pleasant interlude, let's call it. Tryin' to do right by some folks."

You're the folks, Lou, I thought, wishing he'd catch on.

But Lou had a major blind spot where Arnie was concerned; he wasn't going to guess the answer to this one. Arnie would have to come right out and say it. Lou folded his arms. "So, it's for Monica," he suggested. "Your favorite child."

Oh, no, Lou, I told you—

"Monica ain't my child," Arnie said, still enjoying himself hugely. "You're the only one of those I can call my own, son. Monica's like a daughter to me, it's true. But only because I watched her grow up, and I got to worrying about her, up there with all those rich riffraff in Miami. Her dad was worried, too. So we got some balls rolling and moved her down here where folks are real. But no, the house is not for her." Arnie paused, and Lou finally looked like he was caught on his back foot. He had no snappy retort to fling at his father.

Arnie looked relieved. Finally, he said, "Although, if you want to rent her a room up there, I think she'd appreciate it. She don't like that little apartment I found her on Cutlass. But I guess you better ask Katie first. She'll want some say in whether she's sharing her house with a third person or not."

This is it, Lou. Catch his meaning. Figure it out.

Lou blinked at Arnie. "Katie?"

"Your girlfriend," Arnie prompted. "Nice girl, a little bossy—"

"Why would Katie share the house—what do you mean? Did you restore it for Katie?" Lou's voice softened, and I was touched—and a little sad. He was happy enough for Arnie to have done up the house for me; but shouldn't he have at least thought the house was for him, first?

Arnie put his big paw on Lou's shoulder, and then it all came out. "Son, that house is for you. I thought that woulda been obvious by now. But I'm sorry it wasn't. I just wanted to give you something, and it seems like this is your place now...I was hoping you would want to stay on, make it permanent."

Lou didn't answer. His mouth had fallen open, and he was staring at Arnie.

I had hot tears stinging my eyes, falling down my cheeks. I swiped at them impatiently and hoped my sniffling didn't give me away.

"There's only two bedrooms," Arnie went on. "But that's because the third one, I made it into a recording studio. Soundproofing on the walls, extra electricity, all that. So you can make your records with Katie. I know that's important to you two."

Still, no response. I had to cover my mouth before a big, soppy sob escaped and blew my cover completely.

"What do you think, son?" Arnie asked. "Think you'd like to go see the place? Maybe we could go up to Islamorada and get some furniture for it? I know a guy who can get us some good deals—"

And then, without warning, Lou wrapped his arms around his father. It was the first hug they'd shared in many years—maybe it was the first one, ever.

And when it was finished, I wasn't the only one who was crying.

Monica decided she wasn't ready to move to Hell and Dammit Cay yet, after all.

But she sure thought about it. She took a while to come back with her answer. For a while there, I thought we were destined to have a roommate, and I wasn't mad about it. Monica was fun, and our age, and those two items alone made us want to have her around more. But when we asked her a week later if she'd made up her mind, she said she'd decided against it.

"I'm moving to Key West," she announced.

"Monica, no!" I was so disappointed in her. "With everything you know about the real islands, what are you doing moving down *there?*"

"Oh, it's fine. Don't be so prejudiced! I need some nightlife. I need to go on some dates and kiss some boys. You guys come down and hang out with me sometimes, okay?" She smiled, but her eyes were a little watery. "I'll miss seeing you all the time."

"So you're not even going to work here anymore? The Slutty Mermaid will go back to being a free-for-all?"

"I think everyone was happier that way, don't you?" Monica leaned over a paddock gate and gave Ruby a little scratch on her nose. The mare lipped at her fingers. "This isn't a town in need of a bartender. I mean, Arnie just gave me the job to get me out of Key Largo, anyway."

And before that, Miami, I thought. Aloud, I said, "You're going to miss those cinnamon rolls."

"Oh, I know," she laughed. "I guess I'll have to make plenty of pilgrimages back up to grab some."

"And then come here," Lou said. "You're always welcome on our island. I mean that."

We walked back to the truck. Lou was carrying a box of cinnamon rolls for his mother. He set them on the hood of the truck and looked at me. "Did you think for a while that she was my sister?"

"For the longest time," I admitted.

"Sometimes I wish she was," Lou said, rubbing the toe of one sandal in the gravel. "You know? I don't have much family. I have Mom, and I guess she might have some cousins and stuff back up in the mainland, but I don't know them. I've always wondered what it felt like, having a family."

"It feels like this," I told him. "It feels like Hell and Dammit Cay. And sometimes members of your family leave for a while, but you keep in touch...and eventually, they come back."

"I like the idea that they come back," Lou said. "That's a new one for me."

I stepped up to him and wrapped my arms around him, my heart full for the boy he'd been, and the man he was still becoming. "Well,"

I said, "let's make sure Monica doesn't sneak away from us in Key West. She's part of our family now. Whenever we can, we're going to bring her back."

"Deal," Lou murmured.

Epilogue

Waking up every morning in our own house was a dream come true.

I still went over to Crystal's house to share a cup of coffee with her, naturally. I was used to sitting with her at the wicker breakfast table, with the sun spilling through the windows, and talking about the day to come. And Lou still slept through it all, coming outside well after nine o'clock, while I was already down in the barn cleaning up horses and prepping for the day's trail rides. Or, if we'd had guests at the lodge the night before, over at the dock checking in with everyone, making sure they were all set for a fun day in the Keys.

Most weekends that autumn we had a couple of guests, usually snorkeling or diving enthusiasts looking for a unique way to experience the Keys. But there were also a few first-timers who had never been on the water before. We only had one middle-of-the-night panic attack, thankfully, and they were staying on the boat moored to the dock. Monica had cleverly integrated a questionnaire about previous experience with boating into the booking procedure, and we'd known to put the newbie as close to dry land as possible.

And they kept the horses busy! Every booking wanted to go on a beach ride, do a photo shoot, or just hang out around the barn, admiring the horses. My weekends became nonstop saddle time, leading out two morning groups and two afternoon groups. The jungle trail became so trodden by hooves, I didn't need to go out and clear it with a machete anymore. When we added in a festival weekend, I was often so tired on Monday morning that I stayed in bed half the day, and Crystal kindly took care of the horses for me.

But most momentous of all, we had the recording studio. And so nearly every day, we had time to work on our project together. Far more time than we'd have had if we'd been working in rented space at Rivers' studio in Key West. Lou found used equipment and drove around the Keys and Miami, picking up the items we'd need to kit out the space, and then we were off. By the time I got ready to fly from Miami to New Orleans to spend Thanksgiving with my family, we had fourteen perfect tracks—enough for an eleven or twelve song album, and two or three songs to be culled and used as b-sides for our singles.

Rivers was extremely pleased with us. He hadn't bothered to apologize for letting a "high-profile band" book out the studio where we were supposed to record, and I didn't expect him to. For the millionth time, I had to remind myself and Lou that Rivers wasn't a real friend—he was an industry friend who wanted to make money off us. But I was thrilled with his praise, nonetheless. I still liked the guy, and he still knew the ins and outs of the business more than we did.

"Now, all you need is a band name," he told us, lounging back in his chair. We were at his office above Southernmost Jazz. A gentle autumn rain was pattering against the window; Duval Street was subdued and quiet for once. "Tell me you've come up with a killer name."

I looked at Lou. He shrugged.

"No," I admitted. "We haven't."

Rivers sighed. "Get it to me as soon as possible."

I didn't bother reminding him nothing was even due until December thirty-first. We'd gotten this far. We could figure out a band name. "It'll come to us," I told Lou as we trundled down the narrow staircase and emerged onto the wet street. A half-empty Conch Train went by, sightseers in ponchos hunched over against the road spray.

"We could call ourselves Conch Train," Lou suggested, grinning.

"Pretty sure that's copyrighted," I laughed. "But not a bad try."

"We could call ourselves Soggy Cigarette," Lou said, stepping over a little pile of crushed butts; I guessed this was where the servers took their breaks.

"You're getting colder."

"You're not kidding," Lou agreed, tugging his jacket closed as a damp breeze slipped up the street. "What is this, winter?"

"It's seventy degrees, Lou. You lived in Chicago last winter."

"Last winter was a long time ago."

A lifetime, I thought.

"Don't force the name," I said. "It'll come, trust me."

"We could call ourselves Discount Bong," Lou said, looking in the window of a souvenir shop.

I decided to ignore him or he'd just keep doing it. *The name will come,* I told myself.

Everything else had come when we'd needed it. I just had to trust the universe on this one.

And in fact, the name came sooner than I expected. Short, sweet, and simple—the moment I saw the horses waiting for us back at the island, I knew.

"Can we just be The Sea Horses?" I asked.

Lou grinned and shook his head. "It was so obvious. It was *right there,* the whole time. And still you're the one who will get to tell the journalists that you named the band. Life is so unfair."

"Isn't it though?" I laughed and squeezed his thigh. "Isn't life just the worst?"

He leaned over and kissed me. "Unbearable," he whispered. "I don't know how we do it."

Your Next Read

I LOVE WRITING about the Florida Keys!

I plan on returning to Hell and Dammit Cay with a new adventure later in 2023. Stay posted on the latest news and find out when you can go back to the islands — subscribe to my newsletter at subscribepage.io/getbold and you'll be on the list, plus you'll receive a free ebook, *Bold*.

For more books with spunky heroines and gorgeous settings you'll love, check out my other chick lit and women's fiction series, all available from my store and major retailers.

Ocala Horse Girls: A light-hearted and fun-loving trilogy about three friends finding romance as they chase their equestrian goals in Ocala, the horse capital of the world! Learn more and read sample chapters at: https://nataliekreinert.shop/collections/ocala-horse-girls-series

Grabbing Mane: A duet about getting back to what matters in life. Casey has it all: great job, great boyfriend, great friends. So why does she feel so empty? When chance — or fate — brings her back to the farm where she learned to ride horses, she takes the leap and gets back in the saddle. Things get chaotic from there! Join Casey's wild ride: https://nataliekreinert.shop/products/grabbing-mane-grabbing-mane-book-one

Catoctin Creek: For country vibes and romantic feels, visit the town of Catoctin Creek, Maryland, where lifelong friends and newcomers just can't help falling in love. For the Hallmark lover in all of us, Catoctin Creek invites you to brew a cup of tea, pull up a cozy blanket, and read all night. Find book one for free now: https://nataliekreinert.shop/collections/catoctin-creek

Find more, including adventurous friendship sagas like *The Eventing Series*, *Alex & Alexander,* and *Briar Hill Farm,* at nataliekreinert.shop, or wherever you shop for books.

Free Book: Bold

READY FOR SOMETHING new? Saddle up for an equestrian adventure with The Eventing Series.

This tumultuous seven-book series follows Jules Thornton from a tough and prickly twenty-two-year-old struggling to make it as a professional rider to a difficult—but beloved—trainer and riding instructor. Her highs and lows, her good horses and bad rides, and her relationships with fellow equestrians are all shared in stunning detail.

You can begin The Eventing Series for free with the prequel novella, *Bold.*

Bold introduces you to Jules for the first time just a few months after she's left home for her own farm in Ocala, Florida. When she arrives, she thinks the eventing world will welcome her with open arms...but it turns out she's already built a little reputation for herself.

Jules needs her training business to launch and succeed. But if she can't find anyone in Ocala to hire her, she's going to lose everything before she even gets started.

Get *Bold* in ebook format for free now! Visit subscribepage.io/ getbold to get your copy. You can also find the paperback with a special preview of Book 1, *Ambition,* wherever print books are sold.

Acknowledgments

I'M SO HAPPY to welcome everyone back to Hell and Dammit Cay, and so grateful for the patience my readers showed in waiting for this sequel. It took a long time—I know! As I tried to balance my writing schedule with moving, renovating a house, and dealing with some difficult situations throughout the year, things definitely slowed down. But there's no escape quite like my fictional family in the Florida Keys. Writing this book was slow and challenging, but still ultimately satisfying.

Thanks as ever to my Patrons, who support me on Patreon with words of encouragement, incredible enthusiasm, and generous donations. I appreciate you all so, so much. From making my books better every single day, to providing financial support during difficult periods between book releases, your help is immeasurable! I love the guessing what will come next after I post a new chapter, and the spirited conversations about characters in the comments. You're all amazing. I couldn't spend nearly the amount of time I do get for writing without your support!

Want to be a part of it? Visit patreon.com/nataliekreinert to join the family!

Here are the fabulous people you'll be hanging out with: Pamela Allen-Blanc, Raina Kujawa, Kellie Halteman, Jennifer Williams, Natalie Clark, Megan McDonald, Adrienne Brant, Sally Testa, Becca B., April Lutz, Sherry Ogrsm, Julie Koeger, Heidi Schmid, Mel Sperti, SKLamb, Cathy Luo, Elana Rabinow, Laura, Dörte Voigt, Empathy, Gretchen Fieser, JoAnn Flejszar, Nancy Neid, Elizabeth Espinosa, Renee Knowles, Libby Henderson, Maureen VanDerStad, Genevieve Dempre, Jean Miller, Susan Cover, Sherron Meinert, Leslie Yazurlo, Nicola Beisel, Mel Policicchio, Kylie Standish, Harry Burgh, Alyssa, Kathlynn Angie-Buss, Peggy Dvorsky, Christine Komis, Annika Kostrubala, Thoma Jolette Parker, Karen Carrubba, Emma Gooden, Katie Lewis, Silvana Ricapito, Sarina Laurin, Di Hannel, Jennifer, Claus Giloi, Cyndy Searfoss, Kaylee Amons, Mary Vargas, Kathi Lacasse, Rachael Rosenthal, Orpu, Diana Aitch, Liz Greene, Zoe Bills, Cheryl Bavister, Sarah Seavey, Megan Devine, Mara Shatat, Tricia Jordan, Brian Dimmler, Lindsay Moore, Emily Nolan, Caitlin Harrison, Rhonda Lane, C. Sperry, Heather Voltz, and, of course, Kim Keller.

Thanks to everyone for reading! I appreciate you all so very much!

About the Author

I CURRENTLY LIVE in Central Florida. While most of my books are set in Florida, I love writing about places I know intimately, so I also write based on my experiences in New York City and rural Maryland.

I write fiction and freelance for a variety of publications, but my favorite topics are travel and horses. In the past I've worked professionally in many aspects of the equestrian world, including grooming for top eventers, training off-track Thoroughbreds, galloping racehorses, working in mounted law enforcement, on breeding farms, and more.

In my spare time I ride Ben, a clever chestnut pony with a big white blaze, and hang out with my husband and teenage son. My family also includes a foxhound named Sally, who sleeps most of the time.

Visit my website at nataliekreinert.com to keep up with the latest news and read occasional blog posts and book reviews. For installments of upcoming fiction and exclusive stories, visit my Patreon page and learn how you can become a subscriber!

Plus, follow me around the Interwebs for general nonsense:

* * *

- Facebook: facebook.com/nataliekellerreinert
- Twitter: twitter.com/nataliegallops
- Instagram: instagram.com/nataliekreinert
- Email Newsletter: visit nataliekreinert.com
- Patreon: patreon.com/nataliekreinert
- BookBub: bookbub.com/profile/natalie-keller-reinert

You can find my books at your favorite retailer and Taborton Equine Books.

Order signed editions by sending me an email at natalie@nataliekreinert.com